"So, what's your plan for ruining the wedding?"

"I'm not going to ruin any wedding," I say.

"You're driving how many miles and you're just going to chicken out at the end?" Riley asks me, looking incredulous.

"I'm going to take the high ground."

"Come on. You've got to at least have a speech planned for the 'speak now or forever hold your peace' bit."

"No, I don't."

"How about 'I'm a crazy woman who's been in love with you since I was ten. Marry me instead!'"

"No, I don't think so," I say, but I can't help but smile a little. "Besides, I'm not in love with him. That was a long time ago."

"Uh-huh," Riley says, sounding unconvinced. "So that's why you were so desperate to have a stand-in boyfriend tag along for the ride."

"I didn't say you were my stand-in boyfriend," I protest.

"Uh-huh, right."

"Do you have a problem with that . . . being a stand-in, I mean," I say. I am dangerously close to crossing that line from innocent platonic flirting to innuendo flirting.

Riley just looks at me, an impish smile on his face.

I think, suddenly, *he doesn't seem like he'd mind crossing that line at all.*

"No," he says. "I don't mind."

Also by Cara Lockwood

In One Year and Out the Other
Pink Slip Party
I Do (But I Don't)

Dixieland SUSHI

Cara Lockwood

doWn
tOwn
press

New York   London   Toronto   Sydney

An *Original* Publication of POCKET BOOKS

DOWNTOWN PRESS, published by Pocket Books
1230 Avenue of the Americas
New York, NY 10020

ISBN: 978-0-7434-9942-2

First Downtown Press trade paperback edition May 2005

10 9 8 7 6 5 4 3 2 1

DOWNTOWN PRESS and colophon are
trademarks of Simon & Schuster, Inc.

Manufactured in the United States of America

For information regarding special discounts for bulk purchases,
please contact Simon & Schuster Sales at 1-800-456-6798
or business@simonandschuster.com

Acknowledgments

Thanks to Mom and Dad, who give advice nearly as good as Mr. Miyagi's. Thanks, too, to my grandparents, Mitzi and Tom Tanamachi, to Uncle Smokey and Uncle Pro, and all the Nimuras, who may have lost their savings in the internment camps but never lost their sense of humor. Thanks to my brother, Matt, who will always tell me when I'm not being funny and to my husband, Daren, who will tell me when I am.

Thanks to my editor Lauren McKenna whose sharp editing is more nimble than Daniel LaRusso, and to my agent Deidre Knight, who can do a mean crane kick, especially during contract negotiations.

A special thanks to Jerry White, who gave me a crash course in television journalism, to my tireless volunteer copyeditors, Jean Hess and Joanne Lockwood, to my publicist, Susan Schwartzman, and to my volunteer gang of fierce marketing ninjas: Elizabeth Kinsella, Kate Kinsella, Shannon Whitehead, Jen Lane Lockwood, Keith Lockwood, Jane Ricordati, Kate Miller, Stephanie Elsea, Cyndi Swendner, Stacey Causey, Mary Chalfant, the Girls' Night Girls, and everyone else in my honorary Cobra Kai publicity team not afraid to use karate, Tae Bo, or any means necessary to persuade others to buy my books.

For the Tanamachi
and Nimura families

Dixieland
SUSHI

One

To make honey, young bee needs young flower.

—Mr. Miyagi, *The Karate Kid*

The year was 1984, the evening of my tenth birthday, inside the Dixieland Roller Rink, also known as the local Rec Center. The basketball nets were up, the disco ball was down, and it was a Free Skate Friday night.

I wore my brand new Gloria Vanderbilt jeans with the hot pink piping and my favorite lavender-colored roller skates with the clear plastic wheels carefully decorated with sparkly, puffy silver star stickers and tried my best not to fall on my face as I coolly attempted to skate along to Queen's "Another One Bites the Dust," which was blasting through the speakers as the disco ball overhead spun in tune with the beat. I was on the outskirts of the skaters, avoiding the center of the rink, where the teenagers were doing advanced spin moves and wearing satin short shorts.

"Another one down, and another one down . . . Another one bites the dust . . ."

My birthday cake, topped with pink gel icing and a decorative plastic pink roller skate, sat on one of the long tables by the Ms. Pac Man and Frogger video games. I was ignoring (read: desperately trying to get the attention of) Kevin Peterson, my fourth-grade crush, who wore a very cool red Members Only jacket and black roller skates as he leaned against the roller rink rail. He, in turn, was doing his best to ignore me, a sure sign that he, too, felt the unspoken attraction between us. We were so blatantly ignoring one another that it should've been obvious to anyone that we had serious chemistry.

"Another one down and another one down . . ."

Kevin was by the rail where I should be, because it's hard to look cool wobbling about with your hands outstretched like wings, trying to keep your balance. If I fell, my too-tight, pre-the-invention-of-spandex jeans would rip straight down the rear seam in what would become a serious Therapy Moment. Luckily, I had on my training bra underneath my rainbow baseball T-shirt, which, as anyone knows, wasn't so much a support garment as it was a status symbol. It screamed, I don't have boobs yet, but they're on the way.

I glided to an awkward stop about ten feet from Kevin, under the pretense of adjusting my silver laces. I turned my back to him in order to complete my cool indifference, and to offer him a view of the strap through my T-shirt, so that if he was so inclined, he could come and snap it. But Kevin was too cool to resort to bra-strap snapping. He, in fact, had sisters. And a boy with sisters was far more advanced in terms of romantic strategy. He was what you would call a fourth-grade ladies' man.

I noticed for the hundredth time how much he looked like a younger version of Ralph Macchio. I'd seen *The Karate Kid* somewhere in the neighborhood of six times, partly because I had a small crush on Ralph Macchio, and partly because our town's one-screen movie theater played only a single show for two months at a time. Our small Southern town didn't offer the newest movies, or the newest anything, which accounted for the song selection at the local roller rink.

For a whole week, I went about talking in broken English like Mr. Miyagi ("Mama-san, Miyagi no do dishes" and so on), and stopped only after my mother, Vivien, threatened to ground me until I was fifteen. Still, standing so close to Kevin Peterson, I couldn't help but wish that I could conjure Mr. Miyagi and some of his wisecracking advice.

"Another One Bites the Dust" came to a close, followed by that awkward moment of the fade-out of a song, when the skaters paused in their moves, waiting for the next beat. My heart pounded in my small rib cage, and I wasn't sure if this was because of the proximity of Kevin Peterson or the fact that I had downed one too many "Suicides." This was my cocktail of choice at age ten: a mixture of all the fountain drinks at the snack counter. The drink had enough corn syrup and caffeine to keep me awake for three days.

After a second of silence, the opening chords of the theme song to *The Dukes of Hazzard* piped in over the speakers in a triumphant blare. A cheer went up from the free skaters. Everyone loved this song. It was, after all, the unofficial theme song for Dixieland (that is, Dixieland, Arkansas, population 10,230) and current Southern Pride, even if it came from a show that seemed to bolster all the ignorant southern stereotypes. At the Dixieland Roller Rink, it was a hit.

Even Kevin Peterson, stoic, cool, immobile Kevin Peterson, pushed himself away from the wall; he was going to join the skate. As he did so, he caught my eye, a perfect and subtle end to the Ignoring Phase of our courtship. This was a pivotal moment. He looked at me. He was about to extend his hand, to offer me a holding-hands skate, which was practically one step from a declaration of going together.

My mind raced ahead: First, going together. Then, going steady. Then, we'd be married and incredibly wealthy (Kevin would be a self-made millionaire industrialist and I'd be an internationally known freelance journalist—like Robert Wagner and Stephanie Powers on *Hart to Hart*). We'd have a grizzly but lovable butler named Max and we'd tolerate his insolence because he was grizzly but lovable and he talked nonstop about how generous we were. Like on *Hart to Hart,* Kevin would wear expensive suits, and I'd wear impractical heels and big floppy hats, and we'd fly around in our private jet solving murder mysteries with the help of our scruffy dog, Freeway.

I was thinking of us, Max, and Freeway as I reached out to take Kevin Peterson's hand, which would seal my romantic destiny forever, when Grandma Saddie (short for Sayoku) and my mother, Vivien, appeared from nowhere, carrying a giant Tupperware tray full of foul-smelling sushi and pickled vegetables.

"Birthday treats!" Vivien cried, oblivious to the fact that she, wearing her slick black hair in a teased helmet, blue eye shadow on the lids of her almond-shaped Asian eyes, along with pencil-straight jeans, gold platform shoes, and matching elastic gold belt with the butterfly clip buckle, was Ruining My Life As I Knew It. The tray she and Grandma Saddie carried was stacked high with little cucumber rolls and *inari* (what Grandma called "footballs" for their shape)—fried tofu sacks filled with sushi rice—and what seemed like mounds of Japanese pickled cabbage, squash, and ginger, and a good helping of dried fish—ordered especially for the occasion from San Francisco—which all together gave off the powerful odor of toe cheese.

Now, in the privacy of my own home, away from the questioning eyes of Kevin Peterson, I would gladly have devoured the sushi and pickled treats. But under his gaze, as I saw the look of horror and surprise as the pungent combination of smells reached his nose, I found myself frozen with mortification.

"Ew," he breathed, his nose wrinkling, his calm exterior for the first time showing cracks. "WHAT is THAT?"

He could have meant anything—the neon-yellow pickled radish, the dried shreds of fish that look surprisingly like shriveled monkey claws, the "footballs," which, in the roller disco light, looked suspiciously like cat livers.

"Have a bite," my mother insisted, her Asian features hopeful. "Come on, we made all your favorites."

Kevin Peterson looked at the tray of food and then at me and declared, "You eat that stuff? Gross!"

Vivien and Grandma Saddie would've been better off offering me the chilled monkey brains from *Indiana Jones and the Temple of Doom*. As I watched, helpless, Kevin Peterson skated away from me as if he'd been stung, never once looking back, dashing forever my dreams of drinking champagne on our private jet as we laughed over the misfortunes of the evildoer we'd just put in jail.

"What is wrong with you, anyway?" Vivien asked me, when I clambered out of the rink, pouting, my skates catching on the carpet skate-free zone, the voice of Waylon Jennings singing "And that's just a little more than the law would allow" echoing in my ears.

Two

Everything can heal; just take time and patience.
—Mr. Miyagi, *The Karate Kid III*

*I*f fate were kind and sympathetic, the roller rink would have been the last time I saw Kevin Peterson. But fate is neither kind nor sympathetic. Otherwise, life would be like a teen movie, where everything works itself out at prom.

Instead, nearly two decades later, I am going to be standing up at Kevin Peterson's wedding, watching him marry my cousin Lucy, which ranks in the top three list of Things I Never Want To See Before Turning Thirty (it's outranked only by my parents having sex and Mariah Carey in *Glitter).*

As if I don't have enough emotional scarring from being half-Japanese and raised in Dixieland—a small southern town known for fried pickles, an annual barbecue cook-off, and a higher than average teen pregnancy rate—I now have to endure the humiliating event of my twenty-year-old former beauty queen cousin getting married before I do, and to the same boy I first dreamed of k-i-s-s-i-n-g.

It was my mother, Vivien, who broke the news first in an email six months ago that read like a telegram from the *Titanic:*

KEVIN PETERSON AND LUCY ARE GET-TING HITCHED. AUNT TERI WANTS YOU AND YOUR SISTER IN THE WEDDING. DON'T MAKE PLANS FOR JUNE. XOXO MOM

It came as a bit of a shock. It shouldn't have. There are only so many eligible singles in Dixieland, and the odds of your cousin and your former childhood sweetheart dating are only about twenty-five to one.

And while I had thought I long ago buried all my feelings for Kevin Peterson, when I read my mother's email, they all came bubbling up again. Along with a panic I hadn't felt since two weeks before my high school homecoming dance.

Because all I can think about is one single, sad fact: I have only a month to find a date for this wedding.

I realize that I should not care that I don't have a date, or even anything approaching a date.

I am no longer the girl skating along to the theme song to *The Dukes of Hazzard* at the roller rink, desperately hoping for a glance from Kevin Peterson. I am the producer of *Daybreak Chicago* (in fact, the second-youngest producer in the history of the show). I haven't been back to Dixieland in nearly five years, not even for a Christmas visit. My job doesn't allow for much time off, and you don't get promoted by taking holidays. And I want to be promoted. I want to be promoted as high as it is possible for me to go.

That's what separates me from most of my classmates in Dixieland, who generally did not aspire to achieve much beyond covert cow-tipping missions while stoned. Half of my classmates didn't bother to go to college and the two most upwardly mobile people in our class were me and our Homecoming Queen, who had a brief brush with fame after being featured in *Penthouse*. It's no wonder that I've stayed away from home as long as I could.

I wish I could say I'm like Mr. Miyagi in *The Karate Kid II*, and I'm an exile from my homeland, after my true love was forced to marry my evil rival (cue, Peter Cetera's "Glory of Love"—"I am the man who will fight for your honor . . ."). However, I have no such romantic story.

If I'd stayed in Dixieland, I would've had the kind of love story that restraining orders are made of. I would've probably ended up marrying a truck driver who couldn't be bothered wearing shirts with sleeves. When we made our debut on *Cops*, he'd be wearing a white undershirt, a Wife Beater's Special, and I'd be wearing a housecoat and smudged mascara, waving a broken bottle while screaming that my no-good husband stuffed our electric bill money into neon pink G-strings at the local strip club.

Part of me still feels scarred from living in Dixieland. I spent the first year at college wondering if being half-white meant that I could still qualify as "white trash." It's a debate I haven't fully resolved.

I landed my first assistant-producer assignment in a remote part of Arkansas, worked my way up to the Little Rock market, then to Dallas, and now to Chicago, where I am a baby step away from moving up to New York.

I realize I should not care what Kevin Peterson thinks of me. If he even thinks of me at all. I should not be worried about what people will say when I come home, age twenty-eight and single, when most of my classmates are working on Baby Three or Husband Two. In fact, I should be paying attention to my job, which at this moment is heading at high speed toward the next calamity.

"Uh-oh," says my assistant, Anne, as we both watch the broadcast monitors during *Chicago Daybreak,* while the anchor, Michelle Bradley, is interviewing the director of the Lincoln Park Zoo. Said director has brought a small spider monkey, which looks like a big squirrel with a Confucius mustache. Now, having booked enough morning guests to know that animals are always trouble, I should mention that I did it only as a last resort, since two of my guests canceled earlier this week.

Michelle, who never comes in early enough to read her scripts in advance for the morning show, is mispronouncing the director's name, calling him Mr. Vulva instead of Vul-vay. Even worse, she has veered off script entirely and is now asking a question about whether the spider monkey is, in fact, related to spiders.

Some of the crew members are putting their hands over their mouths to keep from laughing out loud. I sigh. I would love my job so much more if it didn't involve working with anchors.

I realize that without anchors, no one would watch the news, and that people do make decisions about which news show they want to watch based on their perceived likeability of certain reporters. And I have worked with the rare breed of anchor, the one who is generous, reasonable, and has no diva tendencies. However, Michelle is not one of them. She is the sort who believes that she is a star and that everyone else working at the station is just one more warm body who can fetch her coffee.

Because she is a star, nothing is ever her fault. Ergo, the fact that she is butchering the zoo director's name is not her mistake but mine for booking someone who has a name remotely approaching a part of the female anatomy. After this broadcast, I'm certain she'll march right into the office of our assistant news director (our boss) and demand I be fired. In the last month alone, she's called for my resignation twice: once because she mispronounced the mayor's name, calling him "Davey" instead of "Daley," and another time because she said I use too many "four-syllable" words in her newscasts, including "interrogate," which she found too difficult to pronounce.

Michelle is wearing sparkling chandelier earrings, which are catching the light and the spider monkey's attention. I told her not to wear shiny jewelry today. I definitely told her.

"Aren't you a cute little thing," Michelle says to the monkey, but the words come out sounding forced. Michelle often complains loudly about her disdain for animals and small children, even though she also believes she has a gift for relating to both. She believes she's Snow White, but in reality she's far closer to Cruella De Vil.

"The earrings," I breathe, just as the spider monkey leaps to Michelle's shoulder, grabbing one of the dangling mobiles of crystal jewelry and giving it a hard tug. Michelle lets out a high-pitched shriek, which causes the monkey to panic, drop the earring, and scream. In its haste to untangle itself, it only wraps its paws deeper into Michelle's hair, probably because there is enough styling mousse in her curls to cement a half-block of new city sidewalk.

There is more wailing, and Michelle leaps up from her chair, struggling with the monkey, flapping wildly at it with her arms. In mid monkey-dance, she falls sideways in her chair onto the studio's blue carpet. Mr. Vulva/Vul-vay, in a panic, jumps up to help, only to get kicked hard in the shin by one of Michelle's pointed gray heels. The monkey, still shrieking, leaps over Michelle and to Mr. Vulva/Vul-vay's now-empty chair, where it jumps and squeals as if it's the host of its own talk show.

And that's when we go to commercial.

This, I think, putting my head in my hands, *is no way to get promoted.*

"HOW am I supposed to work under these conditions?" Michelle asks after the show, as we both sit in the office of our boss, Assistant News Director Bob Marcus.

Bob is a grizzly bear of a man who rose through the ranks of television news back in the days when there was one woman in the entire newsroom and she sat at the front desk and made coffee. His eyes flick back and forth between Michelle and me. He has that panicked look of a trapped animal who is trying to decide whether it's best to stay and wait or chew off its leg to escape.

"Michelle, I realize that you're upset," Bob starts.

"UPSET?" she fumes. Michelle's eyes are flashing. She has the same sort of steely determination that I once saw in the eyes of the mother from Texas who hired a killer to knock off her daughter's number-one rival in a cheerleader competition. "This is well beyond upset, Bob. On *Good Morning, Utah!*, nothing like this would happen."

Michelle is always referencing her last morning anchor gig in the much smaller market of Salt Lake City.

"We would never have stooped to having animals on the show," Michelle says. "My last producer *knew* about good television."

"The fact is, we had two cancellations this morning, and Mr. Vul-vay generously agreed to fill in for us on very short notice," I argue.

"And that brings up another point," Michelle says. "I don't know how I'm supposed to properly address guests if there is no *phonetic* spelling in the scripts."

"Technically, there was a phonetic spelling," I say.

"Well, I don't know what kind of dictionary you are used to using, but mine has those things in parentheses, you know, with the upside down *e*'s and whatever they're called," Michelle fumes.

I cough loudly.

"Okay, Michelle, I think I understand," says Bob, rubbing his temples. "Why don't you let me talk to Jen for a few minutes alone?"

"I want this documented," Michelle demands.

"It will be," Bob says, nodding, as Michelle picks herself up from her chair and walks out the door. She gives me a triumphant look on her way.

"Close that," Bob commands me, which I do.

Bob has on his stern face, and I wonder if he might start shouting now. He's hotheaded and unpredictable, and even though we get along, I'm not sure just how far I am in his good graces. Bob is from the old school of journalism, the one in which drinking on the job was encouraged, and he's amassed a reputation for being a bulldog who makes interns cry. But I am one of the few people in the studio who's not afraid of Bob. He reminds me of my dad, Bubba, who is a good old boy. They both speak in Southern twangs, love to swear, and spend every weekend they can bass fishing.

"Jen, I am disappointed in you," drawls Bob, showing his best stern face.

At least he isn't yelling. Yet.

"Don't you know you shouldn't book monkeys for the show?" Bob pauses, then adds, "We have enough of them running loose through the studio as it is."

I snicker.

"No laughing!" Bob commands, leaning over his desk. "Michelle must think that I'm scolding you, and she'll never believe it if she hears you laughing."

"Sorry," I tell Bob.

"You'd better be. You know I hate to have Michelle in my office. She reminds me too much of my first wife."

Bob has had three wives and is working on a fourth.

"That being said, you know that it's your job to help keep the anchors happy so they don't come bothering me," Bob says, sounding stern. "So, you'd better kiss her ass awhile so I don't have to hear any more of her whining."

"Yes, Bob," I say, nodding.

"You're slipping, Jen. Something like this wouldn't have happened six months ago."

"I'm sorry. I've been distracted," I say. "Family problems," I add. That's just vague enough to be truthful.

"Family!" sighs Bob in disgust. "You know real news people don't have time for families."

This is true. Bob, and the fact that his daughter from his first marriage doesn't speak to him, is living proof of this.

"You'd better get it together if you want what I think might be an opening at the ten slot soon."

The ten o'clock news is the top of the food chain at any local station. This would be a significant improvement in stature. Not to mention saying goodbye to the graveyard shift.

"Really?" I ask, excited.

"You just work on keeping Michelle happy, and we'll see."

Without warning, Bob bangs his hand hard on the desk and tosses one of his stress balls at the window behind my head, causing me to jump.

"For effect," he tells me. "Now, when you leave here you'd better not be smiling. I have a reputation to protect."

"Yes, sir," I say, giving him a mock salute. "You old softie," I tease.

"Who are you calling old?" Bob says, but he smiles at me.

Back at my desk, it looks like a bomb exploded. There are press releases, faxes, old printouts of scripts, and two now-empty cups from Starbucks. It's always a mess at the end of a shift, the result of the panic that invariably precedes a newscast. I sit down and try to get organized, but it feels like trying to tidy up a landfill.

I like my job, even though directing news sometimes feels no different from directing reality TV, except that instead of *Survivor* challenges you have press conferences and weather reports.

My mother says I'm one step away from being Diane Sawyer, but then, she doesn't know how the broadcast business works. I'm about a million steps away from a broadcast network anchor seat and not just because I could never pass for a real blond.

Before I went behind the cameras, I tried being an on-air news reporter. It was a disaster. For one thing, there's something about having a camera pointed at me that makes me lose all sense of grammar, time, and place. The "on-air" light goes on, and I suddenly forget how to speak English. I start sounding like Anne Heche when she's translating for aliens.

And because the networks are always in desperate need of minority faces on air, my boss (then at *News Eleven* in Little Rock) kept telling me to try to "look more Asian," since at the time we didn't have any Asian reporters. He was also the one who said I should go by my mother's maiden name (Naka-mura) instead of my father's name (Taylor).

But I've never felt comfortable playing up my Asian half. Like Tiger Woods, if I embrace one half of my heritage over the other it seems like I'm playing favorites. Besides, I don't even look Japanese—a fact that was pointed out to me on the play-ground by other kids who didn't believe me when I told them my background.

I look as if I belong in the same family with Vin Diesel. My father, Bubba, is blond and pale-skinned, and my mother, Vivien, is clearly Japanese, with dark, thick hair and almond-shaped eyes. I am some mix of the two: dark hair, wide eyes, and skin that tans even in the shade.

So it's difficult to take advantage of race when you don't even really *look* like the race you're supposed to be exploiting, which explains to a degree why I've always felt a little uncom-fortable about race.

In college I had to take a multicultural appreciation seminar, which was required of all freshmen. The seminar spotlighted a different minority group each week, and most of the discussions in class always boiled down to how white, mainstream America was always trying to conform or control minorities by co-opting culture clues and then sanitizing them. Rap being a prime exam-ple. There were two classes devoted to the evil effects of Vanilla Ice (beyond the sheer annoyance of hearing "Ice Ice Baby").

It was in this class that the professor, a white woman who wore a traditional African head wrap, talked at length about the wrongheadedness of metaphors like the Melting Pot. "America," she said, "is far more like a tossed salad."

I wrote a paper on Mr. Miyagi as a Japanese American culture icon and got a C. The instructor said that next time I should pick a cultural hero who wasn't "a fictional character created by the white Hollywood screenwriter responsible for *Lethal Weapon 3*," and that perhaps I should spend more time trying to get in touch with my "authentic" Japanese self.

Meanwhile, my roommate, Carrie O'Brien, got an A on the paper she turned in called "The European-American Experience: Being the Ranch Dressing in the American Salad."

I look up to see Michelle standing in front of my desk.

"I want you to know that there aren't any hard feelings," Michelle says. "I just want us *all* to get better, and we can't do that unless we're properly challenged, you know?"

I give Michelle a closed-lip smile.

"I hope you know that I think you have a *lot* of potential as a producer," she says, sweetly. A backhanded compliment. This is Michelle's tactic. She completely tears you apart in front of your boss but in private she tries to make nice with fake, semi-snide compliments.

"Thanks, Michelle," I say, all the while thinking *be nice, be nice, be nice.*

"Oh, and I need a favor," Michelle says, dropping her four news assignments on my desk. "I didn't get to these, and I've got a waxing appointment I just *can't* miss," Michelle says, her eyes big and pleading.

I stop short of asking her what she plans to have waxed. I imagine that she, like trolls and other quasi-evil creatures, has hair growing in her palms and on the balls of her feet.

"Could you finish them up for me tomorrow?" Michelle asks me.

I want to tell her what she can do with her work, but I remember Bob's warning. If I want my promotion, I need to keep Michelle happy.

"Yes, fine."

"Great, you're the best," Michelle chirps, practically skipping off to her desk, where she grabs her purse and heads straight for the elevator.

"Bitch," Anne, my assistant, hisses when Michelle is out of earshot.

"And then some. But she'll probably be anchoring on MSNBC before the year is out."

"Why don't I stay and help?" Anne offers.

"No, that's okay. Go home. You've been staying late all week."

"So have you. You've had two colds this month, and if you don't go home and get some sleep you're going to be working on a third."

Even though I am her boss, Anne has a mothering instinct toward me. This is because she is a year older and has two kids at home. She can also cook casseroles and quiches, whereas I only know how to dial for takeout. "You really ought to go home and sleep," she cautions.

"I can sleep when I'm a producer on the *Today* show."

*   *   *

Three hours later, after I've done Michelle's work, I stagger home. My condo, which I proudly bought with a down payment I saved after two painful years of depriving myself of department store makeup, vacations, dinners out, and digital cable, is a one-bedroom (technically a studio, except that the half-wall between my bedroom and the kitchen means that it's marketed as a one-bedroom). The best part of my condo is its view of the Chicago River and downtown, and the fact that after ten years of scraping together quarters for the laundromat, I finally have my very own washer and dryer.

By Dixieland standards, my space is ridiculously small. It could, for instance, fit practically in the living room of my parents' house, and for what I paid for it, I could've bought a three-bedroom Victorian house in Arkansas. But it's all mine, and I remind myself that I may live in a small condo but I'm two blocks from Michigan Avenue, and that makes all the difference.

Of course, my twinge of pride at returning to my condo is always tempered by the fact that I spend so much time working to afford it that I rarely have time to clean it. On the whole, my place is a sty.

There are piles of old magazines, dirty clothes, and a few empty cans of Diet Coke on the counter. And, I notice sadly, my third ivy in as many months is dried up and dead on my windowsill for lack of watering. Even the cactus, the plant the nursery owner swore to me I couldn't kill, is looking dangerously close to passing on. It's drooping to one side like a deflated balloon.

Anne says I should get a cat to keep me company, but it would just be one more thing I wouldn't have time to take care of.

The only things thriving in my apartment are dust bunnies, and they're multiplying at an alarming rate.

I once saw a news report in which a man died in his apartment and it took people days to get him out because his body was sandwiched in between giant stacks of old newspapers, magazines, and books. He had a psychological disorder that prevented him from ever throwing anything away.

I have enough old copies of *Time* and *People* to make a nice funeral pyre already. The thought of someone finding my body on top of stacks of old *Cosmos* with articles like "Give the Perfect Blow Job" or "Pick the Right Swimsuit For Your Body Type (Small on Top! Big on the Bottom!)" dog-eared, makes me pick up a trash bag and start to make a clean sweep. I don't get very far before I sink into my sofa and kick off my shoes. I flip through my TiVo listings and settle on the last episode of *American Idol.* I'm a reality TV junkie, and while I'd never admit it in public, I've watched every single episode of *The Bachelor.*

Even though I should at this moment be sleeping, I know I'll have difficulty, as always, falling asleep. It takes me an hour or two or four to unwind from the nervous energy I always have when leaving a shift at the station.

While I fast-forward through the title credits, I half-heartedly try to attack the pile of mail on my coffee table. It's a towering stack of neglect. Bills that need to be paid. Birthday cards from last week I forgot to open. Pleas from my old college to send money. Magazines and catalogs that I probably won't have time to even glance through.

I make it two letters in when I find my cousin Lucy's wedding invitation. I rip open the envelope. It's thick embossed candlelight paper complete with vellum paper overlay. It's just the sort of invitation I would have wanted, if I ever had time to even think seriously about dating, much less getting married. Getting married was always something I thought I'd do "next year" like my plan to go to Italy or France. My target age for marriage was twenty-five, and then when I turned twenty-five, I moved it to thirty, and when I turned twenty-eight, I moved it to thirty-five. I always think, *when my life slows down, then I can think about dating and traveling and doing those things I want to do, like learn how to cook.* The only problem is that my life never seems to slow down.

I run my fingers over the name Kevin Stuart Peterson and remember that when I was ten, I used to write my name over and over again on my Hello Kitty spiral notepad—Jen Nakamura Taylor Peterson.

But that, I think, *was a long time ago.*

I toss the invitation on top of the pile and then lean back to watch TV. I fall asleep to the hum of the television and find myself dreaming of Dixieland.

Three

Balance is key. Balance good, karate good.
Everything good. Balance bad, better pack up
and go home.

—Mr. Miyagi, *The Karate Kid*

1980

My first crush ever was not Kevin Peterson. It was Brian Carlisle, who sat next to me in first grade. According to Vivien, I liked Brian Carlisle because he wore a T-shirt with the number five on it, and at the time, my favorite cartoon on earth was *Speed Racer*. Apparently, to me, Brian Carlisle and Speed Racer were interchangeable. They both had black hair. They both liked the number five. Brian Carlisle drove a Big Wheel instead of a race car, but his Big Wheel was red, white, and blue just like Speed Racer's car.

My crush on Brian Carlisle, however, was short-lived. It ended the day he rolled his Big Wheel up on our lawn, pointed one dirty finger at me, and sang, "You're adopted! You're adopted! You're adopted!"

He was referring to the fact that I did not look much like my blond father, Bubba—who was sitting on the porch swing at the time.

Still, I took Brian seriously. I thought maybe he knew something that I didn't—maybe my life was an Asian version of *Diff'rent Strokes*. I was Arnold, and my older sister was Willis, and instead of being adopted by Mr. Drummond, we'd been adopted by my dad, Bubba Taylor and his Asian wife, Vivien.

Then, I saw *The Empire Strikes Back* with my sister, Kimberly, after waiting in line on a rainy day in May, and I started to think, at age six, that maybe I did have a "real" father out there somewhere. That Bubba was just a stand-in, like Luke's Uncle Owen.

I clearly had my mother's dark hair, but it wasn't obvious that I had my father's genes. He was fair-skinned, blond, and blue-eyed. No one in first grade thought I looked like him. I became convinced somewhere there was an Asian or Latino man in a mask with the voice of James Earl Jones who would come tell me he was my real dad.

My mother says I became so sure of this that in the supermarket I started walking up to complete strangers—usually ones of darker skin tones—and asking them if they were my "real" father.

Eventually, she sat me down for a talk to tell me about the Nakamuras. Grandpa Frank (short for Fujimara) and Grandma Saddie lived in San Francisco before Pearl Harbor, when the FBI came and arrested them.

"Were they spies?" I asked, suddenly excited by the prospect of Grandpa Frank having a phone in his shoe like Max on *Get Smart*.

"No," Vivien said, sounding annoyed. "They weren't spies. They looked like the people we were at war with."

While in the camps, Grandpa Frank got a letter from a man living in Dixieland. This man was the father of a soldier who had written home to say he had been saved from a particularly nasty battle on a ridge in Italy by a special regiment of Japanese Americans. The man's son had written about the particular bravery of Takeo Nakamura, Grandpa Frank's younger brother, who had died helping the man's son in that very battle. In gratitude, the father of that soldier offered Grandpa Frank a job in his small country store in Dixieland.

Without another place to go, Grandpa Frank and Grandma Saddie, then pregnant with Vivien, took up the man's offer and got on a train to Dixieland.

He and Grandma Saddie had two daughters, who they named for famous movie stars Vivien (Vivien Leigh) and Bette (Bette Davis). They were both encouraged to be as American as possible; they spoke in thick Southern accents and, on occasion, forgot entirely they were Japanese.

Vivien dated Bubba, a member of the state championship football team, in high school.

"So now you see that you're not Luke Skywalker?" Vivien asked me, as she spread out before my tiny hands all the many pictures stowed in the collection of shoeboxes in the attic. There were black-and-white ones of my grandparents in the camps; then of Vivien as a baby, and then of Vivien and Bubba standing in the courthouse minutes after they married.

And then, the clincher: Bubba holding me as a baby in the hospital room, grinning from ear to ear. I spent hours looking at the picture of Bubba and looking at my reflection in the mirror.

"You are so vain," my sister, Kimberly, declared, catching me in the bathroom. "And dumb, too. It's obvious to anyone you have his nose."

From then on, I was mostly convinced, although it wouldn't surprise me, even today, to get a call from Jerry Springer for one of his special "Family Secrets" shows. Vivien and Bubba would be sitting on a chair crying, and then they would tell me I was actually the daughter of a circus transvestite and a Darth Vader impersonator.

But then again, Kimberly always said that I was too dramatic and watched too much TV.

Four

Man who catch fly with chopsticks accomplish anything.

—Mr. Miyagi, *The Karate Kid*

"I'm not going to this farce of a wedding," declares my sister, Kimberly, on the phone. Kimberly now lives in San Francisco and for the past year has been in the process of renaming herself Mitsuko, after our great-grandmother, because she thinks "Kimberly" is another tool of the white patriarchy used to oppress her. She thinks this even though her name was selected with care by Vivien, our third-generation (sansei) Japanese mother.

"Why do you care about Kevin Peterson?" I ask.

"Who cares about Kevin Peterson?" Kimberly snaps back. "I'm talking about our cousin Lucy living in that backward town and marrying some guy who can barely read."

"Kevin Peterson can read."

"He's a pig farmer, Jen. I don't think I need to say anything else."

"I thought you were a farm workers' advocate. Sounds like you're talking down to farmers."

Kimberly lets out a long, exhausted-sounding sigh, as she does when she feels she has to explain the complexity of her political agenda, which is somewhere left of Michael Moore's.

"Immigrant sharecroppers in this country are oppressed and have very limited educational opportunities. Kevin Peterson chose to be a pig farmer. I think there's a big difference."

"If you say so," I say. "Anyway, Vivien says it's not just a farm. He runs an enormous plant that partners with Hormel. Vivien says he's rich."

"Even worse. I'm definitely not going," Kimberly says, sounding resolute. "That girl needs to get her head on straight. She could've at least had the courtesy to get pregnant first. Otherwise, I just don't see the point of marriage. She is barely twenty years old."

"She'll probably be pregnant in a year."

"That doesn't make me feel any better." Kimberly sighs. "It was bad enough when she was trying to be Miss Arkansas. But even that was better than *this.*"

Last year our cousin Lucy made it to the top five finalists of the Miss Arkansas contest. She left with a parting gift of a year's supply of Dove soap. Lucy is our dad's niece, the only daughter of his oddball sister, Teri, and has the Taylors' blond hair and blue eyes.

"I suppose this means you aren't going to send her your bridesmaid's dress measurements?" I ask.

Kimberly lets out a snort.

"So what am I supposed to tell Aunt Teri?"

"Tell her she ought to get her daughter to a college, stat."

Mentally, I'm trying to think of how I'm going to explain to Vivien and Aunt Teri that Kimberly isn't going to play ball. Kimberly is always doing this to me—putting me in the middle. Case in point: Christmas 1981, when Kimberly refused to play with the doll Vivien bought her for Christmas: Oriental Barbie. She came holding a folding fan and with the slogan "Learn About the Orient" emblazoned on her box.

Now, Kimberly claims she objected to the use of the word "Oriental," even though all the Dixieland Nakamuras used that word until the summer Kimberly came back from her first year at Brown to inform us that "Oriental" is a term used only for rugs.

Kimberly refused to play with Oriental Barbie and pitched such a fit Christmas morning that neither she nor my mother spoke to each other for a full day. I was the one who intervened, offering up my Paint the Town Red Barbie (inspired by Nancy Reagan) as a kind of truce.

Then again, Kimberly has always had a difficult relationship with Barbie. Two years ago, Kimberly helped organize a boycott of Mattel after the company's 2000 Barbie for President doll came in only three races: Caucasian, African American, and Latin American. A Barbie spokesperson apparently went on the record as saying Mattel decided not to make an Asian American Barbie because their research showed Asian girls prefer to buy white dolls.

Kimberly called this "another example of oppression by the white patriarchy." I called it good luck.

The way I figure it, I can't think of anything scarier than Barbie—of any race—being president. Would she drive around on official government business in her pink Corvette? And during important State of the Union speeches, would Barbie be barefoot—since everybody knows none of her shoes ever stayed on? These were the questions we should've been asking about Barbie for President. I couldn't have cared less what color she was.

Not Kimberly. In general, I think Kimberly (who is four years older than me) is angry because she had a relatively happy childhood in a town that was largely white. She realizes now the horrible injustice of this: she didn't find out until she left home that she was part of an oppressed minority and therefore not supposed to be happy.

"So, I signed your name on the petition. I hope you don't mind," Kimberly says, after she's spoken for fifteen minutes about how she's in the middle of organizing another protest of Abercrombie & Fitch for their production of Wok-N-Bowl T-shirts.

"Isn't that illegal?"

"By this point, I can sign your signature better than you can," Kimberly says.

"Remind me not to let you near my checkbook." I imagine suddenly all of my hard-won savings going to a poor family in Vietnam. "Anyway, that's fine. But what I want to know is are you bringing a date to Cousin Lucy's wedding?"

This is vital information. If Kimberly—who is objectively the prettier sister—doesn't bring a date, then I won't feel so bad about showing up solo.

"Is that all you care about?" Kimberly sighs. "Well, if I were going—which I'm not—I'd bring Matt, since he's been bugging me about meeting Vivien and Bubba."

Matt Chang is one of Kimberly's many admirers. My sister, who believes that marriage is a tool of the patriarchy, does not believe in monogamy, strictly speaking. Somehow this, her random body piercings, her Buddha tattoo, and the fact that she doesn't shave her armpits, manages to attract eligible men in swarms. Granted, Kimberly has always been pretty, even during her phase when she boycotted all makeup tested on animals. She has the dark, shapely look of a Lucy Liu or a Salma Hayek. I'm a little shorter, a little less dramatic and exotic-looking, and irony of ironies, I have freckles on my nose. I'm always the runner-up in cases when we're both in the room. If Kimberly and I are sitting at a bar and two men approach us, the man who gets stuck with me always looks slightly disappointed. It never helps to point out the fact that I'm supposed to be the "smart" sister. This is one of many reasons I've chosen not to live in the same city as Kimberly.

"I assume you don't have a date?" Kimberly asks me.

"Who said I didn't have a date?"

"You never have a date."

"That is not at all fair."

"What? It's a compliment. You're putting your career first. As all women should."

"That doesn't make me feel any better," I say. "I'm going to be forty-five and on Oprah, talking about how my life is empty because I missed my child-bearing window and now I have to make do with the baby I adopted illegally from Cambodia."

"You'll adopt legally and you'll be doing a great service to that baby from Cambodia," Kimberly says. "Anyway, I have to go. Matt's here and we're going to go picket Abercrombie."

Great. Kimberly who doesn't *believe* in monogamy has a date for the wedding she doesn't even plan to attend. Now I have to have one or I'll look like the pathetic sister, the one in need of pity blind dates.

Before I can think more on this, my phone rings. My caller ID says it's a number I don't recognize. *If it's a telemarketer, maybe he's single,* I think.

I pick up.

"Jenny! It's John. Remember me?" John is a guy I met a month ago on *Daybreak Chicago.* He was a guest on the show, an expert in video games, who had advice for parents worried that their kids were exposed to too much video game violence. He asked me out for drinks and we went—two weeks ago. There were no major catastrophes or major sparks, and I have not heard from him since.

"Oh, hi," I say, caught off guard. I have forgotten what John looked like.

"I've been meaning to call you," John says. "Jenny, the time just got away from me."

"It's Jen, actually."

"Right—sorry—my bad."

There's a small pause.

"So, I ran into your assistant, Anne, the other day," John says. "And it came up that you were Japanese. I had no idea."

I wonder how my race came up in a casual conversation but I don't ask.

"Half, actually," I say, thinking that I should wear a name tag on all my dates—one that reads "Hello, I'm half-Japanese" for all the boys who are too polite to ask.

"You know I once visited Tokyo," John is saying.

"Really?" I have never been. In college, I once considered studying in Japan for a semester. I abandoned this plan, however, after an awkward exchange with Hashimoto, our resident Japanese exchange student, who told me that in Japan people like me who are half-white and half-Japanese are thought to have large sexual appetites and do not care about protecting their virtue. He could have been lying, but even so, I figured maybe he knew something I didn't. Maybe people who look like me in Japan walk around with giant red E's on their chests for Easy.

"Listen, this is going to sound weird, but I was wondering if maybe you want to get together sometime." John asks. "Watch a movie maybe?"

I agree to meet John the following Saturday, even though I suspect he has an AO blood type, meaning Asian Obsessed. It explains why he started to take more of an interest in me after he discovered my part-Asian heritage. That happens with a lot of guys.

AO blood types can be all right. After all, I'm not going to attract the same kind of guy whose dream date is Anna Kournikova. At the same time, you want to be sure that the guy you're dating doesn't just see you as a two-dimensional sex fantasy. But given my lack of current dating prospects, an AO blood type is as good as any.

When I arrive at John's apartment a little after seven the following Saturday, my suspicions are confirmed. I discover his apartment is littered with Asian artifacts, which I suspect came from Pier One. Above his fireplace, there's a giant scroll filled with Chinese characters. John is wearing a shirt with Japanese animation on it—which is a scantily clad Asian beauty who is wielding two swords. I am beginning to think that John might not only be an AO blood type, he might also suffer a bit from Nerd Lust. Nerd Lust should not be confused with your garden-variety Man Lust (topless strippers, Man Show Girls on Trampolines).

Nerd Lust involves lusting after women who are largely fictional characters, typically in comic books or cartoons, who have ridiculously unrealistic features (size double-D boobs, but a twenty-inch waist) and who know martial arts or some other sort of deadly hand-to-hand combat. They can also be fairies, vampires, *Star Trek* aliens, or any additional otherworldly creatures, as long as they wear spandex or leather and can fight while wearing stilettos. Nerd Lust has the added feature of putting women on pedestals (i.e., having them kick a ridiculous amount of ass, like Trinity in *The Matrix*). I haven't decided whether putting a woman on a pedestal is better than putting her on a trampoline.

John interrupts my thoughts by handing me hot sake in a cup without handles that has more Chinese characters on the side.

A friend from college once traveled to Japan for a semester in college. She said that half the people walking around were wearing shirts with English words on them like "Toast" or "Hand" or "Spoon." Things that made no sense whatsoever. It's probably the same with all the Chinese letters. The giant framed picture above John's fireplace probably says nothing more inspirational or profound than "Lamp Shade." His shirt might even say something equally meaningless like "Elbow."

I think about Britney Spears, who got a Japanese tattoo on her hip that she thought said "Mysterious" but its actual translation was "Strange."

After I'm settled on his sofa, John immediately presents the DVD box set of *Shogun* starring Richard Chamberlain.

I'm not sure what to say. I haven't seen this since I was ten. All I can think is *I could be at work. I have a million things to do and I'm going to watch* Shogun?

"I thought you loved this miniseries," he says.

I don't think I said "love" exactly. I think I said I thought it was "funny." What I remember of it involves a lot of grunting samurai, giggling geishas, and ritualized suicide.

"I thought we could watch it tonight," John says.

"Okay, great," I say, not at all sure it is.

For dinner, John serves sushi he's bought from God knows where. Sushi these days is as common as hot dogs. He's gotten all the most gruesome raw varieties, too: octopus, eel, squid. Despite being half-Japanese, I am strictly a cooked-meat-only sushi eater (your cucumber rolls, your California rolls) with the minor exception of tuna, which, for some reason is the only fish that doesn't make me gag. The thought of eating anything with suction cups makes me feel a bit queasy. When he offers me a slab of white and purple octopus, I politely decline.

The sushi is stale. Probably bought from a chain grocery store. The rice is hard and the seaweed wrap is far too chewy. John, however, doesn't seem to be aware of the bad taste. If the rice is stale, I can only imagine how the octopus is. I think of Grandma Saddie, who likes to talk at length about how sushi is a gourmet delicacy that shouldn't be consumed casually like French fries.

As I watch, John digs into the worst sushi specimens while I nibble on a few pieces of pickled ginger.

Halfway through the first DVD (of a set of five) John leans over and asks me what one of the samurais who is speaking Japanese is saying. Apparently this miniseries never bothered with subtitles. The idea, I guess, is to view the whole story from Richard Chamberlain's point of view. He is the English sailor who finds himself marooned on the island of Japan in the eleventh century.

"I don't know," I say.

"I thought you were Japanese."

"Half," I correct. "Only my grandma speaks Japanese." Vivien, I don't add, speaks in a thick Southern twang. "But I did take Japanese classes in college."

I omit the fact that I dropped out after only two weeks. I had to learn the hard way that my DNA didn't give me a leg up on Japanese.

"Are you sure you're really Japanese?" he asks me, part-teasing, part-serious.

This time I don't bother to correct him.

I decide then and there to start making up answers when he asks me to translate again.

"He did not just call Richard Chamberlain a white devil," John exclaims, catching me on my fake translating.

"The Japanese words for 'white devil' and 'more sake please' are very close in sound," I say.

John looks at me as if he's not sure whether I'm kidding. But he doesn't ask me to translate anymore.

I decide not to comment when John yells, "Yeah! That's what I'm talking about," when Richard Chamberlain is offered a simpering Japanese consort to fulfill all his household and manly needs.

Every five minutes it seems that someone white in the movie is calling the Japanese "Jappos." If Kimberly were here, she'd set the DVD on fire. But even I find this annoying and say so.

"You've got to cut them some slack, it's just old," John says.

I'm reminded of the time in college when my roommate, Carrie, and I were watching *Breakfast at Tiffany's* and I was try-ing to explain why the upstairs Asian neighbor with the thick glasses and the buck teeth was so offensive.

"But they didn't know better at the time," Carrie had said.

"Then why are you laughing now?"

"Because it's still funny," she said. "He reminds me of my grandma."

"An annoying caricature of an Asian man reminds you of your Irish grandmother?"

"They both hate loud music," she'd said at the time.

Carrie, who calls her ability to hold liquor her Ancient Irish Secret, finds it hilarious when I "get racial." She says I'm the whitest person she knows (which is why in college she used to call me a Twinkie, as in yellow on the outside, white on the inside). I prefer, however, to think of myself as successfully assimilated.

John massages the back of my neck, then starts the not-so-subtle move-in move: the precursor to kissing.

I try not to think that the source of John's ardor may be the fact that we just spent three hours watching geisha consorts baby-stepping around in kimonos.

"You're beautiful," he tells me, out of the blue.

Since I have never been good with compliments, I shrug. Secretly, I love the sound of this, but what I don't love is the smell of octopus on his breath. I pull back slightly.

"Can you excuse me for one minute?" I ask him, squeezing away from him and going to the bathroom to regroup and decide what to do next.

In his bathroom, which is decorated with bamboo wallpaper and has a shower curtain painted with Japanese paper lanterns, I take a deep breath and try to figure out if my sexual drought (going on six months) and my need for a date to Kevin Peterson's wedding outweigh the fact that I am not even remotely attracted to John.

This is why I don't have a boyfriend, I think. I am far too picky. What's wrong with John? Aside from his AO blood-type tendencies. He isn't repulsive, objectively. He's not brain dead. He's average in looks. And yet . . . what am I waiting for? An adult Kevin Peterson?

I realize again why I don't spend much time dating. It's because I just end up feeling that I'm never going to find the right guy. It seems like a waste of time.

I flush the toilet and turn on the faucet to wash my hands. I search around the bathroom for a hand towel. Finding none in obvious places, I open the cabinet below the sink to look for one.

And there it is, a box with one flap closed and the other open and in it, I can see, are stacks of videotapes. I realize I should probably close the cabinet doors, but I work at a news station, for heaven's sake. I have to look.

I pull out the box and take a closer look at those tapes.

The one on top is called *Asian Girls Gone Wild.*

There are others: *Barely Legal: Tokyo, Asian Sluts* (one through three), *Mistress Chin's Asian Academy Part II,* and *Lin Rides the Oriental Express,* which I don't think has anything to do with the Orient Express. There is no white porn here, only Asian porn. And worse, below these tapes are Japanese adult comic books, the kind in which cartoons have sex with other cartoons; on the cover of one book a giant blue monster with four supersize dicks is raping two women simultaneously.

Okay. Asian porn I might be able to deal with. Emphasis on the "might." But the weird X-rated comic books? I have to draw the line there.

"Are you okay?" John asks, giving the door a soft knock.

"Uh, no . . ." I say, putting on my best fake food-poisoning voice and flushing the toilet again. "I think that sushi was bad."

There goes, I think, *my best and last hope for a date to Kevin Peterson's wedding.*

Five

Breathe in through nose. Out through mouth.
Don't forget to breathe. Very important.

—Mr. Miyagi, *The Karate Kid*

1981

I first saw Kevin Peterson at the Presidential Fitness Challenge, a grueling, three-day contest of athletic ability on the grade-school playground not matched until the 1984 Olympic Games in Los Angeles.

Normal recess activities (avoiding bullies while simultaneously attempting to get chosen for kick-ball teams) were suspended for three days, during which we all competed for a coveted Presidential Fitness Patch—the reward for achieving the highest levels of fitness. We were graded in three categories: aerobic fitness (running laps and jumping rope), upper body strength (push-ups and chin-ups), and core strength (sit-ups).

I was in no shape for serious physical sport, since the most exercise I got was fetching Coke from the refrigerator during commercial breaks of *Green Acres* (which I watched religiously after school, along with reruns of *Buck Rogers, Bewitched,* and *I Dream of Jeannie*). That is, when I managed to properly wrestle away the remote from Kimberly, who preferred to watch *Family Feud* and *Good Times.*

There was very little to do in Dixieland, and TV was a real escape, so it's no wonder that I ended up working in television.

As a kid, I'd break from TV only long enough to get my Stouffer's TV dinner and TV tray, and then the whole family would settle in for the main event: Prime Time. Time was measured in sitcoms, not hours. My bedtime fell, technically, at 9 P.M. Central Time, but more often than not, the entire family would be so engrossed in any given CBS or ABC lineup that I'd wind up watching a good fifteen or twenty minutes of *Hart to Hart* or *Trapper John, M.D.* before anyone noticed I was still awake.

Contrary to the belief at the White House, training your body to be still for seven hours a day required a certain kind of mental toughness. I had learned to move beyond numbness in my fingers and toes, shortness of breath, and muscles that were too soft and atrophied to properly pedal a bicycle for more than three blocks. And while the Cokes I drank sucked precious calcium from my stagnant bones, my mind was introduced to new and exotic places like Hawaii and Milwaukee.

Not to mention, I was learning important life lessons from television, including:

How to Properly Slide on the Hood of a Car (*T.J. Hooker* and *The Dukes of Hazzard*).

Be Careful What You Wish For, It Might Come True (*Fantasy Island*).

Voice-overs Are Helpful for Solving Crimes (*Magnum, P.I.; Simon and Simon; Matt Houston*).

Cross Dressing Is Okay if Done for Comic Effect (*M*A*S*H, Three's Company, Bosom Buddies*).

Abject Poverty Can Be Swell (*Good Times, Alice, Sanford and Son*).

I felt sure what I had learned from television could transfer into the know-how I would need to "pass" the Physical Fitness Challenge. Besides, Ronald Reagan said ketchup counted as a vegetable in the school lunch program. A president who saw nutritional value in condiments couldn't be all that concerned with serious physical fitness.

I had never attempted chin-ups, push-ups, or sit-ups before. Nor had I really run for any length of time, except in short sprints to flee Debbie Kenilworth, a notorious playground bully who had mastered the ability to inflict swift and tender bruises by punching your arm with her middle knuckle extended for maximum impact. Aside from that, I hadn't done much running per se. But I had spent hours watching people on television run, and it didn't seem that hard. Thomas Magnum ran all the time and he barely broke a sweat, even though he lived in a tropical climate with 90 percent humidity.

Naturally, the first two days of the contest, Kevin Peterson, who had just moved to Dixieland from Little Rock, dominated the competition. No one could catch him. He was the Bruce Jenner of the Dixieland Elementary playground. And with every contest he won, he racked up more popularity points.

I, on the other hand, barely kept from failing out of the challenge altogether. After coming in dead last in the running competition (note to self: Jelly shoes that make your feet sweat and give you crisscross blisters don't lead to speed on the blacktop), I had only the chin-up event left to prove that I had what it took to finish in second-to-last place.

As luck would have it, Kevin Peterson was assigned to my group. He took to the chin bar like he'd been doing it all his life; as if, instead of sinking into brown shag carpet to watch *Falcon's Crest* or *The Fall Guy*, he actually lifted weights.

His arms began to get a bit shaky only after twenty chin-ups, and even after that, he managed to finish ten more before he dropped from the bar with athletic ease and said simply, "That's it for me," as if he'd just decided he'd watched too much television for one day.

All the other kids around the bar stood and stared. We knew we had been out-done. No one could possibly do that many chin-ups. Nobody.

Miss Owens, our PE teacher, took her clipboard out and scratched down Kevin's number, informing the rest of the class that he had just achieved a school record.

Then came my turn. Now, I had convinced myself that I should at least do one chin-up, and that maybe if I did I might attract the attention or even admiration of Kevin Peterson. I kicked one Jelly shoe toe into the dirt and swung my arms back and forth, willing the muscles in them to come alive, even though the heaviest thing I'd lifted in my life was my Barbie Dream House. And it was made mostly of cardboard.

I reached up and tightened my grip around the bar. I think I could hear the opening chords of Survivor's "Eye of the Tiger" from *Rocky III* starting to play. I checked the stance of my feet and adjusted my fingertips on the grip as if I were a weight lifter at the Olympics. Of course, I was just trying to buy time before I actually had to try to lift myself. I'd never tried lifting my body weight before, and I was fairly certain that I wouldn't be able to do it.

"Whenever you're ready, Miss Taylor," Miss Owens said, tapping her pencil on her clipboard, her voice clearly sarcastic, and while she hadn't added "princess" to the end of the sentence, you could tell by her tone that she wanted to.

It's now or never, I think.

I pulled at the bar with all the strength I had in my softened muscles, fueled by Little Debbie Snack Cakes with corn syrup, praying that the adrenaline surging through my veins from knowing that Kevin Peterson was watching me would push me to new fantastic heights of strength, kind of like the mother I saw on *That's Incredible* who lifted a car to save her son pinned underneath.

My eyes were squeezed tight and I felt my face turn red from exertion, and then I heard the voice of Miss Owens.

"We're waiting," she said.

I opened my eyes.

My feet were still on the ground. I hadn't even budged a centimeter. My arms, like strands of spaghetti, had no strength in them at all.

"I tried already," I admitted to Miss Owens.

"You didn't try," she corrected me. "Now, go on. Don't make me send you to the principal's office."

The principal's office was a dreaded place where children suffered corporal punishment at the hands of a sadistic, grinning maniac wielding a flat wooden paddle. "Spare the rod, spoil the child" was a phrase used in Arkansas for years after corporal punishment went out of vogue.

I tried again, this time adding a little grunt for effect.

Some of the boys started snickering. Debbie Kenilworth called me a dork.

And then Kevin Peterson stepped forward, saving me from a trip to the principal's office and from further public humiliation. Maybe he liked me. Or maybe he just took pity on me. Whatever the case, he stepped out and said, "She just needs a jump start."

Then he wrapped his arms around my waist and lifted me with surprising ease. Kevin Peterson released me, and I hung there, my chin well above the bar, my arms folded at the elbows and straining to hold myself up. I lasted one second there and then awkwardly dropped to the gravel.

Miss Owens said the chin-up didn't count, but by that point it didn't matter. Kevin Peterson, the fastest, strongest, and coolest boy in class, had helped me, and I could feel his popularity rubbing off on me like glitter.

And just like that I fell in love.

Six

Miyagi once had mother, too.
—Mr. Miyagi, *The Karate Kid*

"I know you're there!" Vivien sings into my answering machine Sunday morning. Vivien is a morning person and has probably been up since five. My mother is one of those overly industrious people like Donald Trump who claim to need only four hours of sleep a night. "Answer the phone, Jen. I know you're there! Nakamuras, we always know."

Despite her married name of Taylor, my mother still refers to herself as a Nakamura. Bubba even jokes that one day he'll have his name legally changed. One of the reasons Vivien doesn't want to give up the Nakamura name is that she thinks the Nakamura family is connected by ESP. I call this phenomenon "Nakamura Telepathy"—the ability to sense what's happening in other people's lives without actually talking.

Nakamura Telepathy has never been proven. As far as I know, no one in my mother's family has ever accurately predicted a car crash, an earthquake, or even a hangnail. Why the Nakamuras couldn't just conjure up some useful information like lotto numbers, I don't know. It's like some completely useless superpower. If my mother were a member of the Justice League, her power would be the ability to always point out the obvious. Would she be able to deflect bullets? No. But she'd be able to wear down bad guys just by pretending to know everything they planned to do well in advance.

"Pick up the phone," Vivien commands. "I have BIG news. BIG." Big news for Vivien qualifies as anything she read in the *National Enquirer.*

Vivien continues. "I think I found the perfect date for you for the wedding. Remember Billy Connor? Well, he's single and . . ."

Billy Connor is the boy in fifth grade who once ate an entire canister of goldfish food for a dollar. I scramble out of bed to pick up the phone, which is on the other side of the room.

"Hello? Hello!"

"I knew you were there," Vivien says, sounding smug.

"I am not going on a date with Billy Connor."

"But he's such a nice boy," Vivien exclaims.

"He once ate dirt on a dare," I remind her. "The kids used to call him 'The Hoover' because he'd eat anything if you paid him a dollar. Even worms."

"Really?" Vivien asks, sounding surprised. "Well, he's an Arkansas State Trooper now."

"The state actually gave him a gun?"

"Apparently."

"Another reason not to date him." This is not the first time Vivien has attempted to play matchmaker with someone from Dixieland. It's the diehard Japanese mother in her that's led to the incessant matchmaking. Despite the fact that she's claimed to have forgotten every single Japanese phrase she once knew, there are some things that are far too ingrained in the Asian DNA to avoid. Like the desire for parents to arrange their children's weddings.

"Ya-shee, it was only a suggestion," Vivien says. "Ya-shee" is the hissing sound all the women in my family make. My mother and my grandmother both do it when they're frustrated or startled. I don't know if it actually has any Japanese meaning or if it's just a spitting sound.

"I'm just saying I'm not sure why you and your sister aren't married yet." Given Vivien's love of good weddings (she roused me from bed to watch Princess Di walk down the aisle, and let me stay home from school to watch Luke and Laura get married on *General Hospital*), it's no wonder she's anxious for one of her two daughters to get married. "You're pretty girls."

"Maybe we don't want to be married," I suggest.

"Ya-shee!" Vivien exclaims. "You always have to be a smart alan."

"I think you mean smart aleck." Vivien is always mixing up her metaphors—the result, I think, of speaking only Japanese until age six.

"Same difference. Anyway, speaking of your sister, have you heard from her lately?"

"No," I lie.

"I've been calling her, but I think her phone is broken."

I think this is what's called screening, but I don't say so.

"Anyhow, if you do, tell her we still need her dress measurements," Vivien adds. "The early horse gets the worm you know."

"I think you mean bird. Horses don't eat worms."

"Whatever. Same difference," Vivien says, dismissive. "So? You sure you don't want to go with Billy Connor?"

"No," I say, firmly.

"What about Danny Webber?"

"Absolutely not." Webber is the one who used to drag-race cars in the alley behind the Dairy Queen in high school. In my yearbook, he wrote "Dude—school sucks!" but spelled "sucks" "sux."

"Well, there are plenty of other eligible bachelors in Dixieland. If you lived here . . ."

"Mom, I prefer my boyfriends to have all their original teeth."

"Ya-shee, so much a drama princess. I'm the one who has to live with your Aunt Teri. You know she's been strutting around here like the cat that ate the parrot."

"Canary," I correct.

Vivien barrels on. "She just can't help rubbing it in, you know. About her daughter getting married first. You'd think she was the only mother ever to have a daughter get married."

Vivien is very competitive. The fact that her sister-in-law's daughter is getting married before either of hers is very disconcerting. Vivien is in a constant contest of one-upmanship with

everyone in the family. When I got my master's degree in journalism, the first in the family to go for an advanced degree, she
photocopied the diploma and gave it, framed, to every other
member of the family at Christmas.

"Ya-shee, I'd have an easier time setting you up if I saw you
more often," Vivien says. "I barely remember what my own
daughter looks like! At least Kimberly comes home for Thanksgiving."

Here it is, the Guilt Trip. It happens in every one of my conversations with Vivien, who doesn't understand why I am not
home to visit every three months like Kimberly. Of course, ex-
plaining that Kimberly's part-time work for a nonprofit organization for women's rights in Asia allows her more flexibility than
my ten days of vacation time a year generally falls on deaf ears.

"You know I'm busy . . ." I start.

"Ya-shee—what's more important? Your family should be
more important than anything," Vivien scolds me.

"But—"

"Anyway, I'm going to play bridge next week. I'll find you a
date there. The women are always trying to set up their divorced sons."

Vivien often acts as if finding a boyfriend is as easy as or-
dering takeout. If I could have an acceptable boyfriend delivered, then I would have one by now.

"Mom, I don't want to date a Dixieland divorcé."

"Ya-shee, I've raised such an ungrateful daughter!" Vivien
wails. "When I die—and it'll be soon—you probably won't
even come to my funeral."

"Mo-ther!"

"It's true. You know the women in the Nakamura family don't live long. And I have high cholesterol!"

"You're fifty-seven. And Grandma Saddie is seventy-five. Her mother lived until she was ninety."

"Ya-shee. Still. I have high cholesterol! I'm going to die without grandchildren. And Teri will gloat at my funeral."

"Aunt Teri won't gloat."

"Ya-shee, you just watch her!"

If possible, it's even more imperative that I find a date. There is, I notice at four in the morning on Monday, a woeful shortage of single men at *News Four*. There's Cameraman Barry, recently divorced father of two; Twice Jonathan (twice married, twice divorced, and twice my age), and Dude Chris, the station's nineteen-year-old intern who can't begin or end a sentence without inserting the word "dude."

I shake myself. Now is not the time to be looking for a date. I have work to do.

I start trying to organize which news stories should go first. It's all about flow in TV news. You don't want to have a terrorism story lead into a feature about a waterskiing squirrel. And that's part of what I like about being a producer. I get to take a bunch of bits and pieces of news that don't fit and put them together like a jigsaw puzzle.

I get up and check the fax machine for press releases and see none. I do, however, find Michelle's résumé on the fax, along with a cover letter to one of our competitor stations.

Once again, not a very smart move by Michelle. I take the résumé and cover letter and put them on her desk. *Let her wonder who put them there,* I think.

Back at my desk, an instant message pops up on my computer.

It's from Nigel Riley, who also works at *News Four,* running the station's website. He also has been, at one time or another, every girl's crush in the office. He's fit, dark and handsome, speaks in a clipped British accent, and is known as "The Colins" for his resemblance to both Colin Firth and Colin Farrell. He also happens to be one of my closest friends, and because he has a live-in girlfriend, I have not permitted myself to think of him as anything more. Correction: I haven't *often* allowed myself to think of him as anything more.

Riley is also a raging insomniac and says he needs only three hours of sleep a night so he often catches me online.

Riley was raised in London and has an American-born mother who claims his father's brother is an earl. Riley also has an encyclopedic knowledge of the sport of rugby, of which he is a great fan, including a rather dubious-sounding team called the Harlequins or Quins for short, which, Riley assures me, is a very manly team despite its romance-novel-sounding name. Riley's online name is Rugger, slang for rugby.

RUGGER9: How was your date with John Boy?

Riley's second-favorite hobby, next to playing rugby with a

ragtag bunch of amateurs who call themselves the Chicago Blast, is making fun of the men I date.

JEN76: I found his Asian/monster porn stash. I had to fake food poisoning.

RUGGER9: LMAO (stands for "laughing my ass off" for you nontechnical types).

JEN76: I know what LMAO is, thank you. You've used it enough times in reference to my love life.

RUGGER9: Tsk. Tsk. Bitter? Party of One?

JEN76: Don't make me come over there and hurt you.

RUGGER9: You know that I'm a lover not a fighter.

JEN76: ☹

RUGGER9: ☺ Ah, poor John. You should give the bloke another chance. Every guy has a porn stash.

JEN76: His was ALL Asian porn. Does your porn stash have a "theme"?

RUGGER9: My porn stash is the United Nations of porn. I take all races, creeds, and religions. I feel it's my responsibility to do so, as a citizen of the world.

JEN76: Very nice. Well, his porn stash included Japanese cartoons. Women raped by monsters and such.

RUGGER9: Aren't the Japanese your people? You should be used to the Japanese perv tendencies.

JEN76: You shouldn't judge a culture by its porn.

RUGGER9: Why not? Seems as good a meter stick as any. ☺

"Hi Jen! How are you? We're going to have beautiful weather today!"

This is Fred, our meteorologist, appearing from seemingly nowhere. He's very stealthy. He makes no noise when he walks, and then he's suddenly right over your shoulder piping cheerful accolades. He, like every other weatherman I've ever met, is always far too upbeat for four in the morning.

Quickly, I shut my IM window. It figures Fred would appear during the thirty seconds of my day when I'm not actually doing work.

"How's the weather today?" I ask Fred.

"I'm going to put in an order of sunshine to the Big Guy just for you," he says, sending me his too-white smile that almost looks blue under the station's fluorescent lights. This is what he tells me every morning, even if it's raining. He seems to be on intimate terms with the "Big Guy" since he references him in every other sentence.

"Say, you training for the marathon this year?" Fred asks me. As I never train for the marathon, and I don't see the point of running unless someone is chasing me, I shake my head.

"Oh, you should try it," he says. Fred is a wiry, thin man who is always trying to talk to people about the highs you get from marathon running. "Seriously, try it. I could help you train."

"I don't think so, Fred." I don't know if Fred is just insanely obsessed with running or if this is part of some really lame come-on. He's been trying to get me to run with him for months.

"Well, I'll leave you to it," Fred says. He leaves my cube, whistling.

I pull up my IM window.

JEN76: Sorry. It was Mr. Weather.
RUGGER9: Tell Fred to FOOK off. ☹

When Riley says "fuck" it sounds like "fook," which is what he uses in IM. Along with "shite" for shit and "jaysis" for Jesus.

RUGGER9: Wanker Fred. Wank. Wank. Wanker.

Riley and Fred do not get along. This is mainly because Fred keeps saying "G'day, mate" to Riley, because Fred can't tell the difference between a British and an Australian accent. Being mistaken for an Australian is one of many pitfalls, Riley says, of living in the States. Furthermore, Riley says he is distrustful of anyone who is always so upbeat. His theory is that only serial killers can maintain that level of cheerfulness. "Think about how happy you'd be if you killed anyone who annoyed you," Riley says.

JEN76: Unlike you, I am not the son of an earl's brother. I need this job.
RUGGER9: The second bastard nephew of a bankrupt earl, which means I am 344th in line to the throne. However, you can call me "your majesty" if you'd like.
JEN76: You're in America, now. This is a democracy.

RUGGER9: That's where all you Yanks got it wrong.

JEN76: ☹

RUGGER9: ☺

RUGGER9: So, what are you going to do about the Hee Haw wedding?

JEN76: Take you, if you keep calling it that.

RUGGER9: You should take me. I've always wanted to visit the set of *Deliverance*.

JEN76: You aren't funny.

RUGGER9: Thousands of my loyal (and indentured) English subjects beg to disagree.

I would love to take Riley to Kevin Peterson's wedding, but I doubt I could live with the torture of spending a weekend with him with all my impure thoughts. Riley is all the things I'd want for my grown-up Kevin Peterson. He's funny, smart, and handsome (he's not called The Colins for nothing) and—above that—he seems genuinely interested in me, if only to make jokes about my love life.

Sometimes when I'm standing close to him and I catch that unique Riley scent (something like clean laundry and vanilla), I have to resist the urge to put my hands on him. I know that being together for forty-eight hours means that at some point I'd probably make a fool of myself. And the last words I want to hear are "You're a great girl . . . but . . ." The but, of course, being his practically perfect girlfriend, Tiffany.

I met Tiffany at a bar during a casual happy hour after work celebrating the fact that one of our anchors was nominated for an Emmy. Tiffany was tall, skinny, beautiful, and carried the kind of confidence only tall, skinny, gorgeous women have—the sort that's built up from years of being the target of all the best come-ons in bars, of looking at women's magazines and actually having her self-image improve, and of being able to take a size two into a dressing room and sigh, "This just hangs on me."

In other words, the sort of glamorous life I could only imagine.

I expected to hate Tiffany on principle, but Tiffany was funny. More than funny, crass. She belched. She downed entire beers in one, open-throat gulp. She had an impressive knowledge of Cubs baseball. Worse, I couldn't even say she was dumb, since she graduated from Princeton. There was literally no way on earth I could compete with her. She could be any man's soul mate. And she didn't even have the courtesy to be mean or petty with me. She actually showed interest in me, included me in the conversation, and complimented me on my shoes.

Despite all her obvious attributes, she also had an honest, down-to-earth quality that simply sucked you in. She was impossible to hate. And I hated her for it.

Even worse, she had her own PR firm, and thereafter became responsible for giving me some of my best morning show guests, including Mayor Daley, Kirsten Dunst, and *Bachelor* stars Alex Michel and Andrew Firestone.

I should simply get used to the idea of going to the wedding alone, but something, namely the idea of seeing Kevin Peterson again, makes me feel that if only I could find someone willing to be my date, I could manage to scrape together the dignity that eluded me as a ten-year-old. I am very close to calling an escort service. The only thing stopping me is the image of the stripper that arrived at my friend Carrie's bachelorette party two years ago. He was a greasy, hairy little guy who kept gyrating his pelvis in people's faces, and when he wasn't doing that he was shaking his G-string-clad butt nauseatingly close to the guacamole dip. The thought of some hairy guy slick with baby oil asking Grandma Saddie if she wants "the windmill" during the wedding reception makes me abandon that plan entirely.

I glance over at Fred, the meteorologist. He's doing his warm-up exercises for his face and voice, which make him look like a fish gasping for air. *No,* I think, *I'm not that desperate. Yet.*

Seven

You no look answer in Miyagi. Like bonsai live
inside tree, answer live inside you.
—Mr. Miyagi, *The Karate Kid III*

1982

On Halloween in 1982, I tried to convince Grandma Saddie to let me borrow one of her old kimonos so that I could go as a Kung Fu Princess. This was an idea that I'd somehow gleaned from old Bruce Lee movies and the Hong Kong Phooey cartoon, with the janitor dog who moonlighted as a martial arts expert.

Not to mention I somehow thought being a Kung Fu Princess would impress Kevin Peterson. I'd be both boyish and tough (the kung fu part) but also girly and alluring (the princess part).

Back then, I didn't realize there was a difference between kung fu and karate (for instance, that one was Chinese and one was Japanese), although Grandma Saddie informed me of this fact quickly.

"You aren't Chinese!" she exclaimed when I told her I wanted to be a Kung Fu Princess. Grandma Saddie was even less enamored of the idea of my wobbling around in her platform Japanese sandals, which I started calling "flip-flops on stilts."

"Ya-shee!" she'd exclaim in alarm when I'd wobble out in the family room in her mother's shoes.

Grandma Saddie would often call her mother's heirlooms "ugly" or "not very interesting." She would say, of the kimono that she married in, "Oh, it's so ugly, that thing!"

But I later came to realize that she didn't *really* think they were ugly. It was more of a show of false modesty. The more she called something ugly and useless, the more she really thought it was beautiful and precious.

It turns out that her parents—and many of the issei (first) generation who immigrated to America—believed that bragging about one's possessions or accomplishments was the worst thing you could do. This was a learned behavior and not genetic, since Kimberly would often run through the house with her report card littered with gold stars and demand that Vivien submit her story to Ripley's *Believe It or Not* for "smartest living girl on earth."

After Grandma Saddie told me I could not be a Kung Fu Princess for Halloween, naturally, I set my sights on being Princess Leia. She was the next-best thing to a Kung Fu Princess. Kimberly, however, immediately claimed that *she* had already decided to be Princess Leia, and because she could pinch harder and she outweighed me by thirty pounds, she won. Kimberly suggested I go as Han Solo so that I could be her "date" (a Han Solo that was four inches shorter than his Princess Leia). In the end, I went as a Regular Old Princess, wearing a plastic tiara and a gauzy pink dress made out of ballerina tutus, which seemed highly anticlimatic, although Vivien tried to convince me that Regular Old Princesses still held a degree of mystique.

To prove her point, Vivien decided to dress up as a princess, too. A Real Life Princess: Princess Di. Vivien had been enamored with Princess Di ever since she had roused us all out of bed at three in the morning in 1981 so we could watch the live procession of her wedding to Prince Charles. Somehow, Vivien got her hands on a blond feathered wig and a powder blue suit, but even when she put on a tiara, no one could guess who she was trying to be. She looked like an Asian man in drag.

Kimberly would later call Vivien's insistence on being Princess Di for Halloween "racial amnesia"—which is the ability to disassociate yourself from your true ethnic identity. It's a term that she would later apply to Alan Keyes, Clarence Thomas, Justin Timberlake, and Vanilla Ice. The Nakamuras all had brushes with racial amnesia. It's why they still occasionally used the word "Oriental," and not in an ironic sense.

It was probably developed as a safety mechanism, like a chameleon's ability to blend into its environment and elude predators. If you pretended you weren't Japanese, and tried to look *less* Japanese, maybe people wouldn't notice that you actually were Japanese.

*   *   *

Vivien had her share of prejudice to deal with, after all. Take her in-laws. My father's family disapproved of his marrying what they called "Bubba's Little Geisha" and refused even to attend the wedding under the erroneous assumption that the Nakamuras could not speak English. Eventually, my paternal grandparents overcame some of their prejudices, after Kimberly was born. They even started coming over for Thanksgiving after Bubba convinced them we eat cooked turkey, not giant slabs of raw fish.

Aunt Teri, Bubba's younger sister, was far more open-minded than my grandparents. Then again, Aunt Teri moved to Chinatown in San Francisco in 1977 hoping to find some remnants of hippie free love but instead got a whole lot of disco.

She returned to Dixieland two weeks before Halloween in 1982, very obviously pregnant and unmarried, and claiming to have fallen in love with a man named Patrick Woo, who was wanted in five states for check fraud. It was only later that we would learn, after Lucy was born, that her father's name—Woo—was actually short for "Woodstein." Disowned by her very conservative parents, Aunt Teri came to live with Bubba and Vivien, even though Vivien did not approve of "Aunt Teri's lifestyle" or her being a role model for my sister and me.

While living in San Francisco, Aunt Teri adopted many Chinese customs as her own, including avidly following the Chinese zodiac, drinking green tea, wearing Chinese dresses, and cooking Chinese food. Every morning she'd insist on brewing a giant pot of oolong tea, and when Vivien wasn't looking, she'd read our *I Ching* fortunes. Vivien, who had just gotten her real estate license, also didn't approve of Aunt Teri's "free-loading" and told us on more than one occasion that only "lazy hippies" live in California. Vivien told my sister and me, "See what happens when you go to California?"

Vivien was referring to the fact that Aunt Teri had gotten knocked up by a two-timing pathological liar, but Kimberly and I came to believe that living in California somehow turned you Chinese.

That Halloween, Aunt Teri wore a silk kimono she'd brought back with her from San Francisco, painted her face in kabuki makeup and put her blond hair up with lacquered sticks.

Aunt Teri's labor pains started that very night. Bubba had taken Kimberly and me out for trick or treating, and so it fell to Vivien, dressed in full Princess Di regalia, to drive Aunt Teri to the hospital. The two women arrived in the emergency room—one Asian woman dressed as a white woman, and a white woman dressed as an Asian woman.

Later that night, Aunt Teri gave birth to Lucy, whom she attempted to name Lin Woo, but Vivien persuaded her that the blond baby looked more like a Lucy than a Lin. Aunt Teri compromised and named her Lucy Lin Woo Taylor.

I suggested adding "Kung Fu Princess" to the name, but Vivien said there wasn't room on the birth certificate.

Eight

If karate use to defense honor, defend life,
karate mean something. If karate use to defend
plastic trophy, karate no mean nothing.

Mr. Miyagi, *The Karate Kid III*

Lucy calls me, sounding panicked. "You aren't supposed to bring a date," she breathes into the phone, without preamble, as if she, too, is a subscriber to Nakamura Telepathy. "Your reply card says two people. You weren't supposed to bring two."

"My invitation was addressed to me and a guest."

"But I didn't think you were seeing anybody," Lucy whines.

"Lucy! That doesn't mean I wouldn't want to bring a date."

"It's going to mess up the seating at the head table," Lucy says. She's got that high-pitched, squawking tone reserved for territorial pigeons and brides who are about to have a nervous breakdown while registering for place settings at Crate and Barrel.

"Lucy," I say, slowly and calmly so that I don't shout. I once read that the best strategy when dealing with injured animals and psychotic brides requires speaking in a calm voice and making no sudden movements. "I think you need to calm down."

"Jen. I have less than two weeks, and I don't have my *seating arrangements.*" Lucy sighs dramatically after the sentence, letting it sink in, as if she's just told me she has cancer. When I don't respond, she barrels on.

"This is a disaster!" she cries. "The most important day of my life and it's a disaster!"

I want to remind Lucy that she's only twenty, and if this is the most important day of her life she's going to have a whole lot of boring years ahead of her. But I don't.

I remember suddenly one Thanksgiving when Lucy was three and I was twelve. She threw the mother of all temper tantrums when Vivien refused to serve her pumpkin pie before the main course. She ended up hurling silverware from the children's table and breaking one of Vivien's prized crystal candlesticks.

"You said I could bring a date," I say, trying logic as my weapon.

"I didn't think you'd *take me up on it.*" Lucy sighs. "You don't even have a boyfriend!"

Another Lucy moment of note: her fifth birthday party, with a Winnie the Pooh theme, when she took the plates of cake away from each of her party guests claiming that it was *her* birthday cake and she wasn't going to share.

"Do you really have a date?" Lucy asks me.

I don't, but there's no way she's going to know that.

"Yes, I do," I say, resolute.

"Well, we'll have to get a longer head table." Lucy sighs. "But that means that I don't want you to *say* you're bringing a date and then not bring one, because I don't want empty place settings at the head table. I mean, how will *that* look in the pictures?"

"I have a date, Lucy."

"Are you sure you can't just ask him not to come?"

I bite my lip until it bleeds.

Nine

I say, you do, no question.
—Mr. Miyagi, *The Karate Kid*

1983

As a kid, my cousin Lucy was more spoiled than Blake Carrington's daughter on *Dynasty*. Kimberly and I were given strict orders: Lucy was to have anything she wanted. Viviean said we were to be extra nice to her *at all times* because Lucy's father (Patrick "Woo" Woodstein) was in jail for check fraud, and therefore she didn't really have a father like we did. We were supposed to somehow make up for this cosmic imbalance by letting Lucy play with (and thereby destroy) all of our toys.

When she started to crawl, she got into everything. She bit the heads off my Barbies. She flushed my Legos down the toilet. She cracked the door of my Easy-Bake oven, and she tore the firelike racing stripes off my Big Wheel. With her superhuman baby strength, she scattered and lost all the pins to my

Light Bright and completely demolished the elevator in Barbie's Dream House. Nothing she touched could be played with again, and when I'd go to Vivien to complain, she'd tell me to be patient and remember that Lucy didn't have a daddy.

Lucy had an appetite for destruction that would make Axl Rose proud. Lucy's first word was not "Mama" or "Auntie" or "Grandma." Lucy's first word was "mo" for "more" and this seemed fitting, since Lucy never had enough of anything. She wanted more food. More juice. More hugs. More airplane rides. More tickling. More toys to destroy. More everything. Nothing was ever enough.

And at the very hint that whoever was in front of her was not doing her every last bidding, she would erupt in ear-splitting cries that were guaranteed to make the most hardened man beg her to stop. For such a tiny baby (born at six pounds, one ounce) she had a set of lungs on her I hadn't heard since Patsy Cline. She could wail at a high and steady pitch for twenty minutes if not delivered "mo" of what she wanted, immediately.

Two decades later, I guess I shouldn't be surprised she's about to walk down the aisle with the man Aunt Teri's *I Ching* coins once said I'd marry.

Ten

One day you do own way.
—Mr. Miyagi, *The Karate Kid III*

"No, Jen, I'm sorry, but no, I can't be your date," says Jason, my old roommate. He's gay and has been my stand-by date since we used to live together in a small apartment in Wicker Park after college. Jason is now a corporate accountant who lusts after Carson on *Queer Eye for the Straight Guy* and spends his time keeping up an elaborate charade with his sixty-year-old conservative father about being straight.

"Do I have to remind you of your brother's wedding last year? You owe me one," I say.

Jason took me to his younger brother's wedding in Wisconsin last summer where there was no open bar, cocktails cost ten dollars apiece, and all of Jason's aunts (who were under the impression Jason and I were contemplating marriage) kept asking me whether I planned to breast-feed. At the end of the night, my bar tab was more than my plane ticket.

"I knooow," Jason wails, sounding backed into a corner. "I know. I'm a bad friend. A bad, bad, *bad* friend. If I could, I would. But I've got this business trip, and I can't get out of it."

"I hope this business trip isn't six one with blond hair."

Jason has a thing for blonds. See Carson from *Queer Eye*.

"No," Jason says, primly. "He's technically five ten."

"Jason!"

"I'm kidding. Just kidding. I have to go to Montreal to meet a client. You won't believe what they're asking me to do," Jason says. "But you know me, I'll lick the pole."

"Licking the pole" is Jason's term for being willing to do something extreme to advance your career. It comes from an interview he read featuring Elizabeth Berkley, former *Saved by the Bell* star, who said she won the dubious role in the Las Vegas stripper movie *Showgirls* because she was the only actress who licked the stripper pole during her audition.

"I am so sorry I can't go, though, really. You know I don't really believe you when you say you're from the South."

"I am from the South. Who would lie about something like that?"

"Well, let's look at the evidence. You have no accent. You're Asian, and I have never once heard you use the word 'ya'll.' I'd say that's about as anti-South as you can get."

"I worked hard to lose my accent," I protest. When I was in college, my roommate Carrie burst out laughing every time I said "ya'll," so I just stopped saying it.

"Not to mention, I have never even heard of an Asian person speaking in a Southern twang."

"You've heard my mother's answering machine messages," I

point out. Vivien always says "hiya, darlin'" in her easy Southern drawl.

"Yes, but I'm convinced your mother is white."

"Why would I lie? If I lied about where I'm from, I'd say I'm from Hawaii," I say. Hawaii, after all, is typically where people guess I'm from. "Besides, don't change the subject. I was trying to make you feel bad for not being my date."

"Look, I'll call around and see if I can find a replacement," Jason offers.

"I don't know." I hesitate. Some of Jason's "friends" aren't exactly the sort who would blend seamlessly into a small Dixieland wedding. Three years ago, Jason and a few of his closest friends walked in the Gay Pride Parade in Boys Town wearing only white skivvies, cowboy boots, and brown leather chaps.

"I'll see what I can do, okay?" Jason says. "Don't be mad at me, puhlease?"

Jason, the youngest of a Catholic family of five, lives in mortal fear of being the recipient of anyone's displeasure. This is one of many reasons he's still in the closet with his family.

"I'm not mad," I sigh.

"Good," Jason sings. "What about that guy from work?"

"Who?"

"The one who claims to have a girlfriend but who shows an unnatural interest in your love life."

"We're just friends."

"Um-hmmm."

"We are," I protest.

"Well, I'd bet he'd jump at the chance to go."

"You mean, if his girlfriend lets him," I say.

"If you asked him, I bet you a spa day at Mario Tricocci, he finds a way to go."

My phone conversation with Jason makes me happy, which I realize is wrong, and as instant karmic punishment, my cousin's bridesmaid's dress arrives, sent express from Vivien in Dixieland.

The dress is a hundred times worse than I could have imagined. For one thing, it is pink. In fact, it's more than pink; it's bright magenta. There are more ruffles on it than stretches of smooth fabric, and as I feared, there is no butt, per se, except for a giant flat bow the size of Rhode Island.

When I put the dress on and stand in front of the mirror I think, *Kevin Peterson is going to see me in this and instead of thinking "that's the girl I let get away," he's going to think "her ass is wider than Lake Michigan."*

"What the hell IS this?" Kimberly shouts into the phone the next morning while I'm at my desk at work. It's 10 A.M. and I'm trying to juggle two crises at once: the fact that yet another guest is canceling, this one for Wednesday's show, and Michelle is on the warpath because someone broke the handle off her coffee mug. "It looks like Kathy Lee Gifford threw up all over me."

"Well, at least it's. . . ." I try to think of something nice to say about the dress to calm Kimberly down. "At least it's not . . . uh . . . a Teletubby costume?"

"I'd rather have that," Kimberly says. "At least no one could recognize me in one of those."

"Did you get your plane ticket? We have to be in Dixieland in a few weeks."

"I told you I'm not going," Kimberly says, sounding resolute.

"You have to go."

"I'm trying to abide by my political beliefs. I object to this wedding—and this dress—on principle."

"You're going to the wedding, even if I have to fly you there myself."

"I just want to know how they knew my dress size," Kimberly says. "I've been deliberately avoiding their calls!"

I don't tell Kimberly that I secretly sent Vivien her measurements for the dress—going largely from memory.

"You'd better buy your plane ticket right now, or I'm going to donate twenty dollars to the Republican Party in your name," I say.

Since Kimberly calls George W. Bush, Donald Rumsfeld, and John Ashcroft the Triumvirate of Evil, she reacts to this in a heartbeat. "You wouldn't dare."

"I would. And then I'd email the receipt to all your crunchy granola friends."

"I hate you sometimes," Kimberly says.

"I love you, too."

"Well, try to at least *talk* to Lucy, would you?" Kimberly pleads with me. "We can't actually be expected to wear this."

As much as I'd hate to wear the same dress, part of me wouldn't mind seeing Kimberly have to wear it. I hardly think she can hold on to her hippie-chick charms wearing fuchsia polyester. Then again, Kimberly could make a potato sack look sexy—which is why, I think, she insists on going around wearing cargo pants and combat boots. Even in those she has to fight off men by the dozens.

My IM window pops up on my computer.

RUGGER9: How's your plan coming to bust up your cousin's wedding?

I glance up and see Riley looking over at me. He's arrived, as usual, at 10:15. He wiggles his eyebrows at me. I roll my eyes.

JEN76: Don't you have work to do?

RUGGER9: Noblemen are notorious slackers. So? You have a date yet?

JEN76: Nope.

RUGGER9: That's a shame. Don't you know you're supposed to provide me with entertainment? I'm 312th in line to the throne of England.

JEN76: I thought it was 344th.

RUGGER9: Old royal buggers die off every day.

My phone rings. I pick up the receiver while catching a disgruntled look from Riley. He throws up his hands as if to say "You're ditching me for the *phone?*"

"Hi, Jen," cries the sexy, throaty voice of Tiffany, Riley's girlfriend.

"Tiffany!" I say, unable to contain my surprise. We're certainly friendly, but she doesn't usually call me at work.

"Listen, I told Riley to tell you that we're having a few people over tonight, nothing too formal or anything, but you're more than welcome to come."

"Tonight?" I cry, again off balance.

"Riley didn't mention it?" Tiffany sighs, sounding disappointed.

"Uh, no, he didn't."

I give Riley a look over my computer. He shrugs at me, trying to look innocent.

"Well, there's this guy I work with—he is such a doll, you're going to love him," Tiffany says. "He's from Sydney, and I swear he looks *just* like Russell Crowe. Anyhow, he's going to be there tonight."

Tiffany is trying to set me up. Oh dear.

"Come on, I know you are just going to go home and sleep before your next shift. Why don't you stop by our place for a couple of hours before you go? You'll *love* Paul. I swear."

JEN76: And just when were you going to mention your girlfriend wants to set me up with an Australian?

RUGGER9: I wanted the element of surprise. I knew you wouldn't leave the office willingly, so I had planned on knocking you out with chloroform.

JEN76: You could have just asked me.

RUGGER9: Brits don't like to do anything the easy way.

Riley and Tiffany live in a newly renovated condo in Wrigleyville two blocks from Wrigley Field. Tiffany moved in only a month ago, after a fire in her building caused so much water and smoke damage to her apartment that she could no longer live there. No one was injured in the fire, but Tiffany continues to mourn the loss of her matching white twill loveseat set from Pottery Barn.

Riley's apartment still looks something like a bachelor's pad. His furniture is all dark leather, and he's got black-and-white pictures of old rugby players on his wall, as well as two cricket bats and a British flag (a Union Jack, as Riley would say) above his fireplace. Tiffany's things are still mostly in boxes, which are stacked in his hallway and the far corner of the living room.

The party is in full swing when I arrive at nine.

"You're going to need this," Riley says, handing me a glass of wine and keeping his voice low. "That Australian bloke is a real wanker."

I laugh and take a step around some of Tiffany's boxes as I accept the glass of wine. "He's that bad?"

"Well, he's *Australian.* You know those guys are insane, right?"

"I don't think I should drink," I say. "I have to work in two hours."

"You Yanks, always so scared of getting a little pissed," Riley says.

"Did you say 'pissed'?"

"Means drunk in England," Riley explains. "One drink

won't kill you, and it could make work infinitely more interesting."

"Can't argue with you there," I say, taking the glass.

I glance over to the corner of the living room where Tiffany is talking animatedly with a tall, burly guy who looks distantly like Russell Crowe, but only in size and stature and the fact that he seems to be scowling a lot.

"Is that him?" I ask, nodding my head in their direction.

"Sadly, yes."

"Tiffany seems to like him." In fact, she seems to like him a lot. She is standing very close to him, and she is touching his arm now and again. If I didn't know better, I'd say she was flirting.

"Well, Tiffany has terrible taste in men," Riley says, taking a sip of his drink. "After all, she is dating me."

Just then, Tiffany glances over. "There you are," she says, looping her arm through the Australian's and leading him to me. "Jen, this is Paul. Paul, Jen," she says. "Paul watches *News Four* all the time, don't you, Paul?"

"All the time," Paul says.

"Don't you just love his accent?" Tiffany exclaims.

Riley rolls his eyes.

"You do the *Daybreak* show?" Paul says. "I like Michelle. She's a fine Sheila for sure. She'd make you crack a fat."

"Crack a fat?" I ask.

"You don't want to know," Riley tells me.

"I think I could listen to him read out of the phone book, couldn't you?" Tiffany sighs.

Given that he doesn't seem too bright, I think reading out of a phone book might be all he could manage. He doesn't look entirely like Russell Crowe, although he does have the same thick neck and beefy build. Right away there is zero chemistry. I don't like dumb, muscle-bound types. I go for scrappy, smart, and boyishly handsome guys. Guys like Riley.

Then again, Paul doesn't seem to have any interest in me. He seems to have eyes only for Tiffany. I begin to wonder, *was this setup for me or for her?*

Riley doesn't look happy. He doesn't look happy at all.

I get about five minutes alone with Paul, who talks exclusively about Australia and about how he hates "that drongo" the Crocodile Hunter. "He's got a few kangaroos loose in the top paddock," he says. Then, as if I'm in some sort of farce, he starts talking in the third person.

"Paul would never do something like that . . . and if Paul were in charge, I'd tell you what he'd do to those terrorists. . . ."

I drain my wineglass.

Eventually, when it seems Paul manages to exhaust the topic of himself in the third person, he excuses himself to get another drink, leaving me standing in the living room with my empty wineglass. I watch him trail after Tiffany.

Riley appears at my shoulder a few seconds later. "Would you like a stuffed mushroom?" he says, offering me one from a tray. "I think we also have some that are laced with arsenic if you'd prefer."

"Do I look that bored?"

"Well, it's more like he looks like a big fat wanker. I just assumed you were bored."

"He talked about himself in the third person."

This makes him laugh. "Only bastard cousins of the sons of earls are allowed to do that."

"You know your lineage gets thinner and thinner every day."

"It's only because I'm trying to practice humility. If you'll excuse me, there are some friends of mine in the far corner who look like they're about to starve," Riley says. "Hold that thought and I'll be right back."

Riley slips over to the other end of the room, and I'm left holding my empty wineglass. I walk over to the kitchen, which is empty. I decide against another glass of wine, as I set my glass on the counter and glance at the clock above their refrigerator. It's 10:30. *I should probably be getting to the station,* I think.

I glance around the living room, looking for Tiffany to say goodbye. I walk back toward the bedroom, where I discover two people standing close together. Not kissing exactly, but about to or perhaps having just.

"Oh, I'm sorry," I say, backing out of the room. That's when the man and woman spring apart, and I realize I know them. Paul and Tiffany. If there were a record player playing, now would be the time the music would screech to a halt.

Tiffany and Paul? I can't quite get over what I've seen—or think I've seen. Are they . . . ? Did they . . . ? I feel dirty, as if by witnessing them I'm somehow culpable.

I must look as surprised as I feel, because Tiffany reaches out to me. "Jen—wait," Tiffany says, at the level of a whisper.

My only coherent thought is *I need to get out of here.* "I've got to go to work," I say. I'm out the door, down the stairs, and on the sidewalk before I realize that my hands are shaking and that I left in such a rush, I didn't say goodbye to Riley.

Eleven

Never put passion before principle; even if you win you lose.

—Mr. Miyagi, *The Karate Kid II*

1984

Seeing Tiffany and Paul together makes me think about fourth grade, the year of the Great Betrayal. It was two months after the Roller Rink Debacle of my tenth birthday, and I had only just recovered from the humiliation of Vivien and Grandma Saddie scaring off Kevin Peterson.

My best friend at the time, Christi Collins (proven by our matching baby blue baseball T-shirts with the unicorn on the front and "Best Friends" spelled out in blocky, baby blue velvet iron-on decals) convinced me that perhaps Kevin Peterson had forgotten about the roller rink. After all, it was dark. He might not have even really realized it was me, even though it was highly unlikely that any other family but mine in Dixieland would be consuming sushi.

Christi convinced me by having me consult the paper ora-
cle (a piece of notebook paper folded into a square that could
tell me what kind of car I would drive as an adult and what
kind of house I'd live in) that Kevin Peterson was my true love.

We both went to see *The Karate Kid* and papered our walls
with posters of Ralph Macchio. We also both signed up and
subsequently quit karate lessons when we found out that actual
physical exertion was involved.

Christi Collins was the only girl in fourth grade claiming
not to be in love with Kevin Peterson. She was pining for, de-
pending on the day, either Ralph Macchio or Ryan White, the
boy who contracted AIDS from a blood transfusion and was
banned from school. Like Kimberly, Christi gravitated toward
big social causes. This was why her book covers were plastered
with "Save the Whales" stickers.

We exchanged friendship bracelets to solidify our friendship. I made a pink-and-purple braided bracelet for her, and
she made a pink-and-yellow one for me. They were made out
of needlepoint thread and done usually covertly during math or
reading lessons.

Like friendship pins, friendship bracelets were a coveted
playground item. Kids worked harder than rug weavers in Pak-
istan to make dozens of the bracelets. You didn't want to just
wear one, which would imply that you had only one friend.
You wanted dozens. And wearing them was a commitment.
You tied it on with a double knot, and then there was no getting it off unless you cut it off.

It was Christi's idea that I make a special "friendship"

bracelet for Kevin Peterson. Granted, boys didn't usually wear the bracelets, but Christi still thought it would be a good idea.

We made the bracelet at her house, because Kimberly was on a rampage. She had only just discovered, after being frustrated by months of attempting to solve her Rubik's cube, that I had been switching the colored square stickers when she wasn't looking to thwart her efforts.

I worked for a full hour on Kevin's bracelet. It was red and black, to match his Members Only jacket and his Michael Jackson "Beat it!" T-shirt. Eventually, the time came when I would have to hand it to Kevin Peterson. I decided to fold it up in a note that said:

> Do you want to go with me?
> Yes ___
> No ___
> (Check one)

Of course, I was too chicken to give the note to Kevin myself. That's when Christi volunteered to do it for me. She handed Kevin Peterson the note during recess, and I watched, hiding behind the seesaws.

I saw Kevin Peterson shrug his shoulders, and then attach the friendship bracelet to his arm. I couldn't believe my eyes! He'd accepted! He'd checked "yes."

Then something terrible happened. Kevin Peterson took Christi's hand, and led her away.

I watched them walk, hand in hand, and the cold, hard truth

became clear to me. Christi Collins had stolen Kevin Peterson right under my nose. She'd pretended the note was from her.

Our matching "Best Friends Forever" unicorn T-shirts, our two halves of the same heart charm on our Best Friends bracelets, and the endless rounds of late Friday night Pinkie Swears—all, in that instant, meant nothing. Christi Collins broke the First Commandment of the Girl Code: Thou Shalt Not Brazenly Steal Away My Crush Since I had Dibbs on Him First.

I watched as the two walked hand in hand to the swing sets, and I could almost feel my little heart crumbling to the beat of Bonnie Tyler's "Total Eclipse of the Heart."

Twelve

In Okinawa, honor have no time limit.
—Mr. Miyagi, *The Karate Kid II*

The fact that I caught Tiffany in a compromising situation haunts me through my whole shift at *News Four* and into the next day. Should I tell Riley? Should I not? The Girl Code is distinctly murky on this point. I want so badly to tell Riley, but for all the wrong reasons, namely because I want him to (a) become outraged, (b) break up with Tiffany immediately, and (c) fall in love with me.

This, however, is not what would happen if I told Riley, I'm sure. He would probably not believe me, and even if he did, he'd probably blame me somehow. You never want to hear a person could be cheating on you. Besides, I know what betrayal feels like (Christi Collins/Kevin Peterson). Would I have believed it if I hadn't seen them holding hands with my own eyes? Probably not.

Not to mention, *what* would I tell him? I *think* your girl-friend kissed an obnoxious Australian bloke? I don't even have

any real proof that something happened, other than a dark feeling at the pit of my stomach that something just happened or
was about to. Clearly, something was going on or Tiffany
wouldn't have been so quick to distance herself from Paul when
she saw me, would she?

An instant message pops up on my computer.

RUGGER9: Do I smell?

JEN76: What?

RUGGER9: Your disappearing act. You didn't even say
goodbye. I spent the rest of the night wondering if my
deodorant gave out. It was very embarrassing sniffing
my armpits while trying to talk to our guests.

JEN76: Sorry. I had to work.

RUGGER9: You don't have to lie!

Great. Does he know? Damn Instant Messenger. If he were
here, I could try to read his facial expression, or get clues from
the tone of his voice. *Tread carefully,* I think.

JEN76: What are you talking about?

RUGGER9: The Australian Wanker.

JEN76: What about him?

RUGGER9: Tiffany told me.

JEN76: She TOLD you?

RUGGER9: She told me he tried to maul you in the
bedroom, and that you only just got away.

I read and reread Riley's instant message. So this is how she's getting around it. She's using *me* as an excuse.

JEN76: Wait a second. She said he was coming on to me?

RUGGER9: She said that's why you left in such a hurry. Anyhow, you don't have to worry about that arse. I'll smack him in the head if he tries any more of that bollocks with you.

I am simultaneously touched that Riley would come to my defense and horrified that Tiffany has used me to lie to Riley. I consider telling him the truth. I type, and then delete, and then type again. I take so long Riley thinks something is wrong.

RUGGER9: HELLO? You there?

JEN76: Sorry—it's crazy here. I'll talk to you in a bit.

RUGGER9: K. Don't work too hard. You'll put the rest of us to shame.

My phone rings. It's my friend Jason, sounding far too excited.

"Listen, I have found the *perfect* replacement for me," Jason tells me.

"Jason, it's four in the morning. What on earth are you doing up?"

"You know that a man of my busy social circle never sleeps.

Besides, you're up and at work already so who am I hurting by calling?"

"You have a point," I say. "So what's this about a replacement?"

"I found your gay date for your cousin's wedding. You remember Thom, right?"

"You mean Tom-With-An-H who used to be Cher at the Baton Show Lounge?" The Baton is a notorious female impersonator revue in Chicago.

"He's also willing to go with you, if you pay him five hundred dollars."

"I am not paying anyone five hundred dollars to be my date. Least of all, Cher."

"Look, Thom does a great impression of a straight guy. He's an actor, for heaven's sakes."

I believe, even in my love life, this qualifies as a new low.

A note on my past boyfriends:

Longest relationship to date: Four years, with my college boyfriend, David, who spent almost all the time we dated convincing me that he didn't believe in the institution of marriage—only to go and get engaged six months after we broke up. It turns out he did believe in matrimony, just not with me. Then there was James, who grew up in San Antonio and had a thing for J Lo. I think he often pretended that I wasn't half-Japanese at all, that I really was Latina. He liked salsa and listening to Los Lobos. He got really drunk once and told me that he had never liked the idea of dating an Asian chick because he worried that other people would think he had a small dick. My other boyfriends didn't technically even make it to the "boyfriend" milestone, our relationships dissolving before the three-month mark.

I realize that my sordid dating history should not be a point of embarrassment to me, and that I should not care whether I show up at my cousin's wedding alone, facing my childhood love with only my career accomplishments to impress him. I should, as my women's studies professor in college said, "Let your own inner goddess be your soul mate." But the fact is I do care about showing up alone to this wedding. It's about self-preservation, really. If I don't come up with a date, Vivien will. And I am not about to let my inner goddess be escorted by glue-eating Billy Connor.

"I'll consider Thom," I tell Jason.

"That's about two octaves away from enthusiasm," Jason says. "Why don't you ask The Colins?"

"Riley has a girlfriend. He'll say no. Besides, it seems wrong to ask him. Even if I think I caught his girlfriend kissing another guy."

"Stop everything. Rewind the Ticker. WHAT did you say?"

"I may have caught his girlfriend with another guy." I look at Riley's empty desk. He's not due into work for another several hours, but still I feel he could be listening.

"What do you mean 'may'?"

I explain last night's fiasco.

"That relationship is headed straight to Häagen Dazs,"

Jason says. That's his way of saying it's not long for this
world.

"That still doesn't mean I should ask Riley to be my date."

"Sometimes you're far too honest for your own good."

I met Riley on my second day at work—a Saturday—during
my first weekend shift at *News Four*. Riley came in after a
tough game of rugby by the lake, wearing a soiled jersey and
shorts, smelling like gym socks, with a cut on his nose and mud
on his legs.

It's not at all the sort of thing you'd expect from someone
raised in Great Britain—homeland to James Bond. I assumed
men with British accents all wore suits. Even the cad-playing
Hugh Grant is always seen in a collared shirt. The accent seems
so formal, and it doesn't go with jeans.

"You the new bird?" Riley asked, perching on my desk.

"Did you call me a 'bird'?"

"British slang. The new girl?" he clarified.

"Yeah."

He stretched his legs out from under the table. They were
thick and braided with muscle, "Let me tell you something that
I wish someone had told me when I started," he said, leaning
in. Riley was wearing a baseball cap, with what looked to be a
mime on it—a rope-jumping mime.

"Whatever you do . . ." Riley paused.

My eyes trailed back to his hat. Was that a clown? Then, his
brown eyes drew my attention.

"Don't, for the love of God . . ."

"Yes?"

"You paying attention? Because you don't look like you're paying attention."

"I couldn't be paying more attention."

"Ever, and I mean ever . . ." Riley leaned forward, almost as if putting his hat on display. The mime—and yes, I was pretty sure by that point it was a mime—was staring me in the face.

"Yes?"

"Leave your email open on your computer," he finished, tilting back his hat. "I did that, and before I knew it, someone logged on to my account and sent out emails to everyone at the station saying how I was proud of my ability to fart out the alphabet."

"Can you fart out the alphabet?" I asked him.

"My arse! Do you think I'd be stuck in this dead-end job if I had the talent to fart out the alphabet?" Riley said. "God, no."

"By the way, is that a mime on your baseball cap?"

"YESSSS," Riley shouted, putting one fist in the air. "That's ten bucks you owe me, Larry," Riley said to one of the camera operators sitting in a chair by the coffee machine.

"You bet to see how long it would take me to notice your baseball cap?"

"No, I bet him I could make you say 'mime' in under a minute."

Riley, as it turned out, was wearing a baseball hat for his favorite rugby team, the Harlequins.

After that, we became fast friends. It was only a few months later that I discovered he had a girlfriend.

*   *   *

Anne swings by my desk looking anxious thirty minutes before we go on air.

"Chewbacca is stuck on the Kennedy," she says, alarmed.

Peter Mayhew, the actor who played Chewbacca, is our six-fifteen interview and apparently is caught in traffic. We have to find another guest to fill a two-minute spot, and we have only a half hour or so to do it.

"Why don't you call Tiffany?" Anne suggests. Tiffany, as in Riley's girlfriend, is the last person on earth I'd want to call at the moment.

"I'll take care of it," I say. One way or another.

An instant message pops up on my screen.

RUGGER9: What's happening, hot stuff?

I consider ignoring Riley, but the more you ignore him, the louder he'll get. He'll fill up my screen with IMs until I answer.

JEN76: If that is a reference to *Sixteen Candles'* politically incorrect foreign exchange student, nice work.
RUGGER9: Long Duc Dong. My new cinematic hero.
JEN76: You are disturbed.
RUGGER9: Members of the royal family are called eccentric, not disturbed.
JEN76: I've got to go. Chewbacca is stuck in traffic.
RUGGER9: What? Did the Millennium Falcon break down?

JEN76: Ha. Ha. Chewbacca was supposed to be on the show this morning.

RUGGER9: One guest short of an asylum, eh? I can help you out. Let me get Tiffany.

Even though I protest, Riley insists on involving Tiffany. She manages to land not only a guest but a local celebrity: Rick Bayless, chef and owner of Frontera Grill in Chicago, who normally appears only on national morning shows like *Good Morning America*. Somehow, Tiffany has gotten him into the *Daybreak* studio, on thirty minutes' notice.

Tiffany and Riley stand together next to me as we watch Rick's interview with Michelle, who is a bit starstruck herself.

"I'm going to go to Frontera Grill every Friday from now until the day I die," I say. "Rick's so good to do this."

"He's an old friend," Tiffany says, giving me a winning smile. "He owed me a favor."

She's trying to bribe me, I can't help but think. *She's trying to win me over with grand gestures so I don't tell Riley what I saw.*

"I'm sorry it didn't work out with Paul," Tiffany is now saying.

I can't believe she has the audacity to bring him up. Before I can say a word, Riley speaks.

"What a wanker," he says.

"He's not a wanker," Tiffany protests.

"He is so a wanker. The very definition of a wanker," Riley says. "Anyway, you're better off going alone to your cousin's wedding."

"You still don't have a date?" Tiffany asks me.

I blanch at the word "still."

"It's no big deal," I say, hating the fact I have to admit this in front of her.

"Why don't you take her, Riley?" Tiffany suggests.

"What?" Riley and I say at the same time.

"Yes, take her," Tiffany says. "Make a weekend out of it."

I can't believe Tiffany wants me to spend a weekend with her boyfriend. Either she doesn't consider me serious competition or she'd like the weekend alone to pursue whatever moment I interrupted with Paul.

"Oh, that's okay," I'm quick to say. "Really, I'll be fine."

Is she crazy? Even if she doesn't consider me competition, how can she be so confident that I won't try to convince Riley about what really happened between her and Paul?

"What? Did my deodorant give out again?" Riley asks. "What's wrong with me as your date?"

"Nothing is wrong," I say. "All of my family will be there. It'll be a complete bore."

"Nonsense," Riley says. "The stories I've heard about your family? I've been dying to meet them."

"It's settled then." Tiffany practically beams.

Thirteen

Never stop war by taking part in one.
—Mr. Miyagi, *The Karate Kid II*

1984 STRIKES BACK

*I*n the fall of fifth grade, I saw Christi Collins and Kevin Peterson everywhere. They were inseparable at recess and at lunch, sharing Fruit Roll-Ups and snickering at their own private jokes. After school, Christi would ride on the handlebars of Kevin's bike, or sit next to him on the merry-go-round, or share a box of Nerds candy: Kevin eating the blue ones, Christi eating the red. And all the time he wore that friendship bracelet, my bracelet, the fifth-grade equivalent of a wedding ring.

Kevin Peterson thought Christi Collins was fun, but I knew what she really was: she was a conniving witch, a female version of J. R. Ewing.

Fifth grade was the year I really started to watch *Dallas*

religiously, along with the rest of my family. Meals were planned around the designated start time, and prime seats for the main event (couch and two armchairs with unblocked views of the TV) were reserved far in advance. To me, every Friday became like camping out on the sidewalk in front of the Shrine Auditorium five days before Oscar night in hopes of gaining admission to the stands near the red carpet. It was all about getting an unobstructed view of the stars.

Kimberly and I would fight over the best real estate on the couch. Sometimes I'd stake out couch territory far earlier in the evening, forgoing all beverages to skip trips to the bathroom, which would leave my seat up for grabs. But Kimberly would always manage to oust me, usually by pinching my arm mercilessly, the same tactic she would usually use in the backseat of the family car during road trips when she wanted me to surrender part or all of my stash of Capri Suns.

Everyone in the house, from Bubba to Aunt Teri, intently followed the movements of evil J. R., his long-suffering wife, Sue Ellen, youngest brother Bobby, and Bobby's do-gooder wife, Pam. Even Grandma Saddie and Grandpa Frank (until his death) counted themselves regular watchers of *Dallas*. No one was immune.

Between Grandma Saddie and Vivien's involuntary ya-shee exclamations when J. R. did something particularly evil, and Grandpa Frank's regular declarations that he could run an oil empire better than any of the Ewings, I'm lucky to have heard any of the dialogue.

We saw ourselves in their struggles, even though we weren't rich, white, or from Texas.

If I was going to outwit Christi Collins, I needed to study the movements of the characters in *Dallas*. If I was going to out-scheme Christi, I'd have to see how Victoria Principal handled all the evildoers out to do her wrong.

To start, I practiced the key acting moves in *Dallas,* including:

The Open Palm Slap (see also: throwing drink in face of insulting husband/brother-in-law/rival oil baron)

The Dramatic Pause (used after revelation of husband's affair/brother-in-law's plot/evildoing of any kind usually executed before commercial breaks)

Stage Crying (tears that threaten to spill but never actually do)

Revelation Reaction (stunned look of surprise used upon the discovery the husband you thought had died is still alive and taking a shower, since it turned out you dreamed his death and a whole season of now irrelevant plotting and scheming)

I imagined dialogues between Kevin Peterson and me, with a *Dallas* slant.

Me (wearing rolled, sprayed hair and too much lip gloss): I love you, Kevin. Can't you see that? We are meant to be together.

Kevin (wearing a gray polyester suit, blue shirt, no tie, and a white cowboy hat): I have responsibilities to the family. To Southfork. I can't just abandon them, Jen. I realize it was a mistake to marry Christi. I see that now, but I am wearing her bracelet and that means something.

Me: But don't you see? I made that bracelet! Christi is in league with J. R. They want to take Ewing Oil from you. Let me help you. Together we can stand up to your brother, J. R. Things can be different, Kevin. They can be different this time.

Camera zooms in on Kevin's face. He's pensive, considering. He takes off his cowboy hat, runs his fingers along its rim. He looks up, hopeful.

Kevin: Can they, Jen? Can they really?

Insert Dramatic Pause. Close-up on my face, which is hopeful, yet my bottom lip is quivering. Is that a tear at the corner of my eye?

Me: They can, Kevin. They can. Together we can do anything.

Kevin: Oh, Jen. I was wrong to ever doubt you.

Kevin throws his cowboy hat to a nearby table, then passionately embraces me in a long, lingering kiss, which fades to black and then to a commercial.

Of course, the problem with real life is that it's not scripted, and I never did exchange any meaningful dialogue with Kevin that year. He was always being shadowed by

Christi Collins, who kept him closer to her than Sue Ellen held hard drinks.

But if there's one thing I learned from J. R., it's that double-crossing is something that goes around and comes around. J. R., after all, ended up being shot. So I sat back and learned to be patient.

Fourteen

Sometimes when take trip better know where trip end, otherwise, best stay home.
—Mr. Miyagi, *The Karate Kid III*

The day after Tiffany suggests Riley take me to my cousin's wedding, he does not show up for work. For two days. Then, four. Riley is AWOL on Thursday and Friday, and even the following Monday and Tuesday, which makes me worry that something awful has happened to him. I am tempted to call him at home, but I don't want to risk getting Tiffany on the phone.

When I casually ask Bob if he's heard from Riley, Bob just shrugs, letting slip a tantalizing nugget of information.

"He's out sick, or so he says," Bob answers but says nothing more.

At least he's not in a coma in the hospital, I think.

Still, this doesn't make me feel any better. Bob's answer could mean that Riley's at home nursing a rugby injury, or worse, has discovered his girlfriend is two-timing him and that I knew and didn't tell him.

I tell myself that it's none of my business, but I find my eyes wandering to Riley's desk chair as if I keep expecting to see him there.

When Riley fails to make an appearance in the office on Wednesday, I decide to take the plunge and call his house.

I get his answering machine, and the perky-sounding voice of Tiffany, who recorded the message, using the profoundly irritating "we." I hang up and belatedly remember that he has caller ID. I'm trying to recall whether calls made from the station show up with the extension number when my phone rings.

"Did you just call?" says Riley, sounding a bit groggy and out of it.

"Uh, yeah. I was worried about you."

"Oh," Riley says, going silent for a minute. "What time is it anyway?"

"Four in the afternoon."

"Oh," he says, and then we fall into a small silence.

"Are you sick?"

"No."

"Are you going to tell me what's wrong?"

"Nothing is wrong."

"You took a week off work."

"A week of my sick days were about to expire. I'm not coming back in until next Tuesday, only Bob doesn't know that yet."

"I see." I'm not sure if I believe him. If he's telling the truth, then I have to admit I'm a little hurt he didn't see fit to tell me about his plan. "So I guess that means you're not coming along this weekend for the *Deliverance* wedding?" I try to make my voice sound light and playful, but I end up sounding pouty.

"Shite, I totally forgot," Riley says, yawning. "Yeah, I'll go. When do we leave?"

"You don't have to," I say, profoundly disappointed that he managed to forget the fact that he agreed to spend an entire weekend with me.

"No, I want to, I do."

Which must be why he forgot about it entirely, I think. "No, really," I say.

"Jen, if you don't stop that, I am going to wring your bloody neck."

"Stop what?"

"Being fake polite. I want to go, okay? When do we leave?"

"This afternoon."

"Pick me up. I'll be ready."

There are two ways to get to Dixieland: fly into Little Rock and take a puddle jumper to Texarkana (the other, larger border town, the name a deliberate combination of states Texas and Arkansas, and the closest city with a working airport). Or you can drive. I prefer to drive. By plane it takes no less than three and a half hours. For ten more, I can be assured that I won't have a panic attack in the air like I did the last time I attempted to fly, and spent most of the flight breathing into a sick bag.

Yes, I have an unreasonable fear of flying. That is, if you call unreasonable being uncomfortable with the fact that the only thing that's saving you from plummeting thirty thousand feet to your death is a few thin sheets of aluminum. If you see it as I see it, I have a *reasonable* fear of avoiding heights that could cause my premature demise.

I make it out of the office only after going over two dozen story lists with Anne, who has promised to fill in for me. I deal with a temper tantrum from Michelle, who tries to get me involved in some battle she is having with accounting about having her tanning-bed visits expensed to the station, and then one last meeting with Bob, who is in one of his particularly grumpy moods after spending a half hour on the phone arguing with his fiancée about the cost of the floral centerpieces for the reception.

"In my day, I never went to weddings or even my father's funeral," Bob tells me, sounding disapproving. "Now I'm paying $15,000 for orchids and my best producer is skipping out on me."

"I'll only be gone five days," I say.

"A lot happens in five days," Bob says. "And if I hear one peep from Michelle, no promotion for you."

Bob, I realize, is only partly joking.

"I gave Michelle my mobile number, okay? Everyone has it. So things should be fine."

"Hmpf," Bob grunts, not sounding convinced.

It's no wonder I don't take more trips home. Taking my allotted vacation time always feels like asking for a favor.

"Well, I guess I'll help Anne cover for you," Bob says, reluctantly.

"Thanks, Bob."

I drive to Riley's house in traffic, only to find that he's not answering his apartment buzzer.

I have driven my old Honda Accord—the 1995 white sedan with the bumper so scratched from Chicago street parking that it's starting to look like someone took a coat hanger to it. My car, packed full of my belongings, is double-parked on Riley's street.

I consider calling the whole thing off but then I remember that Lucy will throw a fit if I show up alone and upset the delicate balance of the seating of her head table, and that I'll never hear the end of it for as long as I live.

Not to mention the fact that in person, the guilt-tripping will be immense. I'll be getting a lot of "Why don't you come home more?" and "When are you going to move closer?" and "Little Rock has TV stations—why can't you just live there?"

On the fourth try, Riley finally answers his buzzer. He sounds like I've just awakened him from a deep sleep.

"I'm downstairs," I tell him. "Time to Wax On, Wax Off!"

"It is far too early to be quoting Mr. Miyagi," Riley says into the intercom. The next thing I hear is the front door buzzer.

The inside of Riley's apartment is a mess. More than a mess. A hazardous waste zone. All available surfaces are covered in empty and half-empty pizza boxes, beer bottles, and nebulous brown bags of some mysterious takeout. Dirty dishes are stacked everywhere, including the sofa. His kitchen sink is filled with soapy water and what looks to be a failed or abandoned attempt at washing old socks. His television is on and fixed on the shopping network, where some overly enthusiastic salesperson is trying to sell kitchen knives.

Riley isn't wearing a shirt, and I'm trying not to look in his direction. He's got the chest of a rugby player, and it makes me think of soap operas, and how the guy characters on them use any excuse to remove their shirts and show off their chests. I think I read somewhere that this improved ratings almost as much as supernatural plotlines.

"Are you going to get dressed?" I ask him.

"Are my man boobs offending you?" Riley asks, putting his hands on his pecs. He doesn't, as far as I can see, have man boobs. He has a very nice chest, in fact, one that I wouldn't mind running my hands across.

"No, but we're late."

"So you're saying I *do* have man boobs." Riley has been semiobsessed with "man boobs" ever since we ran a story on *News Four* last month on the increasing rates of breast cancer among men due to obesity.

"You don't have man boobs," I say. In fact, I doubt he has more than 5 percent body fat.

"Don't lie to me just to spare my feelings," Riley says, snatching up a T-shirt from the armchair and wiggling into it. Next, he steps into flip-flops and tames his brown unruly hair under his Quins hat.

"Is that what you're wearing to the wedding?"

"I was thinking of overalls. Without a shirt. Like Jed Clampett from the *Beverly Hillbillies.*"

I glance around his apartment.

"So what happened here?" I ask him, changing the subject. The last time I saw his place it was spotless.

"Tiffany's in Los Angeles," he says, as if that explains everything. I take another look around his apartment and I notice something that's missing: Tiffany's boxes. The ones I nearly tripped over at the party are gone.

"How long is she there for?"

Riley shrugs. "She got a new client there, so she and Paul are going to be working there for a few months. Maybe longer."

I think about Paul and Tiffany and the looks on their faces when I caught them in the bedroom. Chances are they're going to be doing more than just working, I think.

"Are you upset about it?" I ask Riley.

"Eh," Riley says. He doesn't look me in the eye. "We're sort of on break."

"On BREAK?" I nearly shout. "When did this happen?"

"A week ago."

"And just when were you going to tell me?"

"I'm telling you now," Riley says.

Everything becomes clear. His absence from work, and the

fact that he's been distracted. I'd be a little forgetful, too, if I was having relationship problems.

I imagine that he was sitting in his apartment for a week, lights out, listening to "I Will Survive" and crying into his beer. But then I take another look at Riley and he doesn't look devastated. He looks fine, just a bit underslept.

"But when? Why? What happened?" I sputter.

Riley shrugs. "It's no big deal. Let's drop it, all right?"

I give him a look. "You don't really think I'm going to let you drop it, do you?"

"Well, I'm not going to tell you anything, and if you keep at it, then I'm going to have to boycott this little trip."

"Riley! But . . ."

"Nope."

"What about . . ."

"Uh-uh."

"Why . . ."

"NO."

"Wha . . ."

"Zip it!"

I sigh, exasperated. This is going nowhere. He won't even let me ask a full question.

"Are you going to just stand there staring at my man boobs or are we going?" Riley asks me, one corner of his mouth curving up to a smile.

There is something that is always a bit exciting about a road trip, even if you dread getting to your destination. There's the feeling of freedom, of leaving behind everything that's been bothering you, of striking out on clear highways, away from city lights.

This is usually the moment I slip in a Dixie Chicks CD and start singing along to "Wide Open Spaces" but Riley has no interest in hearing country music. Not to mention that traffic doesn't look very wide or very open since we are sitting on the Dan Ryan Expressway lodged in bumper-to-bumper commuter traffic.

"This is why I wanted to leave *early,*" I say.

Riley doesn't answer me. He is busy rifling through my CDs. "Please tell me you have at least *one* Morrissey album," he says. "Bleedin' Christ. Dixie Chicks? Johnny Cash? Dolly *Parton?* What kind of representative are you to your Japanese people?"

"I'm one who grew up in the South," I say. "But I do have a Smiths album. It's on the bottom."

"Phew," Riley says, wiping his brow. "I thought I was going to have to abort this trip." He slides in the *Louder than Bombs* CD and sighs, content. Morrissey's voice singing "Is It Really So Strange?" washes over us.

"So, tell me again why we're driving instead of flying?"

"I do not like airplanes. It doesn't seem natural to hurl yourself three hundred miles an hour forty thousand feet in the air."

"Oh, but driving seventy miles an hour, listening to the Smiths while in an air-conditioned car is the natural state for humans," Riley says, then pauses. "So, are you going to tell me the backstory on this Kevin Peterson tosser or what?"

"He's not a tosser."

"Sure," Riley says, sounding skeptical.

"I've had a crush on Kevin Peterson since the third grade. He barely knows I exist. That's pretty much the story."

"There you go again," Riley says.

"There I go again what?"

"Idealizing men. It's your fatal dating flaw."

"My what?"

"We all have fatal dating flaws and yours is that you love the ideal of man so once you really get to know him, you're always going to be disappointed. All blokes appear better than they are until you get to know them and realize they're all the same. They all like fart jokes and porn."

"I like you, and I already know you like fart jokes and porn." This slips out before I can stop it. Luckily, Riley doesn't even skip a beat.

"Well, you aren't dating me, are you?"

"No," I say. "But . . ."

"But nothing. If I were serious dating material, I wouldn't last two weeks with you. Take the last guy you dated . . ."

"John had an Asian porn stash!" I cry.

"The guy before that. You broke up with him because he chewed his food funny."

"I did not. He peed in the shower. I cannot realistically date someone who pees in the shower. I'm sorry."

"You have just made my case for me," Riley says. "ALL guys pee in the shower. Your standards are just too high."

"That's ridiculous," I say. "And anyway, if everyone has a fatal dating flaw, then what's yours?"

"I am an irresistible bird magnet, so my girls always get jealous," he says, flashing me his Colins' smile.

I have to laugh.

The traffic before us finally eases, as we slip onto Interstate 55, which will take us most of the way south.

Riley starts singing along with Morrissey. "I went to a Morrissey concert once," he says. "I'll never do that again."

"Why?"

"I spent half the show trying to lose a little boy who seemed to be in love with me. Or at least in love enough with me to rub himself against me at every available opportunity."

"Maybe it's your man boobs," I suggest.

"Hey! Leave my man boobs out of this," Riley protests, shielding his chest with one arm like a girl whose bikini top just washed away in the ocean surf.

"Okay—time for a car game," Riley says. "Who do you think would win in a fight? Mr. Miyagi or David Carradine from *Kung Fu?*"

"No contest—Mr. Miyagi."

"Why?"

"Because he's the master!" I say. "He may be short and old, but he's got the moves. And, when I was ten, I idolized him. I spent an entire summer practicing crane kicks and trying to catch a fly with chopsticks."

"Your love of all things Miyagi is frightening. Anyway, your turn."

"Okay, uh . . ." I can smell the distinctive Riley scent: vanilla and clean laundry. For a second, I lose my train of thought. "Who would win in a fight, me or Tiffany?"

"Hmmmm. Tough one," Riley says, thinking. "You," he says finally.

"Why?"

"For someone who claims to have seen *The Karate Kid* a hundred times, I bet you picked up a few moves," Riley says.

"So are you going to tell me about being on break or what?" I ask him.

"There's nothing to tell. Tiffany said she wanted a break, and so we're taking a break. I think it's all Paul's doing, if you want my honest opinion."

I perk up at this.

"Why do you say that?" I ask, cautiously.

"He's moving to L.A. and he's going to start some free lance PR firm."

"Oh." *Should I mention the bedroom scene from his apartment?* I wonder.

"Anyway, I think he's pressuring her to go with him," Riley says. "And I think she's considering it. She's always wanted to live in Los Angeles."

"I see. And how do you feel about it?"

Riley shrugs. "I'd be really upset if she went," he says. "But what I can I do? It's her life. She knows I don't want to move to California."

This doesn't sound like Riley at all. It's not the rugby player in him to let something of his go so easily. Then again, things would be a lot better for me if I didn't have Tiffany as competition. It's not like I have any hope of getting Riley's attention when he's dating a five-foot-nine, model-thin babe who can eat three hot dogs at a sitting and still fit into low-riding Lucky jeans.

"Anyhow, she thinks I'm not serious enough about her," Riley says.

"And are you?"

Riley shrugs. "I don't know," he says. "Sometimes I think maybe I am, but then, I think if I really was then wouldn't I know it? I care for her a lot, but I haven't been as upset as I thought I'd be about the prospect of a break."

"You haven't?" I want to hear more about this.

"Well, I just don't know, sometimes I think there's something missing."

"Like what?"

"If I knew what, then I would know what it was that's missing," Riley says.

"So you wouldn't be willing to marry her—even for the green card?" I ask, partly joking.

"I don't need a green card," Riley says. "Technically, I'm an American citizen. I was born in Dallas, which, by the way, was a very popular show in England."

"No!" I shout, glancing over at him.

"I'm afraid it was very popular."

"No, I mean you—an American."

"Yes, I know. It's a disgrace to the royal family. My American-born mother came home to her parents to have me. Then, she flew back to London when I was about a year old."

"So you're a Yank! The thing you despise most in the world."

"Don't remind me. When I was in kindergarten, my teacher told the class I was a Yank from America and had me stand up in front of everybody and explain what Thanksgiving was. I had no idea what Thanksgiving was about. All I ever remembered was living in England. From then on, all the kids picked on me. They called me 'Yank.'"

I think back to when I was teased on the playground for being half-Japanese. I know what that feels like. "And now you live in a country where people mistake you for being Australian."

"Bunch of bollocks," Riley says. "Well, what can you do, eh? The scars give me character and character makes me deep. And birds love deep blokes."

He flashes me a playful smile. I remind myself that if I were wise, I would not read anything into that smile.

"Likely story," I say.

"Now it's my turn to ask a question." He sends me another intense look. "Why on earth are you driving so slowly?"

"I am not driving slowly."

"For someone so career-driven, you drive slower than my granny."

"I do not!"

"I bet the Queen Mum is a race car driver next to you."

"I'm going five miles above the speed limit."

"Everyone else is passing us like we're standing still."

"Would you rather drive?"

"I thought you'd never ask."

Riley speeds as if we're on the Autobahn, and when challenged about his driving skills, he says that the driving tests in England are a hundred times more difficult than in America. He makes it sound like you have to fry up an egg while parallel-parking.

Two hours later, Riley declares it's time to stop and eat, and in honor of our trip to the South, he insists on stopping at a Cracker Barrel.

"You know, this is not authentic Southern cooking," I say.

"But that's what the sign claims," Riley says, pointing to a hand-carved decorative sign above the hostess station.

"This is a chain," I add.

"A damn good one, too, if this sort of shopping is available while you wait for a table," Riley says, taking in the country store, filled with scented candles and a frightening array of collectible dolls. I stop Riley from asking how much it would cost to buy Lil Miss Oopsie Pants, a doll whose pants are falling down, which Riley insists on calling "Lil Miss Poops Her Pants."

"Did anyone ever tell you that you're the most immature person alive?"

"Only Tiffany. About a hundred times," Riley says.

The hostess who seats us has a distinctly Southern-sounding drawl. While we're only five hours outside Chicago, it feels like we've crossed into another dimension.

"We're not in Kansas anymore," Riley says to me, as we're seated below an old tractor, which seems to be hanging precariously from the ceiling above us, along with some other country knickknacks like a hoe, a rusted rake, and some old pans.

"Do you even know where Kansas is?"

"Yes, for your information," he says. "Unlike you Yanks, I am a product of a school system that *teaches* geography."

"Ha. Ha."

"So, what's your plan for ruining the wedding?"

"I'm not going to ruin any wedding," I say.

"You're driving how many miles and you're just going to chicken out at the end?" Riley asks me, looking incredulous.

"I'm going to take the high ground."

"Come on. You've got to at least have a speech planned for the 'speak now or forever hold your peace' bit."

"No, I don't."

"How about 'I'm a crazy woman who's been in love with you since I was ten. Marry me instead!'"

"No, I don't think so," I say, but I can't help but smile a little. "Besides, I'm not in love with him. That was a long time ago."

"Uh-huh," Riley says, sounding unconvinced. "So that's why you were so desperate to have a stand-in boyfriend tag along for the ride."

"I didn't say you were my stand-in boyfriend," I protest.

"Uh-huh, right."

"Do you have a problem with that . . . being a stand-in, I mean," I say. I am dangerously close to crossing that line from innocent platonic flirting to innuendo flirting.

Riley just looks at me, an impish smile on his face.

I think, suddenly, *he doesn't seem like he'd mind crossing that line at all.*

"No," he says. "I don't mind."

My mobile phone rings. It's the Dixie Chicks playing "Cowboy Take Me Away."

"That is not really your ring tone," Riley says.

"Told you I was a country girl," I say, picking up my cell and walking away from the table.

"I didn't get my expense check this week, and I don't appreciate the delay," says Michelle on the line. "I thought you were going to take care of this for me."

I don't remember agreeing to take care of Michelle's expense reports.

"I put the receipts on your desk this afternoon," Michelle whines.

"Michelle, I haven't been to the office since this morning," I say.

"Well, this is just not acceptable."

"I'll make some calls and see what I can do, all right?" I say, through clenched teeth. *Michelle is going to be the death of me*, I think.

I make a quick call to Anne, but she's not at her desk, so I leave her a message asking her to try to run interference for me with Michelle until I get back.

Back at the table, the waitress sets down our food, and Riley studies his plate.

"Bollocks!" Riley cries, looking at his food. "What is this?"

"I have no idea," I say, poking at the black-eyed peas that are swimming in some unidentifiable sauce that looks like a mix of gravy and butter.

"I think we'd be safer eating at McDonald's next time."

In the afternoon, Riley insists we stop in Amish country so he can have me take a picture of him with a bearded man in a buggy, one of his lifelong ambitions. While we're there, Michelle calls twice more, and I take the calls under the disapproving gaze of an Amish man making candles.

Back in the car, Riley starts a game of Jump the Shark in which we try to name the exact point a famed television series went down the tubes. "Jump the Shark" refers to the episode of *Happy Days* when Fonzie jumped a shark on water skis wearing a leather jacket.

"The dream shower sequence on *Dallas,*" Riley says.

"You watched *Dallas?*"

"Fookin' everybody watched *Dallas,*" Riley says. "You thought you were the only ones with TV sets? And *The Dukes of Hazard* was big, too."

I can only imagine the image of the American South being broadcast to hundreds of countries across the world. It's probably only one of many issues we have with international relations.

Riley attempts to put the Smiths back in again.

"Oh, no—we're in the South, so it's time for some country music," I say.

"Lord, help us," Riley mutters.

Fifteen

Daniel-san, trust quality of what you know. Not quantity.

—Mr. Miyagi, *The Karate Kid*

1985

The one thing about growing up half-Japanese in the South is that I often forgot I was Japanese at all. I wasn't immune to racial amnesia. It didn't help that I didn't really look Japanese, or that my Japanese American mother spoke in a southern accent and said "ya'll" about as often as she said "yashee."

During a particularly bad episode of racial amnesia, I thought I could be a country western star.

Bubba had been taking us to school, and so we'd been hearing a steady rotation of his favorite artists: Alabama, the Oak Ridge Boys, and George Strait. So I had plenty of inspiration.

After school, Kimberly and I watched the reruns of *Barbara Mandrell and the Mandrell Sisters* religiously (it was the one show we could be sure to watch without Vivien's running commentary, which usually revolved around asking what we thought were silly questions like "If the A-Team is supposed to be undercover, why does Mr. T wear all that flashy jewelry?").

I'm not sure when I decided to become a country western star, but at some point it became clear that I took the Mandrell Sisters far more seriously than Kimberly did. Secretly, I thought Nashville would be my ticket to winning the heart of Kevin Peterson. By Halloween, Christi and Kevin Peterson were still an item and going strong, and I knew I needed to do something big to get Kevin's attention.

It didn't occur to me that I had two major stumbling blocks to my Nashville dreams: namely that I can't sing and that I was half-Japanese. There were no Asian people in Nashville. Of course, since I was suffering racial amnesia, this fact didn't concern me too much.

I had a threefold plan to reach Nashville stardom.

First, I started to grow my hair (I wanted it ankle-length like Crystal Gayle's). Next, I practiced singing "Don't It Make My Brown Eyes Blue" in the shower religiously every day. Thirdly, I watched reruns of the *Mandrell Sisters* with my trusty Hello Kitty spiral notepad opened in front of me so I could carefully record notes on their costumes (some variation of sparkling sequins), hair (always rolled, sprayed, with feathered bangs), makeup (lots of lip gloss and silver blue eye shadow), and their dialogue (puns and hand puppets are hilarious!).

With any luck, I would be the next Louise Mandrell,

spokeswoman for White Rain, who not only played the clarinet *and* the banjo but was a famous markswoman, taking highest honors in her high school clay shoot competition. All I needed was some White Rain, a banjo, and a rifle and I'd be the next Nashville Sensation.

Vivien soon shot down my dreams of the banjo and rifle (but allowed me the bottle of White Rain shampoo), and, sensing my interest in music, and perhaps even the potential of my crossover appeal (Half-Asian sings Country Western), Vivien suggested I take piano lessons.

The problem with cultivating musical talent was that it required a significant amount of work. I expected to sit down at the piano and begin playing "I'm a little bit Country . . ." during my first lesson. I didn't anticipate the fact that it would take me six weeks to learn "Twinkle, Twinkle Little Star," which would hardly win me a spot on *Star Search,* and then, instead of playing tried and true country hits like Dolly Parton's "Nine to Five" I wound up practicing scales every day.

Granted, my talent was not that strong. Kimberly's gentle prodding (yelling, "Mom! Make her stop that god-awful racket!") inspired me to look for other ways of improving my talent.

After all, scales by themselves wouldn't get me closer to sequined gowns, big hair, and Lee press-on nails. I started spending more time practicing my singing face in the mirror. Scales seemed pointless, whereas my "singing face" was crucial. For one thing, you had to plan in advance just when you're going to shut your eyes tight (during the most poignant lyrics like

"Working nine to five . . . It's enough to drive you crazy if you let it!"), and when you're going to lift up the microphone and tilt your chin back (usually during the high notes), and how you're going to hold the microphone (two hands or one, and when to alternate).

Note to self—Singing Hands should not be confused with Jazz Hands. Singing hands are to be used not at the end of a song but during particularly emphatic moments. How to execute: pull fist into side, then sweep hand slowly up from hip to above head to help audience visualize voice going up an octave.

I kept imagining that one day Kevin Peterson would see me on my very own variety show. He'd travel all the way to Nashville to visit me backstage. Our conversation would go something like:

Kevin: I've never seen Singing Hands like yours before.
Me (*feigning humility*): These old things? Oh, I don't know.
Kevin: And I haven't seen hair like yours since Crystal Gayle.
Me (*flipping long hair from face*): I use White Rain.
Kevin: I can tell. Say, I know this is sudden, and that you're famous and all, but do you want to go together? I've been dying to ask you.
Me: Oh, Kevin. John Schneider, the actor who plays Bo Duke on *The Dukes of Hazzard*, asked me to go with him already. (*Pause, watch Kevin's face start to fall.*) But, I don't think he's so hot anyway.

Kevin: Really? Oh, really?

Me: You've always been the boy for me.

(*We share a passionate embrace.*)

Ms. Lowery, my piano teacher, however, had no appreciation of my Singing Face or Singing Hands (granted the hands
were negated as I had to use them to play piano). But still, anyone could see how much emotion my hands were conveying
when I pressed down the keys.

Ms. Lowery, who wore bottle-thick glasses and her grayish
hair in a tight, spiral perm, spent almost every piano lesson
using what I only imagined was her highly developed ESP to
discern that I had not practiced piano at all the previous week.
Attempting to explain the importance of practicing Singing
Face or Singing Hands fell on deaf ears.

Eventually, Vivien stopped paying for my piano lessons,
after Ms. Lowery told her I wasn't practicing enough to make
real improvement. Ms. Lowery also said she was worried that
there might be something wrong with me, since every time I
played, I squinched up my face and looked like I was either in
pain or constipated. Ms. Lowery suggested that if I practiced
more, I might not feel so much pain when I played.

"But that's my Singing Face!" I cried.

"Ya-shee, I'm not throwing money away so you can make
faces at the teacher," Vivien scolded.

That ended my dream of being a country western star.

Sixteen

Stupid but fact of life. Win, lose, no matter. You
make good fight, you win respect.

—Mr. Miyagi, *The Karate Kid*

"You would have made a bloody fantastic country
western singer," Riley tells me when I've finished my
story. Riley is driving again and has his eyes on the road.

"Is that sarcasm?" I ask him.

"No, absolutely not. Speaking of country music, what do
you say about stopping in Graceland? That sign back there said
we're only twenty minutes away."

"I don't think so."

"But it's *Graceland*," Riley sighs. "There is nothing more
American than Graceland."

"What about the White House? The Grand Canyon?
Mount Rushmore?"

"Not even close seconds," Riley declares. "Have you been to Graceland?"

"No," I admit.

"Me neither, and I think as American citizens, it's our duty to go."

Riley starts humming Paul Simon's ode to Graceland.

"Stop that," I say.

His humming gets louder, and then he adds lyrics. "We're going to Graceland . . . to Graceland . . . to Graceland."

"Please stop singing."

"I won't stop unless you agree we're taking a detour."

"No."

"Don't make me start singing 'Walking in Memphis.'" When I say nothing, he starts to sing. "I put on my blue suede shoes and . . ."

"Stop! Please. You win." I look at my watch. A little detour, I think, won't hurt us too badly on time. "Okay, but we can only spend an hour there," I say, sounding like someone's mother.

"Whooppee," Riley says, clapping his hands together.

"Keep your hands on the wheel," I admonish. "What's that?" I point to the red engine light, which has just flicked on.

"Nothing to get your knickers in a knot over, most likely," Riley says.

Ten minutes later, a steady stream of white smoke starts wafting up from the hood of my car.

"Uh-oh," Riley says, pulling into the first gas station we see, next to the sign that says "This way to Graceland."

In the gas station parking lot, my car hisses and then dies, and Riley opens the hood to a theatrical show of steam and smoke that billows out.

"I bet it's the radiator," Riley says, looking at my engine and sounding confident. "Bet your fan went out."

"What's that?"

"One of many things that keeps the engine cool," Riley says.

"You overheated my car," I exclaim.

"I didn't overheat anything."

"You were driving. My car never has any problems when I'm driving."

"You never get above fifty." Riley raises his voice.

"This is your fault."

"It is not my fault. It's your car's fault. Anyway, it's a waste of time to argue the point."

"Can we just stop arguing and find a mechanic?"

"That's what I was *saying* in the first place. That it's a waste of time to argue."

"You weren't saying that."

"I did so say that."

"Can we please stop arguing now?"

"I'm not the one arguing."

"I think you are the one arguing, because I'm certainly not the one arguing."

"STOP! Enough," Riley says, sounding exasperated. "Jaysis Bleedin' Christ. Women's logic."

Riley stomps off from the car and heads into the gas station. I follow behind him.

Inside the small store, there are just two glass refrigerator cases, a counter, a freestanding display of car air fresheners, and the sweet, thick smell of marijuana.

"Wow," Riley says, then coughs. "Strong."

"Hello?" I shout, for good measure. "Anyone here?"

"Does it look like anyone's here?" Riley asks me.

"Always the smart-ass."

"That's Sir Smart-Ass to you."

"Say, you don't think this place was robbed, do you?" I ask, suddenly feeling that the place has a creepy air.

"No," Riley answers matter-of-factly.

"This is always how some horror movie starts. Stranded motorists. A weird gas station, and before you know it there's some guy wearing a mask made of human skin wielding a chainsaw."

"You do realize you're certifiable, don't you?"

"Innocent travelers are almost always the victims in horror movies. All the *Friday the 13th* movies. *The Shining. Psycho.*"

Riley snorts. "Completely insane."

"Well, if I'm so crazy, why don't you check behind the counter, just to make sure there's not a dead clerk back there."

"It smells like weed in here, not like a crime scene."

"I don't see you moving."

Riley leans over the counter. "You see there's nothing to . . ."

Suddenly a guy pops up, as if he'd been lying on the floor. He's wearing a mechanic's jumpsuit, and his hair is oily and flattened in weird places.

Riley shouts in fright, causing me to scream, and we both jump back five feet.

"Can I help you?" says the bleary-eyed clerk, who is swaying a little on his feet. His eyes are bloodshot, and I am positive he's very high. He is clearly the source of the pot. He reeks of it.

"Our car broke down," Riley says. "We need it fixed."

"Huh?" says the clerk.

"Our car," Riley repeats.

"What?"

"Our car," I say this time.

"Huh?" The clerk says. His eyes are having trouble staying focused. They keep wanting to cross over his nose.

"OUR CAR," I shout. "IS BROKEN."

"Broken," Riley echoes.

"What you say?" says the terminally stoned car mechanic.

"Mate, look, our car. See? Car?" Riley makes the international sign for car by pretending to drive an imaginary steering wheel.

"Yeah," the high car mechanic says. He sounds like he's starring in his own Lil Jon video.

"It's overheated."

"What?"

"Over. Heated."

"OVERHEATED!" I shout.

"Oh? Yeah?" The high car mechanic's tone is one of polite surprise.

"Can you fix it?" Riley asks him.

"Can I what?"

"Fix it," I say again.

"Fix what?"

"The car," I say.

The car mechanic blinks a few times. "Oh, yeah, yeah, sure. Not a problem."

"Can I talk to you a second?" I ask Riley, tugging him by the arm away from the mechanic.

"I don't think I should leave my car here," I tell Riley in a hushed whisper.

"What's the worst that happens?" Riley asks me.

"He completely trashes my car."

"Last I looked, it *was* trashed," Riley points out, glancing over to the car, which is still hissing and has steam and smoke puffing from the sides of the hood.

"Good point."

"I don't see that we have another choice, even if this guy is mashed."

"Mashed?"

"High," Riley explains.

We both turn and look at the mechanic, who is staring intently at a piece of lint on the sewn-on name tag patch on his mechanic jumpsuit.

"I don't know." I hesitate.

Before I can say anything else, my cell phone rings. This startles the mechanic, who looks about for the source of the sound. Riley rolls his eyes. "Bloody cell phone—again." He sighs. "Don't you ever turn that thing off?"

It's Anne, my assistant.

"I am SO sorry to bother you," she starts. "It's just that Michelle is a bit on the warpath and . . ."

"Say no more," I say. "Just tell her to leave her expense report on my desk and I'll deal with it when I get back."

"I did, but she doesn't seem very happy about it," Anne says.

I sigh, just as I watch a giant bus pull into the gas station. It has Elvis painted on the side doing a famous hip swivel and singing into an antique microphone. On the back of the bus are painted the words "Follow Us. We're Going to Graceland."

We both watch as the bus driver gets out, inspects a wheel, and then hops back on the bus.

"That's our ride," Riley says, taking me by the arm.

"Anne, I've got to go," I say, hanging up. "No way," I tell Riley, shaking my head.

"What else have we got to do?" Riley asks, a mischievous look in his eye.

"Find a sober mechanic for my car, for one . . ."

"Come *on,* we're going to miss it," Riley says, tossing my keys to the mechanic and tugging me in the direction of the bus.

On the shuttle to Graceland, a retired couple on the seat behind us informs their neighbors that this is their fifth trip to the home of Elvis Aron Presley, and the tour just gets better every time. While Riley and I pretend not to listen, they slip into what sounds like a familiar argument—which room is the most impressive: the rec room (with three wall-embedded televisions), the jungle room (with the working waterfall), or Elvis's racquetball court/hall-of-fame room?

"Elvis played racquetball?" I ask Riley.

"And you call yourself an American," Riley says, disapproval in his tone. "You don't even know anything about Elvis."

"Are there Elvis impersonators in England?" I ask Riley.

"Oh, tons of them. Elvis is huge in the UK. My uncle moonlighted as Elvis once. The fat Elvis. He saved up his money for five years to take a trip to Graceland."

"Did he think it was worth it?" I ask, eyeing the front gates, complete with music notes carved into the wrought iron, with some skepticism.

"Every shilling, he said."

Graceland is packed wall-to-wall with impersonators. There is some sort of impromptu vigil happening outside the mansion, and we are very lucky to get inside after being jostled through the onlookers.

"What's going on?" I ask Riley.

"I dunno. Maybe somebody has spotted the King? In Vegas, they have running odds that the King is still alive. They're a thousand to one."

"Well, maybe this time he made an appearance in a tortilla like the Virgin Mary."

"He'd prefer fried banana and peanut butter sandwiches."

"Why fried banana?"

"Don't you know your American history? That was his favorite."

"You know a frightening amount about Elvis," I say.

We walk through the doors of Graceland, and I feel like I've stepped back in time. The year is 1977. There is plenty of shag carpet and earth tones—avocado green, banana yellow, and brown. And, for some odd reason, lots and lots of white ivory monkey statues.

Riley takes in the "jungle room"—the monkey statues, the exotic animal shag couches, the antler skull, the cascading waterfall down the gold brick wall—and then leans over to me and says, "This is fabulous. I can't believe you wouldn't let me buy the audio tour."

"It's horrible," I say. "And," I add, noticing the shabby look of the shag carpet, "it's a bit run-down."

"This," Riley says, eyes gleaming, "is the most American place on earth."

"Do you think the King played racquetball in a sequined jumpsuit?" I ask as we walk into his personal racquetball room, which is decorated wall-to-wall with gold records.

"God, I hope so," Riley says.

In the rec room, where there are three televisions embedded in the wall—one for every network station so that Elvis could watch all three network news stations simultaneously—Riley leans closer to me.

"You think if Elvis were alive today, he'd have one television for every major cable channel? He'd have to fill up the whole room with TV sets."

"He'd have to trade in his Colt .45 for an Uzi to keep up with blasting that many televisions."

"Look, if you were incredibly rich, very eccentric, high on Mother's Little Helper and a steady diet of fried foods and carbs, I think you'd want to shoot out your television sets, too."

We brush by a gaggle of Japanese tourists with cameras.

"Your people," Riley whispers to me, as we watch a hundred flashbulbs go off as they take a picture of his wall of gold records.

"Very nice," I say. "I'd point out your people, except I think even you can recognize the people with really bad dental hygiene."

Riley gives me a smile full of mischief. "If Elvis were alive today, I think he'd be the spokesperson for stomach-stapling surgery and he'd spend two months out of the year campaigning for ultraconservative Republicans."

"I think he'd be the spokesperson for Viagra and Doritos."

"There would be plenty of Elvis to go around, I'm sure," Riley says.

At the end of the tour, Riley insists we buy fried banana and peanut butter sandwiches at the souvenir diner, along with a bumper sticker that reads "I've died and gone to Graceland" and an "Elvis Lives!" T-shirt.

"I got a gift for you," Riley says, outside the diner.

"I don't even want to see."

"I picked it out just for you."

Riley presents me with a red velvet box. I open it up to see a plastic Elvis head on an adjustable ring.

"His head spins around, see?" Riley says, putting the ring

on and spinning Elvis's sunglass-wearing face around and around.

"Does this mean we're engaged?"

"Only if we can get married at Graceland," Riley says, flashing me his impish Colins grin.

At the garage, the mechanic, still bleary-eyed and, if possible, even more disoriented, doesn't recognize us for a full fifteen minutes, even after I stand by my own car in the garage and point to it.

"I haven't gotten a chance to look at it," the mechanic says.

"What do you mean you haven't even looked at it?" I am livid.

"Merv called in sick, and we're swamped," he says, shrugging.

I look around the completely deserted gas station. There's no car here but mine and one other, an old pickup truck that is sitting on blocks.

"I can probably fix it tomorrow," the stoned mechanic says.

Great. We're already a half-day behind schedule. At this rate, we could be in danger of missing the rehearsal dinner in two days. Vivien is going to be furious.

"Come back tomorrow, around eleven," says the stoned mechanic. "Should be done by then."

"This is all your fault," I tell Riley.

"You sure you don't want me to drive Old Red up to get you?" Bubba asks me on the phone. Old Red is Bubba's prized vintage Chevy pickup.

"No, Dad. We'll be fine."

"We?"

"Riley is with me," I say.

"Who's Riley?"

"The boy I told you about. The one who's coming to the wedding."

"Hmmmm. Well, if you like him, I like him. But if he tries anything funny, be sure to tell him about my gun safe."

"I will."

"Now, here's your mama."

Vivien is even less understanding about my little detour.

"Ya-shee," she sighs, sounding despondent. "You're just trying to make things difficult for me."

"I'm not deliberately trying to make things difficult." I want to remind her that I am not the difficult daughter. That title usually falls to Kimberly.

"Even Kimberly is flying. Why couldn't you fly?"

"You know why," I say.

"Just like your father. He's scared of flying, too! You are just like your father." This is the worst insult Vivien can think of, and she uses it only when she's really frustrated, like the time when I was seven and left a half-eaten Dairy Queen dipped ice-cream cone to melt in between the cushions of her backseat.

"I'm doing my best to get there," I say.

"Ya-shee. Try harder. What are you trying to do? Step on a crack—give your mother a heart attack?"

"Break your mother's back," I correct.

"That, too," Vivien says and sighs. "Well, you know there is nothing more important than family. You need to be here. This is *family.*"

This is one of Vivien's favorite lectures. She likes to speak about the Nakamura clan as if we're part of the Japanese syndicate.

"I know, and I'll be there," I say.

"I'm sorry, but we're all booked up," says the man behind the Motel 6 counter, where Riley and I have ended up after walking two miles from the gas station. "In case you haven't noticed, it's Elvis Week."

"What does that mean exactly?" I ask.

"We're celebrating the Twenty-fifth anniversary of the King's death. Didn't you see the candlelight vigil outside Graceland?"

"That would explain the busload of Elvis impersonators," Riley says.

"Anywhere you think we might be able to get a room?" Riley asks him.

"Well, my cousin works over at the Heartbreak Hotel. He said they had one room left about fifteen minutes ago," the clerk says.

"Did you say Heartbreak Hotel?" I ask him.

The lobby of the Heartbreak Hotel looks like Barney on acid: there's bright purple, red, and blue everywhere, and animal print trim on everything. In the lobby, we nearly collide with a pack of Elvis impersonators.

"That's all right, mama," says the one I nearly slam into. He's wearing a white jumpsuit open to his navel, a purple scarf, and giant gold Elvis sunglasses.

"Are you lonesome tonight?" says another, this one wearing a gold jumpsuit and silver sunglasses, and very large, oddly real-looking muttonchops.

"Aye, but she's a hunk, a hunk of burning love," says the third, except it comes out sounding less like Elvis and more like Scotty from *Star Trek*.

"I think they're from Scotland," Riley whispers to me. "Look at the fourth one," he says, nodding his head in their direction.

As I watch, a fourth Elvis joins them, only he's wearing a plaid skirt with his leather jacket.

"There are so many things wrong with that, I can't even begin to start," I say.

"Now, this is the America I'm talking about," Riley says, taking in the tiger-print-trimmed carpet in the lobby.

"I think I'm going to go blind."

"Where's your sense of adventure?" Riley asks me.

"You're in luck," says the woman behind the counter. She's dressed surprisingly normally, in a mauve polo shirt. "We have one junior suite that just opened up. The couple canceled this morning. It's The Burning Love Junior Suite."

"The Burning Love Suite?" Riley echoes.

I am certain that I turn bright red.

We share the elevator ride with a man who has a parrot on his shoulder dressed like Elvis. The parrot is wearing a red cape and a golden medallion and fake Elvis boots on its clawed feet.

"Six please," the man with the Elvis parrot tells us.

Riley presses the button and the parrot caws "Thank you, thank you very much," sounding eerily like Elvis.

Riley is looking straight ahead in the elevator trying not to laugh. I am staring at the parrot, which is gnawing on its owner's shirt and periodically barking out lyrics to "Love Me Tender."

The parrot sounds so sincere that I lean a little closer in, only to have it snap its beak at me.

I jump back. Riley snorts.

We get off at our floor, and the parrot shouts after us "Thank you, thank you very muuuch." This could not get worse. Then we open the door to the room.

Everything is red velvet and heart shaped—heart-shaped bed, heart-shaped ottomans, couches, and red carpet. There are also gold drapes, gilded mirrors on every wall, and wall-to-wall purple-and-red-heart carpet. There's champagne chilling by the bedside, which is, coincidentally, a king-size heart. Distracted by the flamboyant colors, I don't immediately see the worst problem of the room: there's only one bed. A king-size bed.

"I feel like I should be carrying you over the threshold," Riley remarks.

"I think I need a drink."

"Dead right."

*   *   *

Riley flags down a cab and asks to be taken to the place where they make the strongest drinks, and we end up at one end of Beale Street, lined with neon signs for dozens of bars, and the cabdriver says, "Take your pick."

We go into the closest one, which also happens to be promoting "the largest karaoke stage south of the Mason Dixon" and seems to be ground zero for the Elvis Invasion.

"Question: What do you get when you mix karaoke night and Elvis Week?" Riley asks me.

"This?"

"I was going to say your idea of hell."

We take our seats next to a throng of Asian Elvises, who rival only William Hung in sheer talent. They're cheering for one of their members, who is on stage singing "Ain't Nothing But a Hound Dog" in a screech so terrible it makes me yearn for the cat-strangling sounds of "She Bangs."

The karaoke bar looks like a Benetton ad. There are black Elvises, white Elvises, Asian Elvises, Hispanic Elvises, even female Elvises. Scottish Elvises, Russian Elvises, You Name It Elvises. Elvis in his early days. Elvis in his late days. Elvis in sequins with giant gold belt buckles and Elvis in his military uniform. Even, I see in the crowd, one Elvis in drag.

"To think that all it took to unite us as a world was polyester sequined jumpsuits with butterfly collars," I say.

"Mock this all you want, but *this* is America," Riley says. "It doesn't get more American than this."

"It could if we added a Wal-Mart, a McDonald's, and a civil law suit."

"So jaded," Riley says, shaking his head. "Look at all these people. Look how happy they are."

The Asian Elvis onstage is windmilling his arms at a dangerous speed, getting ready for his finale.

"I still think I need a drink," I say. "Preferably one with lots of vodka."

"Two All-Shook-Up martinis coming up," Riley says.

Two martinis later, I begin to relax. I realize that it's probably a bad idea to drink two martinis on an empty stomach, since I'd long since burned through those peanut butter and banana sandwiches, but these are desperate circumstances. If being in a room full of Elvises doesn't make you want to drink, I don't know what will.

"I dare you to get up there and sing one song," Riley says. "Let's see this famous Singing Face of yours."

I laugh and shake my head. "I am far, far too sober for that."

"One song! What? Are you afraid of being shown up by Yoko Ono's brother over there?"

"No," I say. "Why should I sing? Why don't you sing?"

"Because if I sing, you'll fall madly in love with me. I have that sort of power over women."

I snort. But internally my heart does a little jump. Does this mean he'd *want* me to fall in love with him? There's that flirting territory again.

"It's a fact. My song voice is in a frequency that directly correlates to the emotional center of a woman's brain."

"This I have to see."

"Fine." Riley finishes his martini with a flourish. "I'll sing, but you've been warned."

"You aren't really going to sing," I say, still not believing him.

"Watch me."

He marches straight up to the line of karaoke singers and pretends to flip through the songbook. I am almost certain it's all for show.

It's at this point that an unusually hefty Elvis pushes his way through the crowd on his way to the restroom and bumps my arm, sending me nearly on top of Mini Elvis—an Elvis impersonator wearing a red cape and gold jumpsuit who is no taller than my waist.

"Hey, darling, watch where you put those blue suede shoes," he says, pushing up his Elvis sunglasses with one finger and giving me the trademark Elvis sneer.

"Sorry," I say.

"You seem sadder than a hound dog, sugar," says Mini Elvis.

"I'm fine, really."

"You wanna see my Elvis Pelvis? Chicks dig my Elvis Pelvis."

"Uh, no thanks. That's okay." My eyes slide to Riley, who winks at me from his position near the stage.

"Come on! I don't bite," says Mini Elvis. He hops up on a nearby chair and starts gyrating his hips. "One for the money . . ." he says.

"How about you stop for the money?"

"Two for the show. Three to get ready, now go, cat, go . . ."

Mini Elvis's shiny rhinestone belt buckle is a little hypnotic; still, I think I am too sober for this.

I look up and see that the current karaoke performer, Elderly Elvis, is having difficulty finish up his version of "All Shook Up," because he is in danger of losing his dental partial.

"Do you want to be my Priscilla, baby?" Mini Elvis is asking me.

"I'm sorry. I'm with someone."

"Who?" he asks me. "You show me my competition."

Just then, Riley takes the stage, his back to the audience, microphone in hand.

The beginning chords of "I Can't Help Falling in Love" come blaring over the speakers. Riley does a slow half turn. I see that he's borrowed someone's Elvis sunglasses, complete with muttonchops that hang from the earpieces. Every time he moves his head, the muttonchops sway from side to side. He flips up the collar of the Hawaiian shirt he's slung over his Smiths T-shirt, and I can't help it, I laugh.

"Him," I say, pointing to Riley, who is starting to sing.

"Wise men say," Riley sings. "Only fools rush in . . ."

He can actually sing. Really sing. Not just one of those weak, barely on key voices. He can *sing*.

Onstage there's something even more magnetic about Riley. No one can take their eyes off him. Some of the women in the audience start cheering. He points to one woman in the front, and she joins him onstage. "Shall I stay? Would it be a sin? If I can't help, Falling in love with you . . ."

She does a little happy dance, and then Riley moves on to another woman. He's working the crowd like a pro, getting them into it, and I find myself wondering what else I don't know about Riley.

Then he points to me and motions me onstage.

I shake my head.

He points again.

"No," I mouth.

"Yes," he nods, more vigorously this time.

The crowd starts to cheer. Hands push me to the front of the stage, and then I'm standing there, in front of a room full of Elvises, and Riley is looking right at me and singing, "Take my hand. Take my whole life, too. 'Cause I . . . can't . . . help . . . falling in love . . . with yoooou."

Riley finishes on his knees, his head slumping forward, and nearly loses his Elvis muttonchops. My heart is pounding. This, I think, is most *definitely* flirting.

The crowd goes wild, and someone yells, "Encore."

"What did I tell you?" Riley says to me.

"I'm impressed," I say. My head feels a little fuzzy, either from the proximity of Riley's face to mine, or the fact that the All-Shook-Up martinis are taking effect.

"No," Riley corrects. "You're in love."

Riley flashes me a grin, and I wonder if he might be right.

I consume three more All-Shook-Up martinis, and by the end of the night have:

1. Danced with Mini Elvis
2. Sung "Heartbreak Hotel" badly with Riley

3. Got a lei from Blue Hawaii Elvis

4. Judged a muttonchop contest

5. Joined in an Elvis conga line.

By the time Riley can drag me back to our hotel, I am laughing so hard that I have given myself the hiccups. I am leaning heavily on Riley, as my legs don't seem to be working properly.

In the lobby, we stumble into an all-Elvis wedding. That is, an Elvis impersonator marrying an Elvis impersonator and a Priscilla Presley look-alike.

Elvis is saying, "I do—Thank-you-very-much."

"Maybe we should get married," Riley says. "You could arrive at your cousin's wedding already married, and wearing Elvis muttonchops."

"It would almost be worth it just to see the look on her face," I say. "I doubt, though, an Elvis marriage would hold up in court."

"We do have the Hunk of Burning Love Suite," Riley says. "It would make a perfect honeymoon spot."

I stumble and Riley catches me. We are flirting. Yes, definitely flirting. In my muddled state, however, I am having a hard time remembering why this is a bad thing.

In the hotel room, Riley tries to sit me down on a chair but I take him down with me, so that he's nearly sitting on top of me. I hiccup again—loudly.

"This must be your half-Japanese side at work."

"What?" I say, playing with the collar of his shirt.

"Your inability to hold your pints."

"I can hold my liquor just—*hiccup*—fine," I slur.

"Ummm-hmmm," Riley says, doubtful.

"I can," I protest.

"You wouldn't last two hours in a pub in England," he tells me. "Besides, your face is bright red."

I open my mouth to answer but end up hiccuping again. Riley laughs and shakes his head at me.

"It's a good thing I'm a gentlemanly bastard son of the cousin of an earl," Riley says. "Or else I could take advantage of you."

Flirting! My heart sings.

"Your lineage changes daily," I say.

"That's what my mum says." He starts to throw some pillows and a blanket on the floor next to the giant heart-shaped bed.

"What are you doing?" I ask him.

"Making my bed."

"What? I have cooties or something?" I ask him.

"If by cooties you mean an alluring female form, then yes, you do," Riley says.

"Alluring?" I echo, coming close to him, except "alluring" comes out more like "allurringed" in my drunken state.

I throw my arms around him and say, "You're cute."

"Thanks," Riley says.

"I mean it. You're cuuute."

I am too drunk to heed the dull warning bell at the back of my head. The one that's trying to remind me that even though he's on *break* from his girlfriend, it doesn't mean that he doesn't have one, exactly.

The little devil who sits on my right shoulder is telling me to take off his pants, and the angel—the one on the other shoulder, the one who is normally the voice of clear morality and reason—is drunk and shouting for Jell-O shots.

"I think we both have had too much to drink," Riley says. "And by 'we,' I mean 'you.'"

"I'm just fiiine."

"I think maybe you should sit down."

"You're no fun when I'm drunk. I mean, you're no fun when you're drunk."

"I'm not drunk."

"Right, that's what I meant."

"Careful," Riley cautions.

"Why?"

"Because you're jumping on the bed, and I think you're going to hit the golden chandelier."

"I'm not going to fall," I say, just as my foot slips off the bed and I hit the floor with a *thunk*.

Riley dives after me, and somehow we're both rolling on the floor, and when we come to a stop the room is still spinning, and so is Riley's face, which is now just inches from mine.

We sit there, nose to nose for what seems like eternity. Then Riley's face gets even closer to mine, and suddenly we're kissing, which soon progresses into a full-on teenage make-out party, with roving hands over rumpled clothes.

I'm not sure if it's Riley's lips on mine or the All-Shook-Up martinis, but the room is definitely spinning.

Riley lets his hands wander down into the waistband of my pants and into X-rated territory. I realize I shouldn't be enjoying this so much.

"Riley . . ." I start thinking that while he's on break from his girlfriend, it implies he might be getting back together with her. "Is this a good idea?"

"No," he says. "It's definitely not a good idea. But I don't think I want to stop, do you?"

I laugh. "No."

"Good," Riley says, giving my butt a good squeeze. "God, I've been wanting to do this for ages."

And then we're tearing at each other's clothes in such a frantic hurry to get to where we're going that all I remember is a whirlwind of arms and legs and smooth bare patches of skin.

Two explosive—Disney World Fireworks Finale—orgasms later, we lay curled together, panting and slick with sweat, and the room isn't spinning so much as doing a slow dance.

I'm happy for the first time in a long time, happy and giddy and still a little drunk. And Riley's arms are around me, and I feel safe and snug and high on the smell of him so close to me.

"Riley," I sigh, tangling my hands in his hair. He is laying scrumptious kisses down the sensitive part of my throat. I close my eyes, feeling the strong pull of alcohol, the lead call of sleep, and even though I battle violently to keep awake, I think I am losing. It's what happens when you go without sleep for as long as I have. Even one martini could put me under the table. Never mind five.

And just as I am sure I am going to pass out, three words pop out.

"I love you," I sigh.

And that is the last thing I remember.

Seventeen

Sometime what heart know, head forget.

—Mr. Miyagi, *The Karate Kid II*

RETURN OF 1985

By Valentine's week of 1985, I got the best news ever. Kevin Peterson and Christi Collins had broken up—at last. It was rumored that Christi Collins wanted to go with Jacob Langford, whose parents had a pool in their backyard and a time share in Orlando, Florida.

For the first Valentine's Day in two years, Kevin Peterson was once again a bachelor. And I wasn't about to let an opportunity like this pass me by. It was now or never.

Every Valentine's Day since third grade had been pretty much the same. Everyone in class would get their own paper bag stapled to the bulletin board, and then classmates would fill up that bag with mini valentines bought from the five-and-dime.

I used extra care in picking out my valentines from the drugstore. I passed on the Mickey Mouse and Scooby-Doo (too obvious) as well as Care Bears and Rainbow Brite (too cutesy). In the end, I went with Garfield. He was trendy but not too trendy.

I laid out all twenty-four valentines, looking for just the right message I wanted to send to Kevin Peterson. I nixed all the Odie cards—they were the type I'd save for the Billy Connors of class—the carefully neutral lame ones like "Happy Valen-ARF-tine's!" I also nixed the one with Garfield saying, "I love you almost as much as I love lasagna."

It took me a solid hour to decide on which valentine to send. I had narrowed it down to a simple but coy "Happy Valentine's Day" with Garfield opening his hands for a hug, and the more direct, and more risky, Garfield holding out a big red heart and asking the question "Will you be mine?"

I went with the more direct approach, deciding now was no time to be timid. I sealed the little envelope and the next morning looked for an opportunity to deliver it to Kevin Peterson's bag.

Unfortunately, Kevin Peterson's bag was already full to bursting with notes from Strawberry Shortcake ("You're Sweeter Than Strawberries!") and Cabbage Patch Kids ("We're a Match Made in the Cabbage Patch"). It looked like some of the girls in the class may have put in more than one. Apparently they had the same idea I did. Still, I found room and stuffed my envelope down one side of the bag and hoped for the best.

After I'd delivered the valentine, I started to panic. Was it too much? Was I being too forward? I considered digging my valentine out of Kevin Peterson's bag, but then he wouldn't get one from me at all and, even worse, I'd look like I was trying to steal from his pile. No, what was done was done.

I sat at my desk, butterflies in my stomach, too nervous to eat the Valentine's Day cookies that Kevin Peterson's mom brought to class. I watched our teacher, Miss Gordon, pass out our respective Valentine's Day bags. She took forever to get around the room. It didn't help that she was pushing seventy.

Kevin Peterson got his bag first, and he looked like a rock star sorting through fan mail. I half expected to see a few training bras stuffed in his sack, but when he turned over the paper bag, only envelopes flew out. Envelopes and the occasional messaged lollypop.

I still did not have my bag, so I watched as Kevin Peterson casually went about opening cards. I saw him open two Bugs Bunnies and a Strawberry Shortcake, and then came what looked like mine.

Yes, there was Garfield, orange hand-paws extended, offering a big red heart. Kevin Peterson read it and put it down. I watched as he opened the next Valentine, and again—there was Garfield, hands extended, asking, "Will you be mine?"

I watched as Kevin Peterson opened five straight identical valentines. The valentine I had so carefully chosen had been the exact same one chosen by four other girls in class.

Miss Gordon finally got to my desk, where she plunked down my valentine bag. There was still hope that all was not lost. Kevin Peterson could have given *me* a valentine. Hastily, I began ripping through my envelopes.

The one I longed for—hoped for—was the last one I

opened, addressed simply "from KP." I ripped open the tiny envelope, and pulled out the tiny paper card. It was a Transform-
ers theme. It had Optimus Prime, the transforming red semi
truck on it and below the picture, typed in big block letters,
was "You're Optimal!" Kevin Peterson had signed it simply
with his first name. No hearts, no declaration of love. I read
and reread it.

What did that mean? Was he trying to tell me I was his soul
mate, or was he trying to tell me he barely even knew who I
was? "You're Optimal." It sounded like something I'd read on a
poster in the dentist's office. My stomach hurt and my mouth
went dry, like I'd eaten too many of those message candy hearts.

And as I watched, Kevin Peterson swept most of his valentines—even his Garfield ones—into the trash bag Miss Gordon
offered. My valentine, along with the hope of making Kevin
Peterson mine, was soon buried under crumpled napkins and
sticky Valentine's Day cupcake wrappers.

Eighteen

It's okay to lose to opponent. Must not lose to fear.
—Mr. Miyagi, *The Karate Kid III*

I wake up in the heart-shaped bed, my head throbbing and my mouth tasting like glue, with Riley's arm around me. I am wearing Riley's Smiths shirt and nothing else. I take a second to soak in the cozy warmth of Riley's body next to mine. Then I remember the night before.

I sit up in bed. Well, more like spring up in a panic. Oh. Dear. God.

I love you. I dropped the L-bomb and then passed out. This is what happens when I drink too much. I start playing free and loose with my emotions. I'm not the sort of person who EVER says I love you, at least not first, and certainly not two seconds after rolling off a guy who has said nothing about his own feelings.

I don't have to read *Cosmo* to know that the fastest way to get a guy out the door is to use an indiscreet L-bomb. I might as well have asked him to pick out china patterns.

The key thing here, I think, is not to panic. Jason, who has his own share of one-night-stand stories—including the time when he locked himself out of a guy's apartment when he mistook the front door for the bathroom door—always says not to panic. He, after all, found himself in the hall naked, and he had no idea what the guy's last name was.

"If you act as if you're supposed to be where you are, then you *are* supposed to be there," Jason says of how he marched into the lobby of the apartment building naked and asked the doorman to ring apartment 21B.

Riley shifts next to me. He'll be awake soon. What was I thinking? First, jumping into bed with a guy who is only "on break" from his girlfriend, and then saying, "I Love You," the three most terrifying words in the English language to the male species next to "I am pregnant."

Don't panic, I think. Slowly, cautiously, I extricate myself from Riley's arm. *Maybe,* I think, *he didn't hear me.* That's a distinct possibility. He didn't shout "Dear GOD!" when I said it, so maybe, he didn't hear me. In fact, what did he say? I can't remember.

Riley groans and comes awake, peering at me through one open eye. "Bollocks. I feel like shite," he says, grabbing his forehead. "I need coffee. You?"

Riley and I have breakfast in total silence, since I am having problems looking him in the face. I'm not sure if it's because

I'm too embarrassed about the L-bomb, or if it's because Riley is wearing a neon yellow rugby jersey and my hangover makes it difficult to stare too long at bright colors.

My phone starts beeping. It's trying to tell me I have new voice mail. I don't bother to check them. The very thought of hearing Michelle's voice makes my head feel it's going to explode.

"Your blasted phone is chirping."

"I know," I groan.

We fall into a silence, both staring at our coffee cups. I realize we're in that delicate part of a new relationship. It's like the first five minutes after takeoff in an airplane. Statistically, most plane crashes happen shortly after takeoff. If you last through the first part, chances are you're going to make it to your destination. Now is the time you start to think: *Is this going to be a relationship, or are we going to make an emergency landing in a cornfield?* You just don't know.

"Are you going to wear those sunglasses through the whole meal?" Riley asks me. He's referring to the gold plastic Elvis sunglasses that I picked up from our karaoke adventure. They're the only sunglasses I could find in the hotel room, and since my head is throbbing and I feel like my pupils can no longer dilate by themselves, I figured there are worse things than wearing Elvis sunglasses in Memphis during Elvis Week.

"I'm just trying to fit in," I say.

The breakfast diner is full of Elvis impersonators, even though it is not yet eleven. The singles counter is the Rainbow Coalition of Elvis.

"I appreciate your newfound affection for the King," Riley says. "But I can't talk to you seriously when you look like that."

I stroke one of the fake muttonchops hanging from the glasses. "I have no idea what you mean."

"Stop that! You're supposed to be the stoic, conservative one. I'm supposed to be the wild and crazy one."

"That sounds like an insult."

"I'm just saying you're the one who's petrified of getting up in front of people on camera or anywhere else, and suddenly you're getting drunk, doing karaoke, and wearing Elvis glasses in public. It's a lot to process at once. Not to mention that the fake facial hair is a bit disconcerting."

"What? You don't like a woman with muttonchops?" *That's right*, I think. *Be Light. Airy. Pretend that you did not just jump into bed with him last night, declare your love, and then pass out like a college coed.* I'll be just like Grandpa Frank, who never acknowledged anything awkward, including the time he opened the bathroom door when I was eleven only to find me trying to learn to operate his beard trimmer on my new underarm hair growth.

"You look a little too much like the King for my own liking," Riley says.

"Fine," I say, taking off the glasses. I squint like a mole seeing sunlight for the first time. "Are you happy now?"

Riley makes a face. "You look terrible."

"I told you so," I say, putting the glasses back on.

*   *   *

I can't seem to shake the blanket of shame that's covered me since I woke up that morning. I wonder if Riley can sense it. I feel like I've just woken up after a night of tequila shots to discover that I'll be featured in one of the "private hotel scenes" in a *Girls Gone Wild* video. Why did I say "love"? Why? Why? WHY?

I wonder if this is what happens in your late twenties. You stop feeling guilty about sex and you start worrying about emotional indiscretions.

"I think we should talk," Riley says next.

This conversation is heading dangerously close to that conversation I'd been dreading the moment I met Riley. The one that starts out with "You're a great girl . . . but I have a girlfriend, and I'm in love," and blah, blah, blah . . . Except that this time it'll be "You're a great girl, but I'm on the rebound," and blah blah blah or even worse, "You're a great girl, but it turns out that break with Tiffany is over." Blah. Blah. The end.

This is what you call relationship turbulence. I can almost hear the ding as the fasten seat belt sign comes on just as there's a loud clanking sound over by the right wing.

"Look, I'm not sure what happened exactly," I say, cutting him off at the pass.

"You were so turned on by the thought of shagging me for a second time that you fell asleep," Riley says.

Clank. Clank. Clank. Our flight has just lost the right engine somewhere over O'Hare International Airport and the plane lurches dangerously to the left. Put your tray tables in the lock-and-stowed position.

"I was drunk!" I exclaim. "I didn't fall asleep. I passed out. There is a small but important difference."

"You snore, by the way," Riley tells me.

I'm glad I'm wearing the muttonchops, because my face turns bright red.

"I do not snore."

"Like a bloody chainsaw. You kept me up half the night."

"Maybe you shouldn't have given me so many martinis."

"You were the one screaming for another one. Right after you started the Elvis conga line last night."

Assume crash position, I think.

"Forget last night," I say. Yes, this is my only option. I have to jump in, end things first, and then walk away with whatever pride I have left. "I just want you to know that I don't expect anything from you. It was a crazy night, okay? It was all some crazy mistake that we can both chalk up to Elvis Week."

Okay. Now, this is some way to make up for the L-bomb. *I'm* telling *him* it's a one-night stand. *Nice,* I think. This is what's called parachuting out of a plummeting 747.

But is this what I mean? I'm not so sure. Am I in love with Riley? It's a thought I've not fully considered before.

"Oh," Riley says. He looks disappointed. Sad, even. "Right. If that's how you feel."

The pang of disappointment I feel at hearing him agree with me so easily makes me think that I've made a terrible mistake. Maybe it was something more than a postcoital brain malfunction. I think I do have feelings for him—strong ones that are shouting at me to quit being such an idiot and say something before it's too late.

"You're right. It's probably best this way," he says, but he doesn't look at me.

And in that moment, I want to say something. To take back the one-night stand provision. To be honest about my feelings. But I can't seem to form the right words. And before I have a chance to try, my cell phone lights up and starts playing the Dixie Chicks again. I know without answering that it's probably Michelle.

"You'd better get that," Riley says. "I'll go pay the bill."

By the time I finish my phone call with Michelle, who is upset because she claims another reporter stole her investigative story about reckless pizza delivery drivers, Riley has gotten us a cab to take us to the mechanic's. And whatever chance I had to share feelings with him has passed.

He's got on the Elvis sunglasses and he's back to his goofy, nonserious self. "Look on the upside," Riley says. "A day that starts with checking out of Heartbreak Hotel has got to be a good one."

"What do you mean you can't fix my car?" I ask the stoned mechanic, who is staring intently at a spot somewhere above my left ear.

"You are really wigging me out," the stoned mechanic says.

"No. You are really wigging *me* out. I need my car."

I am hungover and in no mood to deal with another setback.

"Dude," he says, putting up his hands. "I'm just the messenger, all right? One or two days, tops, I'll have it fixed."

At this point, the only way to feasibly make the rehearsal dinner tomorrow night is to fly. I know it, and Riley knows it.

"I can't do it," I say, as we stand before the automatic sliding glass doors of the Memphis airport.

"Of course you can," Riley says, taking me by the elbow and guiding me into the air conditioning.

"You don't understand. I nearly threw up the last time I got on a plane."

"Well, you're in luck then, because I hear they have air sick bags right on board."

"Riley, that isn't funny."

"You know, you spend so much time telling me that I'm *not* funny that I'm beginning to think you actually do think I'm funny."

"Look, let's not do this," I say, digging in my heels a little before we get to the ticket counter. "I mean, I've made a good faith effort to get to this wedding. It's not my fault my car broke down. I've done everything I could to get there."

Riley keeps pulling me. "Bollocks. You haven't done everything."

"You're going to make me do this, aren't you?"

Riley nods. "It's for your own good. Besides, it'll be two hours that Michelle can't call you—doesn't that sound nice?"

On the plane, I sit with my eyes squeezed shut trying to visualize a calm and soothing place, like my sofa at my apartment during a marathon weekend of *Queer Eye for the Straight Guy.*

There's a horrifying clatter against the side of the plane, and my eyes fly open.

"What was that?" I cry.

"The luggage," Riley says, pointing outside the small circular window to my right. "We haven't taken off yet, you know. They're just loading the luggage."

"Oh." I relax a bit.

"You really weren't kidding, were you?" Riley asks me. "You really are scared of flying."

"Why would I lie about something like that? Of course I am." It's times like these I wish I were Catholic and carried around a rosary.

I open the little side window shade and then shut it again. There's an announcement over the PA from a disembodied voice that tells us to stow our luggage and prepare for takeoff. I double- and triple-check my seat belt. I let out a long breath and try to remember the calming techniques I once read about that are useful in staving off a panic attack. Was taking off your shoes and pushing your toes in the carpet one of them? Or was that only in *Die Hard*?

"Here I thought you just wanted to get me away for a romantic road trip," Riley says.

I turn to look at Riley. I can't believe he's said that.

"What in the world are you talking about?" I demand.

"Well, it's clear to anyone with eyes you fancy me."

"That's ridiculous," I say, but my face is turning bright red.

"Last night *you* were the one who kissed *me* first if I recall."

"I was drunk. I would've kissed a seal." *Please,* I think. *Please don't let him mention my L-bomb.*

"As much as it pains me to hear that, I have to tell you that I've noticed you've been flirting with me for weeks," Riley says.

Now, I'm really starting to get angry. Just because this may be true doesn't mean he should point it out. "Look, I'm sure *some* women like the whole 'I'm related to an earl' come-on line, but I for one don't. Besides, *you* were flirting with *me,* too."

"I was just being polite," Riley says. "We royals are taught to be appreciative of adulation."

It occurs to me suddenly that we're moving, more than moving, booking it down the runway. We're about to take off.

"And, I don't think I need to remind you," Riley says, "but just in case, you were the one who told *me* you *loved* me last night. Which I could have predicted, since no woman can resist my karaoke skills."

My mouth drops open. "I was drunk. I didn't know what I was saying. And besides, it doesn't matter now, does it?"

"I think it does matter."

"I didn't mean it."

"You can try to take it back if you like, but you said it and we both know you said it."

"Your ego is completely out of control."

"I think it's sweet," Riley says, and then he starts to sing the Beatles' "All you need is love. . . . Love, love, love . . ."

"Stop that," I say, looking around the plane. "People are starting to stare."

"Still worried about what everybody thinks?" Riley asks me, shaking his head. If possible, he starts singing louder. "There's nothing you can sing that can't be sung . . . There's nothing you can do that can't be done . . ."

"SHH."

"But you can learn to be you in time . . . it's easy . . ." He winks at an elderly woman from across the aisle who sends him a puzzled look. "All you need is love . . ."

"I am going to call the flight attendant."

"All you need is love . . ."

"I'm seriously never going to speak to you again."

"All you need is love, love. Love is all you need."

"You'd better be quiet. I need to concentrate for the take-off."

Riley stops singing. "Actually, I believe we've already taken off."

The PA system dings above our heads. The captain's voice comes over the speakers announcing that we've reached our cruising altitude.

I whip open the window shade next to me and stare out the window. I see only clouds. Then, slowly, I realize that Riley did that on purpose. He was distracting me so that I wouldn't be scared. I'm struck by the fact that this is incredibly sweet.

"Riley . . ." I start, but he's pulling his baseball cap over his eyes, preparing to sleep.

"Don't mention it. And by the way, would you mind shutting that shade? I'm going to take a nap."

Riley falls instantly asleep and midway through his nap, he puts his head on my shoulder. I let it stay there.

My hangover is not improved by the dry air in the airplane, and after trying to down as much water as possible, I find my head is still throbbing and I can't concentrate on anything, even the possibility of plummeting to my untimely death. Before I know it, I've fallen asleep, too.

I come abruptly awake with a jarring kind of panic and realize that we've landed.

"You've got some drool on your chin," Riley points out to me.

Hastily, I wipe my face.

"Gotcha," Riley says, giving me a sly smile.

We collect our bags quickly from the two-gate airport terminal. Riley is still humming "All You Need Is Love" and I'm trying to ignore him, but it isn't working. I turn on my mobile phone and check to see if I have any messages, but I can't get a signal.

"What are you doing?" Riley asks me, as I hold up my phone in various directions, then freezing when I get a single bar on my cell phone.

"I can't get a signal."

"About bloody time. Maybe now you'll finally let go a little."

"Funny," I say. "The Elvis conga line wasn't enough letting go for you?"

"I happen to like the Elvis-conga-line Jen. I'd like to see more of her."

I give him a look. "I bet you would."

Outside, we're greeted by a blast of hot humid air and Grandma Saddie's silver Buick.

"Uh-oh." I sigh.

Grandma Saddie is honking and waving from the driver's side like she's in a parade. A few of the people milling about the airport entrance stop to stare. "Praise Jesus!" she's saying. "Praise the Lord!"

Grandma Saddie is the Nakamura family's religious zealot. In 1986 she wandered into a Baptist tent revival by accident, thinking she was at the flea market. She had been on the lookout for some new serving plates, but instead she got eternal salvation.

Grandma Saddie, who is four feet tall, comes out of the driver's side door and hugs me. She pulls away and looks at Riley. "Praise Jesus, you must be The Boyfriend," Grandma Saddie says, sounding like I never have boyfriends. I watch to see if Riley flinches at the word "boyfriend." He doesn't seem fazed.

"His name is Riley, Grandma," I say. "Nigel Riley."

Riley glances at me. He likes being introduced last name first like James Bond. "Riley. Nigel Riley. Nice to meet you, Mrs. Nakamura." He offers her his hand, but she gives him a hug instead, and he stoops down to hug her back. Her head barely meets his elbow.

Released from Grandma Saddie's hug, Riley walks around to the back of the car to put our suitcases in her trunk. I hope he doesn't notice Grandma Saddie's bumper stickers. She has one that reads, "Honk if you love the Lord" and another that reads, "Jesus is my co-pilot."

When I was younger, I would always joke about accidentally sitting on Jesus when I rode shotgun. Grandma Saddie never found it funny. "Ya-shee, but you're getting skinny," Grandma Saddie says, looking me over. "Those pants are hanging off you."

"Grandma, they're low-riding jeans. They're supposed to sit down low."

"They look like they're falling down."

"Pants at your knees, it's the latest fashion statement," I quip.

"Ya-shee," Grandma Saddie says, laughing. "You always want to be like Johnny Carson."

"Ah, it's been so long since we've seen Jen," Grandma Saddie tells Riley as we climb into the car. "So long. Years, even. She's so busy with her work."

Here it is, I think. *The first guilt trip. I'll hear some variation of this from all the members of my family.* While they're proud of my accomplishments, they don't understand why I don't take vacations like a normal person, or why I can't spend two weeks at Christmas and a week at Thanksgiving like Kimberly does.

In the car, Grandma Saddie turns up the radio and sings along to a Christian rock ballad about turning the other cheek.

Grandma Saddie, who is eye to eye with her steering wheel, has jet black hair and only a single streak of gray running down the middle like a skunk. She is propped up on a telephone book, and she still has difficulty reaching the gas or brake. I'm sure that to other drivers it looks as if Riley and I are in the car alone.

Grandma Saddie is a notoriously bad driver. She's killed two possums, four raccoons, and one armadillo with her Buick. The armadillo she didn't even know she hit, even though it rolled up on the hood, hit the windshield with a crack, and went flying off over the car roof.

When a giant semi barrels by us, honking, I suggest that maybe she should consider giving the car more gas.

"I'm going the speed limit," she tells me, even though the speedometer says 35 mph.

I've told Grandma Saddie before about the stereotype regarding Asian women drivers. She doesn't seem concerned about reinforcing prejudices.

"The Lord, in his blessed mercy, has prevented me from ever being in an accident," she says.

"Are you sure you can see?" I ask her. It seems to me she has to look up to see the speedometer.

"Praise Jesus, my eyes are as good as ever."

Her tires spin a little in the gravel on the shoulder of the highway, and she makes an exaggerated adjustment of the wheel that nearly sends us careening into a Jeep full of teenagers. They honk angrily at us and then one of the passengers gives us the finger.

"Praise Jesus!" Grandma Saddie exclaims. "So many people love God."

I've long since tried to explain that people aren't honking because of her bumper sticker, but Grandma Saddie simply prefers to think she's surrounded by God's faithful followers.

I glance back at Riley. He sends me an amused smile. He is clearly being entertained.

"Are you sure you won't let me drive?" I ask her.

"Jesus is looking after us," she says. "There's no need to worry."

Jesus, I think, *may be looking after Grandma Saddie, who gives her entire Social Security check to the church, but I doubt he's looking after me, since I haven't been to church in ten years.*

A UPS truck driver beside us lays on his horn with five rapid bursts that almost sound like he's trying to play *Dixie*. Grandma Saddie gives him a good-natured wave and exclaims, "Praise, Jesus!" as he passes.

Forty minutes of honking later, we cross the city line of Dixieland, which is marked by a hand-painted wooden billboard that welcomes us "to the home of Fried Pickles and the Best Barbeque in the South."

Dixieland consists of a town square and a Dairy Queen and other coffee shops off the main Interstate. It has some old small-town charm, but Dixieland would never be chosen for the setting of one of those endearing Southern movies like *Steel Magnolias* or *Fried Green Tomatoes*. For one thing, you couldn't get a shot of the town square without one of those bothersome signs in the distance, the giant golden arches, or the supersize highway signs for Burger King and Dairy Queen.

Added to these modern franchises, I notice, are a couple of signs indicating new construction of what looks like an outlet mall. "What's all this?" I ask Grandma Saddie.

"Praise Jesus, we're a big suburb now," Grandma Saddie says. "A lot has changed since you've been here last."

What hasn't changed, I see, as we pull up into the driveway of my childhood home, is my mother's house. It's a vintage shingled Victorian two-story with a giant wraparound porch, complete with porch swing. It looks just as it did the last time I saw it five years ago. The only thing that's different is the line of white trucks and trailers parked out front. It looks like her house has been turned into a movie set, since there are so many men walking around with cords and pieces of a tent they're trying to erect on the lawn.

Even from the driveway I can hear Lucy shouting from inside the house. Apparently the tent men are abusing the lawn.

Aunt Teri comes out first. She's still blond, and she's wearing a signature red Chinese dress, as well as three different Chinese zodiac pendants hanging from her neck. They're all some version of a Tiger, her zodiac sign. I never took to the Chinese zodiac, in large part because I'm an Ox, which is hardly flattering.

Aunt Teri—sensitive to recent claims by Vivien that she's a "fake Oriental"—has started taking tea ceremony and flower-arranging classes (Ikebana) at the Little Rock Community College. Last summer, she tried building a Japanese garden behind

Vivien's house, including a small pond with carp, but the Arkansas summer was so hot the fish died of heatstroke.

"Jen!" Aunt Teri says, giving me a hug. She steps back and takes notice of Riley. "You must be The Boyfriend."

Why is everyone saying "The Boyfriend" as if it's a title of dubious distinction?

"I'm Riley, nice to meet you," he says, extending his hand.

Aunt Teri shakes his hand distractedly. "What year were you born?" she asks him right away.

"1976."

"I didn't know you were younger than me."

"Ah-hah!" Aunt Teri says. "A Dragon. Very special. You're popular, intelligent, gifted, but a bit demanding. You want everything to be perfect. But, most importantly, you're well suited for our stable Ox here. She'll help ground you, while you help loosen her up."

"Teri!" I exclaim.

"What?" she asks me.

"Ox?" Riley says, sending me a sly grin of amusement.

"Ya-shee!" cries my mother, Vivien, in excitement. She barrels into me with all the force of a steamroller. She crushes me in a hug as if I've just been released from a hostage situation.

"I thought I wouldn't see you till my funeral," Vivien says, releasing me after nearly crushing the wind out of my lungs. "What are we all doing standing outside? We're going to get heatstroke."

Vivien ushers everyone inside. She, being the older sister, is also bossier. Since Grandma Saddie never had a son, Aunt Bette calls Vivien the de facto patriarch of the family. Despite the fact that she is often inadvertently alienating her sister or sister-in-law, Vivien is always the one who claims to believe most in the importance of family.

"Go easy, Viv," Teri says. "You're so typically a Pig."

"Pig is her zodiac sign," I explain to a startled-looking Riley.

Vivien looks the same—her big-helmet hair is in place, as well as her blue eye shadow. She gives me another big hug and tells me I look too skinny.

"What are these pants?" she asks. "They're falling down."

"They're *supposed* to be low riding," I tell her.

"So this is the Mystery Man we've been hearing about," Vivien says, giving Riley a once-over and walking around him like he's a used car. I half expect her to ask him to show her his teeth. She doesn't. Instead she offers her hand.

"Vivien," she says. "Nice to meet you."

"Riley," he says, and shakes her hand. "Pleasure to meet you, too."

Lucy comes out next, and she's carrying a bridal veil in one hand and a bridal magazine in the other. As usual, Lucy is stunning. She's got her mother's blond hair and big blue eyes. She is the only one in the family that people regularly mistake for a model. At twenty she manages to exude a deadly combination of innocence and sex, even though she's wearing a seemingly casual outfit of yoga pants and a tank top, her honey gold mass of curly hair swept up in a loose bun at the back of her neck.

"Mooom!" she whines. "This veil doesn't look like the one in the picture at all."

Lucy stops talking once she sees Riley and me, although it is Riley where she focuses more of her attention.

"Hi, Jen. When did you get here? Who is this?"

"I'm Riley," he says, extending his hand. I watch his face. Usually when it comes out that I'm related to a five-foot-ten blond model, people never believe me. Riley doesn't show surprise. I secretly like him even more for that. In fact, he doesn't even seem overwhelmed the way most men are who meet Lucy for the first time. Most of them are trying to figure out where to look first, and it's usually not Lucy's face.

"I'm the bride," she answers and then starts giggling in her flirty way. "But I guess that's obvious, huh?" she says, holding up the bridal veil.

"Nice to meet you, Ms. . . . Uh . . . Bride?" Riley says. This causes Lucy to laugh.

"Oh my God. I love your accent!" Lucy exclaims. "G'day, mate!" she coos at him.

Riley sends me a wry glance. "Uh, I'm from the UK, actually."

"Oh, how silly of me," Lucy says. "Isn't that where they filmed *Lord of the Rings?*"

"That's New Zealand," I say.

"Do they eat Vegemite in the UK? I hear that stuff is loaded with fat," Lucy says. She's still not getting it. I doubt she knows what UK stands for. This is one of many reasons she ought to be going to college instead of getting married. Then again, Lucy never did well in school. I think this is because there was always a boy willing to do her homework.

"He grew up in London," I say.

"Oh! Right. I'm so silly," she says, giving Riley her patented coy look. I know she's practiced this look because years ago I caught her doing this face, among many others, in the bathroom mirror. Her main staples are: Coy, Pouty, Flirty, and the Miss America Smile. The whole family believes that had she used her Coy look instead of her Miss America Smile she would've won the title of Miss Arkansas. Normally, even men double Lucy's age will start to melt at the mere hint of Coy.

I watch Riley carefully to gauge his reaction. Again, Riley doesn't show any new emotion. He treats Lucy with the same friendly, polite expression he used for Grandma Saddie. I send Riley a grateful smile.

"Jen has told me so much about you all," Riley says. "I'm glad to meet you in person."

"How long have you been dating?" Vivien asks us.

"Is anyone else hungry?" I interrupt. "I, for one, am starved."

"Oh dear. Where are my manners!" cries Vivien. "Come on, ya'll, sit, and I'll get you both a snack."

Seconds later, Vivien presents us with a giant plate full of *inari* and her signature cooked tuna rolls (tuna marinated in soy sauce and sugar and rolled up in sushi rice). "But save some room. We're having stir-fry tonight."

Beef stir-fry is another Nakamura signature meal. Vivien and Grandma Saddie load beef and all sorts of vegetables into their giant wok and out comes the most tender, tasty concoction you've ever eaten. No matter how often I try to imitate this, I fail. I'm convinced it's my Southern genes at work.

I look at the sushi and the pickled vegetables and think of the time at the roller rink with Kevin Peterson. I glance up at Riley, almost daring him to eat something. Riley takes hold of the most exotic thing on the plate, dried fish, and takes a big bite.

"Not bad," he says, mouth half-full. He goes for the pickled radish next. And then the sushi rolls. He has no one to impress, not like John the Asian Interloper. He has nothing to prove by eating my grandma's odd assortment of Japanese foods, but he does so with gusto. In fifteen minutes, the two of us have wiped the plate clean.

"I'm glad you're back to liking Oriental food," Grandma Saddie notes.

"You had this stuff all the time, and you *wouldn't eat* it?" Riley asks me, amazed.

"I was going through an Identity Crisis."

"She didn't think she was Oriental," Vivien says.

"Mom, you know if Kimberly were here she'd tell you the correct term is '*Asian.*'"

"Ya-shee, same difference," Vivien says. "You see, the kids at school were telling Jen she was adopted. And so she started thinking maybe she was. She'd go up to different families at the supermarket and ask, 'Did you give me up for adoption?' For months she went around convinced she was from Central America." Vivien and Grandma Saddie have a laugh at my expense.

"It's actually tragic when you think about it," I say in my defense.

"Well, you know what I say," Vivien adds. "You can lead a duck to water, but you can't make him drink."

Riley looks from both of them to me, with a quizzical expression on his face.

"Um . . . where is the groom?" I ask, changing the subject and trying to be casual, but my voice shows some of my nerves.

Riley gives me a sidelong glance.

"He's in Little Rock tonight," Lucy says. "But he'll be back tomorrow. He had some kind of business to take care of, he said."

"We think he's getting a special gift for Lucy," Vivien says.

"Oh, go on," Lucy says, but she's clearly thrilled by the idea. The fact that I won't be seeing Kevin Peterson fills me with both disappointment and relief.

"You two thinking about getting married?" Grandma Saddie asks suddenly of Riley and me. I nearly spit out my iced tea.

"Grandma!" I gasp.

"Well, everyone was thinking it, I just asked," Grandma Saddie says. "The joke around here is that Jen will show up at Thanksgiving one of these days married with four kids."

"She never tells us anything, and we're lucky to even see her once in a blue moon. We're so neglected," Vivien explains. "And you know I have a heart condition."

"Mom, you don't have a heart condition."

Vivien ignores me. "How long did you say you were dating?" she asks Riley.

I look at Riley but see no panicked look on his face, and not even the blush of uncomfortable embarrassment.

"Not nearly long enough," Riley says, without losing a beat.

"Aw, that's so sweet," Grandma Saddie says, giving Riley's face a loving pat. He's won Grandma Saddie's and Vivien's approval in under ten minutes and I want to hug him.

Our conversation is interrupted by what sounds like a gun firing in the yard. Riley jumps. Everyone else barely looks up. It's the familiar sound of Old Red, driven by Bubba.

"He still hasn't given up his truck?" I ask Vivien.

Vivien rolls her eyes to the ceiling. "And he won't either, even though that piece of junk barely runs," she says. "But you know a man and his pickup truck. He'd rather give up his wife than his truck."

Bubba has had Old Red, his vintage Chevy, since before I was born. In the South, there's something sacred about a man's pickup truck. And there are fierce debates about which brand is better: Chevy or Ford. Bubba won't even tolerate a discussion of Ford in his presence, so deep is his loyalty to Chevy.

"The man of the house is home!" Bubba calls, clambering in, wearing an old faded T-shirt and cut-off khaki shorts, and smelling like fish. "And I caught us some sushi."

Bubba offers up a line of freshly caught bass. Bubba's favorite pastime next to working on Old Red is bass fishing.

Bass fishing is practically a religion in Dixieland. Every year there's a bass fishing tournament at which hundreds of men from across the state gather to fish on one of many nearby lakes. The team that catches the most fish in three days wins a trophy and bragging rights for an entire year.

"This must be the boy you were telling us all about," Bubba says, taking in Riley. Bubba is no slouch of a man. He's tall, broad, and when angry can be quite intimidating. Riley, however, does not flinch. He simply extends his hand for a shake.

"Nice to meet you, sir," he says.

"You're not from around here, are you, boy?" Bubba asks Riley, hearing his accent.

"He's from England," I say.

"Brit, eh?" Bubba says. "I was stationed in London for a few months when I was still in the air force. I went to a rugby match or two, and let me tell you, y'all are a bunch of crazy characters, playing football with no helmets."

"Well, let me tell you a bit about rugby," Riley says, his face lighting up at the prospect of discussing his favorite sport. He and Bubba quickly strike up a conversation that involves the ins and outs of rugby.

"Where's Kimberly?" I ask Vivien.

"She flies in tomorrow morning. She got hung up at some mall protest," she says.

"But she is coming, isn't she?"

"Well, I've had Bubba talk to her, and you know he's the only one who can handle her," Vivien says.

Bubba is, in fact, the only one who can really convince Kimberly to do something she doesn't want to do. Despite all of Kimberly's feminist ravings, she's still a little bit of a daddy's girl.

*   *   *

We make it through dinner with only one attempt by Grandma Saddie to convert Riley, who's an Episcopalian (who are about as exotic as Buddhists in Dixieland, where the Methodists and Baptists feud almost as heatedly as Catholics and Jews). And after dinner, Vivien shows us our "sleeping arrangements."

I'm bunking with Grandma Saddie and Riley gets the couch in Bubba's "study," which is his gallery of all manner of bird, deer, and bass caught or shot by him over the last fifteen years. Kimberly calls it The Death Room, but Riley doesn't seem fazed.

"Be sure to ask Bubba about Bud," I say.

"Who's Bud?" Riley asks.

"His prizewinning fifteen-pound bass. It's on the wall, you'll see."

Bubba caught Bud during a bass-fishing contest five years ago, and it landed him in the list of Top Five Biggest Bass ever caught in Arkansas.

"Why is the fish called Bud?" Riley asks.

"'Cause I caught it with a can of Budweiser," says Bubba, giving us an exaggerated wink.

Grandma Saddie's room, where I'm sleeping, is covered in pale pink frills. Everything in the room has a strong perfumed scent, with only the barest hint of Ben Gay. On Grandma Saddie's bedside table is an oversize picture of Grandpa Frank when he was still young and handsome. This was taken at the internment camp during World War II, and behind him, you can barely make out a fence of barbed wire.

I pick up the picture of Grandpa Frank that I've studied a hundred times before. He looks so young and full of life. It's hard to imagine the Grandpa Frank I knew young.

"Grandpa was the most handsome man in camp, ya-shee," Grandma Saddie says, a note of longing in her voice.

"You've mentioned that," I say. The story is one I love. Grandma Saddie was a beautiful young girl and every guy asked her to dance at the sock hop. Grandpa Frank was the best-looking boy in camp, the one all the girls wanted to date. Grandpa Frank proposed to Grandma Saddie near the mess hall. He got down on one knee and said, "You'd be crazy to marry me, so here's hoping you're a little loony toons."

"I knew then he was the only man for me," Grandma Saddie says.

If Perv John and I had started dating, what sorts of stories would I have told my grandchildren? "I knew I loved your grandfather the afternoon I found Asian porn hidden under his bathroom sink"?

"Of course, he always wanted sex, you know," Grandma Saddie adds now. "Even to the day he died—he never slowed down!"

This is Grandma Saddie's trademark. Despite being born-again, she has no shame in sharing extremely personal details of her life, from sex to bowel movements.

"I kept thinking he'd get tired of it," Grandma Saddie continues, oblivious to my obvious discomfort. "But that man was the energizer bunny, even till the day he died."

I try, unsuccessfully, to get out of my head the image of Grandma Saddie in her bejeweled jogging suits and Grandpa Frank in his polyester shorts in the throws of passion.

"That's more information than I need," I say.

"Ya-shee. It's natural, you know," she says.

Nineteen

First learn stand, then learn fly. Nature's rule,
Daniel-san, not mine.

—Mr. Miyagi, *The Karate Kid*

1986

After Kimberly and I saw *The Karate Kid II* in the theater, I asked Grandpa Frank, since he bore a passing resemblance to Mr. Miyagi, if he knew any karate.

"No," he said, pretending to look thoughtful. "But I know kick-in-the-shins-run-like-hell. You want me to teach you my technique?"

This shattered forever my hopes that the knowledge of killer hand-to-hand combat might be hiding within the Japanese half of my DNA, ready to unleash itself at a particularly timely moment, say when Kimberly insisted on stealing my Dr. Pepper Lip Smacker.

This was the first in a long line of disappointments about my Japanese DNA. It didn't, as I hoped, give me a proficiency in math, the ability to get A's without even trying, inherent knowledge of a foreign language, or the skill to remain expressionless and inscrutable.

It was during this same summer—after I tried, but failed, to convince Vivien to let me take karate lessons—that I refocused my attention on something entirely different: L.A. Gear tennis shoes.

At that time, anything remotely related to California was cool. There was OP wear (Ocean Pacific), Valley Girl Speak (gag me with a spoon), and the video of *Fast Times at Ridgemont High,* which Kimberly had stolen from her boyfriend's car after she discovered that he liked to watch the topless scene of Phoebe Cates over and over and over again.

While I dragged Vivien to store after store in search of the perfect L.A. Gear shoes (pink and white with pink and black laces), Kimberly kept trying to convince our parents that she needed a pair of real Ray-Ban sunglasses like the ones Tom Cruise wore in *Risky Business,* or barring that, the ones Tom Cruise wore in *Top Gun.* Either one, she said, would do. Vivien and Bubba, however, were not about to spend two hundred dollars on a pair of anything, much less sunglasses for Kimberly, who had become notorious for losing her valuables (she'd gone through two retainers already, had lost Grandma Saddie's pearl earrings, and once, when she and Bubba went out to practice driving a car, she misplaced Bubba's car keys when they stopped for ice cream).

"Ya-shee," Vivien would say to me. "You hit fifteen and you lose your brain. Remember that."

It was that same summer, while Kimberly tried pulling double babysitting shifts around the neighborhood in order to save up for her Ray-Bans, that Grandpa Frank had a heart attack. He was mowing the lawn on a particularly hot August day, even though Grandma Saddie had warned him to come inside and quit trying to prove he was "stronger than Jesus" that he collapsed and died on the way to the hospital. He was only sixty-one.

On the day of Grandpa Frank's funeral, all the California Nakamuras flew in to pay their respects. They were the branch of the family (descendants of Grandpa Frank's sisters and brothers) who moved back to San Francisco after World War II. I had never seen so many Japanese people in one place before. There were enough to start our own Little Tokyo right in the heart of Dixieland.

I later learned that many of them came to help pray for Grandpa Frank's spirit. While Born Again Christian Grandma Saddie believed only in Christian doctrine, many of my Buddhist California relatives believed that you needed to pray to help guide the spirit of the dead in the right direction. That's why so many Nakamuras descended on Dixieland: to hold a Buddhist prayer vigil.

I remember Vivien's kitchen being overrun with homemade Japanese goodies. Mochi, sticky rice cakes that were usually reserved only for New Year's celebrations, were stacked in trays in our refrigerator. There was enough sushi and pickled radish to last us months.

I'm sure that the First Baptist Church had never seen so many Japanese visitors in one place. Some of them who were still practicing Buddhists lit incense at Grandpa Frank's grave site, and, apparently, there was some commotion among California relatives because Grandma Saddie chose not to have Grandpa Frank cremated.

At the funeral, several of the California Nakamuras spoke about Grandpa Frank. Until then, I had known him mostly as a man who never missed an episode of *Wheel of Fortune*. But it turns out he had a lot of other events in his life that didn't include Pat Sajak.

His brother, Sam, told a story about him before World War II. In 1941, six months before Roosevelt signed the order to intern all Japanese Americans, Grandpa Frank had graduated from high school and had been accepted to study at Berkeley with a full scholarship. His father, proud of his eldest son's accomplishments (the first of his family to go to college), offered him a choice of graduation gifts: either a convertible car or a trip to Japan. Grandpa Frank, as any young American boy would, took the car.

Six months later the FBI seized it, along with all other major Nakamura assets, including the family's house and grocery store. And Grandpa Frank, who had dreamed of being an architect, never went to Berkeley—since his four-year internment forced him to forfeit his scholarship—and he never saw the convertible again.

"But he never complained, not once," Sam said.

I can't imagine what it would've been like for Grandpa Frank and Grandma Saddie, who are as American as I am, to have been suddenly rounded up like criminals and locked away because of what they looked like. It made me angry to think about, but a diffuse, aimless kind of anger, the same thing I felt when something unjust happened that I couldn't control, like when a kid on the playground discovered my middle name was Nakamura, and started the chant "Nakamura, Sakahura, makes me wanna hurla."

If I had lived at that time, I would've been interned, too. The War Relocation Authority took anyone who had more than one-eighth Japanese blood. Even seven-eighths white was not white. The smallest concentration of ethnic chromosomes turned a whole person that color, sort of like highly concentrated food dye.

During and after the funeral, I realized that I had a lot to learn about my Japanese half. For instance, I couldn't wield chopsticks with half the skill of my California cousins. And every time I spoke, they made fun of my drawled *a*'s and the use of the word "ya'll." None of the California Nakamuras had the distinctive drawl; in fact, the Dixieland Nakamuras stood out like sore thumbs. I swore I could hear Vivien's sharp twang from across the lawn. Not to mention, every five seconds, inexplicably, Vivien kept saying "I'm just a good old southern belle" even though I don't know of any southern belles who look like Vivien, and neither did the California Nakamuras, who would nod politely but say nothing.

Then, of course, there was blond, blue-eyed Aunt Teri, who was decked out in her best Chinese attire and kept asking everyone their Chinese zodiac signs, and offering them fake paper money to burn at Grandpa Frank's grave. Given that Japanese Buddhists don't adhere to the Chinese tradition of giving spirits of the dead money for their travels, and that Teri was about as ethnic-looking as Loni Anderson, none of the California Nakamuras were quite sure what to make of it. Then there was Aunt Bette, who came back to Dixieland after three failed attempts at college (at age twenty-five she decided she probably wasn't going to graduate), during her Early Madonna Phase, when she had her hair teased and wore large spandex leggings over a thin, lacy skirt and rubber bracelets up and down each arm.

And, last but not least, there was Born Again Grandma Saddie, the only person who wore more crosses around her neck than Aunt Bette in her Early Madonna Phase. Grandma Saddie kept trying to convert the California Nakamuras to Christianity at every available opportunity, going on and on about hellfire and damnation and about how Grandpa Frank's soul was safe "at the right hand of Jesus" because he'd taken the Lord into his heart two days before his death.

The California Nakamuras, on the other hand, were well dressed, dignified, and decidedly Asian. It was clear when the Dixieland Nakamuras stood next to the California Nakamuras that we were the poorer, less dignified side of the family.

This was further proven after Grandpa Frank's funeral, when my great-aunt Yuki's husband apparently told Grandma Saddie that all the Dixieland Nakamuras held their chopsticks like peasants. We, apparently, moved both chopsticks simultaneously to grab hold of food. In Japan, only the peasants did this. Samurai and noblemen would hold one chopstick completely stationary, moving only the other.

Then, to make matters worse, I poured a heaping helping of soy sauce on great-aunt Yuki's rice, which made her cry for an hour, since adding salt or soy sauce to cooked rice, I would later learn, is one of the most dire insults you can inflict on a Japanese cook. But how was I supposed to know? Dixieland Nakamuras put soy sauce on everything, even chicken fried steak and mashed potatoes.

While I was feeling less Japanese, Kimberly started to feel more. At the susceptible age of fifteen, she became enamored of one of our older male cousins, Mitch, who wore his hair in a ponytail and talked incessantly about his work with PETA and a small political group that had helped lobby Congress to get reparations for Japanese Americans from the U.S. government. Mitch also discussed his prolonged trip to Asia, where he found our distant relatives still living on a rice farm in Japan. Apparently, despite the fact that he didn't speak Japanese (aside from the single phrase he'd learned, "I'm your cousin from America"), the Japanese Nakamuras put him up for an entire week.

"The Japanese value family above all else," he told us.

Cousin Mitch opened our eyes to a lot of things we never knew. For instance, L.A. Gear was *not* cool in Los Angeles. And OP was practically on the way out. Rumor had it that Kmart would soon be selling it, and while not the kiss of death in Dixieland, it was in California.

Kimberly hung on Cousin Mitch's every word, even going so far as to take down all her posters of Rob Lowe and replace them with the racially intriguing Benetton ads she cut from magazines, as well as a Rising Sun Japanese flag.

Kimberly later told me that Cousin Mitch said the crane kick in my beloved *Karate Kid* movie was not based on any real martial arts, and that the role of Mr. Miyagi reinforced all the worst stereotypes about Asian Americans, since Pat Morita could speak flawless English, but in the movie Mr. Miyagi spoke with a thick accent and incorrect grammar and was, amazingly, the only Asian person seemingly living in California, where the movie was supposed to take place. Cousin Mitch also pointed out that Mr. Miyagi would never have used "Daniel-san" since "san" is a suffix of respect only attached to last names in Japanese society.

"Technically, it should've been LaRusso-san," Cousin Mitch said with some disdain. In fact, first names are used in Japan only between lovers, which led to a long line of jokes from him about the real nature of the relationship between Daniel and Mr. Miyagi.

Kimberly listened, rapt, but I thought it was all a bit ridiculous. I couldn't see why Mr. Miyagi was the problem. I couldn't see what was wrong, exactly, with a Japanese character who was wise, funny, and could kick serious butt. But I never shook the feeling that maybe by liking Mr. Miyagi I was somehow selling out my roots.

Twenty

Not matter who stronger. Matter who smarter.
—Mr. Miyagi, *The Karate Kid II*

I'm awakened the next morning by the indignant voice of Kimberly demanding to know why Vivien has not stocked Second Generation recycled toilet paper in the house.

"Do you *know* what global warming is doing to our planet?" Kimberly shouts.

"That stuff is too rough for Grandma Saddie," Vivien counters.

When I make my way down the stairs, I see Kimberly, wearing cutoff jeans, a faded Greenpeace shirt, and flip-flops. She has highlighted her jet black hair so that there are a few streaks of red in with the black. She's wearing her staples: a nose ring, her Buddha tattoo over her left ankle, and something new—a red string Kabbalah bracelet around her wrist.

"Can you believe these people?" she asks me, giving me a big hug. "I've forgotten how antienvironment this place is."

"You could always save the toilet paper you use and use it over again," I suggest.

"Don't be gross," Kimberly says. "Double ply!" she wails, looking at the roll of toilet paper in her hand. "This one roll of toilet paper could have housed a whole family of tree monkeys in the rain forest."

Just then, a tall, handsome Asian man walks into the room. "I can go get Second Generation bathroom tissue if you need it," he says. This, I think, must be Matt Chang.

"Don't bother. They don't sell it for another four counties, at least," Kimberly says.

"I don't mind, really," he says. He looks sincere. *Poor Matt,* I think. *He's probably going to be yet another one of Kimberly's admirers too eager to please.* Kimberly never falls for men who show her too much attention.

"Hi, I'm Matt Chang," he says, extending his hand to me. "You must be Jen. Kimberly's told me so much about you."

"Uh, nice to meet you," I say, taking his hand.

Riley appears at the stairs then, his dark hair ruffled, wearing only a T-shirt and jeans, looking every bit like his nickname, The Colins. Even though we're not really dating, I find myself dreading introducing him to Kimberly. She is always supercritical of men. She's the first one to seize upon a flaw and not let it go. When I introduced her to my prom date, she told me she thought his nose was too big.

"Morning, luv," he says, coming near me and giving me a peck on the cheek. I'm surprisingly glad for that.

"This is my sister, Kimberly." I watch as she takes in Riley, assessing.

"Nice to meet you," Riley says, shaking her hand.

"Ditto," Kimberly says. Riley yawns and then turns to me.

"And this is her . . ." I trail off, wondering if "boyfriend" is the correct term here. Chances are the very word would throw Kimberly into a feminist fit. "Uh . . . friend, Matt Chang."

"Good to meet you," Riley says. He stretches and adds, "I hate to be a pest, but is there only one loo in the house? I believe the upstairs one is in use."

"Jen didn't tell me you were from England," Kimberly says.

"She probably didn't want you to think I had bad teeth," Riley jokes. "Now, about the loo?"

"It's over there, by the kitchen," I say.

"Thanks," he tells me and squeezes my shoulders.

When he's out of earshot, Kimberly grabs my elbow. I expect her to tell me that I shouldn't be dating a British guy because Brits were responsible for the subjugation of the population of India, as well as half the globe at the height of the British Empire. Instead, she says, "Not bad." This is as close as Kimberly gets to giving her approval.

"You think so?" I say, not sure.

"If he's a pity date, I'd like to see one of your real dates."

I shrug.

"JEEN! KIIIMBERLY," shouts Lucy from the top of the

stairs. She looks down at us. "Good Lord. Why aren't y'all dressed? We're late for our appointment at Lulu's Bridal Wear."

"What about the boys?" I ask her, referring to Riley and Matt.

"Bubba is taking them fishing," she says. "Now come on. We're LATE."

Lulu's Bridal Wear is the only bridal shop in Dixieland. It's been on the square since the fifties, and its mannequins, with their fifties style coifs and slightly yellowed hues, are still in the windows.

"Well, I don't believe my eyes. Is that *Jen Nakamura Taylor?*" cries the woman behind the counter at Lulu's, Miss Maggie Lane, who bears a frightening resemblance to Minnie Pearl. She lacks only a straw hat with the price tag still on.

"How are you, Maggie?" I ask her.

"Jen, I'll be damned, but you sound like a Yankee," she says.

In the South, anyone failing to use the word "ya'll" and to stretch out their vowels is automatically labeled a foreigner.

Like Kimberly, I've spent years trying to shed my accent, a deliberate decision to leave behind my Dixieland roots. When people in other places tell me I don't sound like I'm from the South, I take that as a compliment.

"And is that . . . Kimberly?" Maggie asks, tentative. Kimberly's nose ring, her red Kabbalah bracelet, and her tattoo of Buddha above her left ankle might go unnoticed in California.

But in Dixieland, she might as well be traveling with the circus.

Maggie is temporarily speechless. "Good to see you again, darling," she finally says.

"You first," Vivien tells me, handing me my bridesmaids' dress and sending me back to the dressing room.

"Why me?" I whine.

"Because I said so."

Once on, the dress is even worse than I feared. I'm covered from head to toe in frosted pink tinfoil like some sort of human Hershey's Kiss: Special Pink Valentine's Day edition. If I raise my arms, I suspect that I might be able to pick up Satellite XM Radio.

"Have you gained some weight?" Lucy says, frowning and stepping back and studying my reflection in the mirror.

There are so many ruffles and poofs in this dress that it would make even a chopstick look like it was putting on weight.

"I don't think I've gained any weight."

"You *have*," Lucy declares, sounding ever more alarmed. "You've clearly gained more weight."

My sister and I exchange glances. Kimberly rolls her eyes.

"I'm going to have to take offense at the word 'more,'" I say.

"We're going to have to let it out." Lucy sighs, shaking her head and rubbing her temples with her fingers.

"It's fine," says Vivien.

"Aunt Viv. It is NOT fine. She looks like a sausage in tinfoil," Lucy mutters.

"She just needs some nice control-top hose," Grandma Saddie offers.

"I'm still here," I point out. "I can hear you."

"They have full body suits at Victoria's Secret," Grandma Saddie says.

"How do you know what they have at Victoria's Secret?" Kimberly asks her.

"Ya-shee, I may be old but I'm not dead," Grandma Saddie says.

"I heard duct tape might work," Vivien is musing.

"That's only for better cleavage," Lucy corrects.

"I can hear you, ya-shee," I sigh.

"Did you just say 'ya-shee'?" Kimberly asks me.

I shrug. Desperate situations call for desperate measures.

"It's your turn now," Vivien tells Kimberly.

"No way am I wearing that," Kimberly declares.

The shop bell dings. "Yoo-hoo," calls a familiar voice. It's Aunt Bette, the top saleswoman for Mary Kay in southwestern Arkansas. She's the one responsible for introducing Grandma Saddie to bejeweled jogging suits and for getting most of the women in the family hooked on coral lipstick. Aunt Bette often says she's just a few cases of blush away from winning the coveted pink Cadillac, which, in her mind, will mean she's arrived. Bette has on her weight in makeup and her signature color of pink. She's a long way from her Material Girl phase.

"Kimberly—beautiful as always," Aunt Bette says, passing inspection.

Then she turns to me. She gives me a tentative hug, careful not to break her French-manicured acrylic nails. She studies my face, putting her hand on my chin and turning it back and forth. Aunt Bette has been doing this since I was eight.

"I have something that will help reduce the size of those pores," she tells me. Her silver eyeshadow on her almond-shaped eyes glitters under the gleam of lights at Lulu's Bridal.

"Aunt Bette," I whine.

"I'm just saying, you're so pretty, sugar," she says. "Why not take it to the next level? I've got some *great* new spring shades of eye shadow, too."

It's comforting that no matter what the occasion, Aunt Bette is always ready with a sales pitch. It's clearly why she's the largest single retailer for Mary Kay in southwestern Arkansas.

Still, I owe Aunt Bette quite a debt. She's the one, after all, who introduced me to Nair, eyebrow shaping, and tampons. Kimberly did not have the inclination or the patience to try to teach me about the female arts. In high school, she was too busy trying to raise money for Amnesty International.

There's something quite different about Aunt Bette. It takes me a moment to realize she's blond. "You're blond," I exclaim, before I can help myself.

"Do you like it? You know Picasso had his blue period. I'm going through a blond period," Aunt Bette says.

"Did you just quote Hugh Hefner?" I ask her.

Aunt Bette waves her hand, dismissively. "So what do you think?" she asks me.

She looks like a forty-something Asian woman who is wearing a blond wig. I have flashbacks of Vivien dressed up like Princess Di.

"Um, nice," I say.

"Your mother says I look *just* like Michelle Pfeiffer, but I like to think I'm more of a Pamela Anderson type," Aunt Bette says. *The Nakamura racial amnesia at work,* I think. Kimberly rolls her eyes.

"Definitely Pamela Anderson," I say. Aunt Bette doesn't have the D-cup boobs, but she does have the penciled-in eyebrows and the collagan-injected lips.

"I thought so," Aunt Bette says, and beams. "So? I hear you have a *boyfriend.* Is it true?"

Why is my love life the topic of such widespread family discussion?

"We're all so proud," Aunt Bette says, as if I just announced I'd won the Nobel Prize. "Your mother thought you might be a lesbian like Cousin Gillian. Not, of course, that there's anything wrong with being a lesbian."

"I never said that," Vivien says, giving Aunt Bette a stern look. Aunt Bette ignores it.

"But I'm nothing like Gillian!" I exclaim. Gillian is a California Nakamura cousin who shaved her head when she was fourteen, pierced her tongue, became a Sid Vicious groupie, and then went through a series of identity changes, including becoming a Hare Krishna, then a Scientologist, and most recently, a follower of Wicca, which is some version of modern-day witchcraft.

Five years ago she announced she and her life partner—her roommate, Paula—were going to have a commitment ceremony on the solstice, where everyone in attendance would be required to shed their clothes and participate in some sort of ritual under a full moon. Being gay is fine, but being like Gillian—that's an insult.

"Well, you just never know," Aunt Bette says.

"Vivien really thought I was gay?" I ask. This is very clearly another failing of Nakamura Telepathy.

"You don't talk much about your boyfriends," Aunt Bette says.

"Just how much time do you guys spend talking about my sex life?" I ask.

"Did you just say 'yose guys'?" Aunt Bette asks me, putting on her best mobster accent. "You sound like a Soprano. I guess up North you don't use 'ya'll'?"

"If she visited more often, maybe she wouldn't sound like a stranger," Vivien says, giving me a pointed look.

I sigh.

"Praise Jesus!" I hear Grandma Saddie emerging from the back of the store. "Bette's here to do our practice hair."

"Practice hair?" I ask Bette.

"You wouldn't go into the vaulting competition for the summer Olympics without practicing first, would you? Same with wedding hair. I even brought you some falsies," Aunt Bette says, whipping out from her shopping bag what looks like a small schnauzer, only it's fake hair.

"You will not put that on me," I say.

"How about these?" Aunt Bette says, showing me two silicone pads shaped like boobs. "They'll bring you up a full cup size."

"No way," I say, shaking my head.

"Let's see what the bride says." Aunt Bette winks at me.

An hour later, I find myself standing in front of the three-way mirror at Lulu's Dress Shop. My hair is enormous and at least three-fourths fake, my eyelashes are fake, my nails are fake, and even my boobs are fake.

Aunt Bette is now beaming at me. So is Vivien. Kimberly is looking at me and silently thinking, "sucker." Kimberly has refused even to try on the dress, and since Bubba isn't around, there's no one to make her do it.

"My lovely granddaughter!" exclaims Grandma Saddie.

"Definitely an improvement," Aunt Bette remarks.

I frown at my reflection in the mirror. If possible, I look even less Japanese than Aunt Bette with her streaky blond hair.

"Why are you taking off your eyes?" Grandma Saddie cries, when I begin tugging at my fake eyelashes. "They're so pretty."

"Grandma," I sigh. "They itch."

"Beauty," Aunt Bette tells me, "is *always* worth suffering for."

Aunt Bette, it should be said, sometimes wears a light layer of makeup *to bed* just in case her house catches on fire in the middle of the night and she has to run out with no time to put on her face.

The bell on the front door of the shop dings again, and I

look up, praying it isn't Riley. He'd never let me hear the end of my fake hair.

But the visitor to the shop isn't Riley. It's much worse than Riley.

I find myself staring at an adult Kevin Peterson.

Twenty-one

Lie become truth only if person want to believe it.
—Mr. Miyagi, *The Karate Kid II*

1986 AND THE TEMPLE OF DOOM

The summer between sixth and seventh grades, Kevin Peterson grew five inches, therefore becoming one of only a handful of boys eligible for dating in Dixieland Middle School, where most of the girls had outgrown the boys. So now, if possible, Kevin Peterson had even more admirers, as the populations of Dixieland Elementary School and Robert E. Lee Elementary School (in the neighboring town of Noxville), merged into one middle school for grades seven and eight.

I, however, had fate on my side when I landed a locker five down from Kevin Peterson, where I could hover and work up the nerve to say hello. By November, it was clear Kevin Peterson was headed toward the sort of superstardom popularity reserved for the Brat Pack and middle school football stars. His locker was jammed with notes from admiring girls, covered in pink hearts and smelling like Exclamation perfume. Every day after fifth period, I'd watch him come to his locker, pocket the four or five admiring notes without even looking at them, tend to his spiky hair (which he seemed to be modeling after Simon Le Bon) and if I was very, very lucky, he'd see me, nod his head in my direction, and simply say, "Hey."

If I didn't have much of a chance of winning Kevin Peterson in grades fourth through sixth, I really had a less than zero chance of getting his attention in seventh. Kevin Peterson's list of ex-girlfriends soon became larger than MC Hammer's group of backup dancers. His basketball letterman's jacket was passed through the population of cheerleaders faster than frosted lip gloss.

In the South, cheerleaders and drill team girls were the royalty of the popularity hierarchy. Girls trained for years in gymnastics only with the hope of becoming a cheerleader in middle school and then high school, because it was a well-known fact that you couldn't be homecoming queen without being a cheerleader; and homecoming queen was the highest honor a girl could hope to achieve in her entire life if she lived in Dixieland.

One mother once told Vivien at a PTA meeting that she was "ruining my life" because she had not insisted that I take gymnastics lessons at age three.

Cheerleaders were worshipped in Dixieland Middle School. They were given the best table in the cafeteria; hordes of honor students rushed to do their homework for them, and even teachers would give them passes out of class without question.

I resented cheerleaders, because I couldn't understand why

the ability to do the splits in two ways meant you were somehow better than everyone else. At age twelve I didn't understand the power of sex appeal, obviously.

There were emergency tryouts held midyear after Christi
Farnsworth broke her leg falling down from a cheerleader pyra-
mid, and nearly a hundred girls tried out for the one spot. I
was one of them, but only because Kevin Peterson had, in a
roundabout way, asked me to.

One afternoon at the lockers he'd said, "Hey, you trying out
for Christi Farnsworth's spot?"

And while I had no desire to do so—after all, I am not at
all athletic (see Presidential Fitness Challenge)—I decided
maybe Kevin Peterson was trying to tell me something.

With my twelve-year-old ears, I heard "Hey, Jen, if you became a cheerleader, *maybe* we could date."

So that's how I ended up wearing flannel boxer shorts,
standing in a group of one hundred girls who were trying out
for the same position, trying to figure out how the hell I was
going to manage the splits.

I was at a distinct disadvantage. Some of these girls had
been to cheerleading camp and knew all the ins and outs of the
drill team voice (like every single routine began with "READY?
O-KAY!" and a loud clap) and many of them could do backflips, front and side splits, and a series of cartwheels ending in a
double flip.

I, on the other hand, didn't even know the proper vocabulary.

I didn't know the difference between a "Half T" and the
"Liberty Position" much less how to go about doing a "side

hurdler" jump or a "toe touch." Every other one of the one hundred girls at tryouts seemed to not only understand these commands but also talked about the perfect "form" based on some summer cheerleading camp trainers I'd never heard of. Apparently cheerleading was an art form, even though up until then I'd thought it involved nothing more complex than shaking pom-poms and then, at the end of the routine, throwing your fists in the air and shouting, "GO, TROJANS, GO!"

The first leg of the competition was called "Show Your School Spirit." This involved running down a padded mat and doing a cartwheel and some kind of combination of hurdler jumps and a backflip and shouting some version of "Go, Trojans, Go! Yeah!"

Kevin Peterson and his friends wandered up to watch, probably because Kevin was scoping out new girlfriend material.

When my turn came, I stood at the end of the mat trying to figure out what I should do. I sucked in my stomach and tried to think peppy, cheerleading thoughts. I closed my eyes and tried to summon the spirit of Tawny Kitan doing cartwheels and splits on the hoods of cars in White Snake's "Here I Go Again" video. I opened my eyes and started running, hoping that my body, despite a complete lack of training, might somehow curl itself into a backflip naturally, without any sort of instruction.

According to Kimberly, who had wandered into the gym looking for me, since she was picking me up from school, I had a good running start with lots of momentum. It seemed like I was gaining speed for a serious move. A multiple backflip, maybe, or a series of midair flips. Something big, since I was running at full speed.

I raised my hands up, like I was going to start a tumble. Only, I didn't start tumbling. I just ran—hands up—until I reached the end of the mat. When my feet hit the solid gym floor, I skidded to an abrupt stop and made a little, almost three-inch jump off the ground with my hands still in the air. Then, instead of shouting "Give me some spirit" or "Go, Trojans!" like the girls before me had, I mixed up the two phrases. I shouted at the top of my lungs, "GIVE ME SOME TROJANS!"

Since I sounded like I was asking for condoms, the entire gym burst out laughing, including Kevin Peterson.

Needless to say, I didn't make the first cut of the cheerleading tryouts. On my scorecard, I got a possible one out of ten for School Spirit.

Twenty-two

Concentrate. Focus. Power.

—Mr. Miyagi, *The Karate Kid*

*I*t takes me a moment to recognize Kevin Peterson in Lulu's Dress Shop. I am, after all, clinging to the memory of the last time I saw him—his Members Only jacket slung over one shoulder. His red parachute pants, which were then *IT* in terms of style, and his cutting-edge asymmetrical hair cut too short in the front and too long in the back—a 1980s mullet.

What throws me at first is the fact that he seems to be wearing the same stuck-in-the eighties clothes: Ice Ice Baby pants that were pleated in front and tapered down to a tight fit around the ankles, sockless expensive-looking crocodile loafers, an Izod pastel polo shirt, and—horror of horrors—a white blazer with the cuffs pushed up to his elbows, à la *Miami Vice*.

I blink a few times, wondering if my imagination is playing tricks on me. No. It's Kevin Peterson. Older, taller, broader, a little heavier around the middle, and a little thinner up top, and looking like he should be pursuing coke dealers on a speedboat with Crockett and Tubbs.

Kevin gives Lucy a hug and a kiss on the cheek, saying, "Hi, darlin'," in his Southern drawl.

I don't even have time to be embarrassed by what I'm wearing. I can't stop staring at Kevin Peterson's white blazer. I know fashion trends move slowly in Dixieland but this is ridiculous. I think I would have preferred to see him in the Dixieland male uniform of choice: a bass-fishing T-shirt and frayed jeans.

I am divided between two distinct but separate emotions: stunning disappointment and enormous relief. The man I once thought was my soul mate is wearing Z Cavaricci's. I think even in the cosmic, eternal world of love that means I'm free to move on.

"Sweetheart, you remember Kimberly and Jen—my cousins?" Lucy says to him. He turns then and looks at me for the first time. And to my surprise, his eyes light up and he knows who I am.

"Jen! Jen Taylor! The girl I practically shared a locker with in middle school, how could I forget," he says. He wraps me in a tight hug, and for a second I'm stunned.

He *remembers* me. I'm temporarily blind to the fact that he's wearing a white blazer over a pastel blue Polo shirt. Kevin Peterson *knows who I am*. For a second, I'm twelve again. I feel the same bubbly excitement I did when he used to give me a casual "hey" at the lockers.

Kevin's hug goes a beat longer than a casual greeting. I am still reeling from the fact that he remembers me. It feels like being known by a celebrity—a badly dressed one, but still a celebrity of sorts.

"I didn't think you'd remember me," I say, before I can stop myself.

"How could I forget the prettiest girl in school," Kevin exclaims.

Me? Pretty? For a second I see in him the old Kevin Peterson. The irresistibly cute, cool Kevin Peterson. He hasn't lost all his charms, I think.

For a second or two he holds my eye, and I can feel a blush start to creep up the back of my neck. He probably says that to every girl he went to school with, but I still can't help but think maybe he really means it.

"Are those *alligator?*" Kimberly cries, aghast, looking at Kevin's shoes. Kimberly, who is a vegan and owns several "Meat Is Murder" T-shirts, looks like she's about to take Kevin's loafers and beat him about the head with them.

"Gen-you-ine alligator," he drawls.

Has he always sounded like a hillbilly—or have I just been away from Dixieland too long?

"They're from New York City," he adds.

He says this as if it's supposed to impress us. Clearly, he doesn't understand that Kimberly, a card-carrying member of PETA, is looking about the store for something that might substitute for red paint.

"So are you going to say something about my getup or what?" Kevin asks me.

"Your what?"

"My outfit," Kevin beams, proudly. He pulls on the lapel of his white jacket. "I am trying to fulfill a bet with my Lucy."

"He's trying to get away with not throwing out any of his old clothes," Lucy explains. "I told him he could only keep in his closet anything he wore within the last month—so he's dragging out all his worst clothes. Yesterday, he wore an 'I'm a Bass Man' T-shirt and galoshes."

"Oh—*oh,*" I say, finally understanding.

"I can see you think I walk around wearing a getup like this all the time?" Kevin Peterson asks.

"Um . . ." I pause.

Kevin Peterson throws back his head and laughs. "We're not all that backward around here, Miss Big City Girl. I just wanted to prove to Miss Lucy that I can still fit into the clothes I wore when I was eighteen."

"We all know how adorable you are," Lucy says. "Next thing he'll start telling you about how he got $150 during the bachelor-for-charity auction last fall."

"I seem to recall that $150 was your bid," Kevin Peterson says. "You insisted on outbidding Laura Cody, who was pretty determined to win me, as I remember."

"You can see why I want to get a ring on his finger," Lucy says to me.

"Until then, she's got to dress me in terrible clothes so no other woman runs off with me," Kevin Peterson says. "Speaking of women, you know how I remember you, Miss Jen Taylor?"

I shake my head.

"You were the first girl I ever wanted to kiss," Kevin says, giving me an honest smile.

I can't think of anything to say.

"Really?" Lucy says.

Kevin is giving me the kind of extended eye contact I would have killed for in seventh grade. He's off the charts in terms of flirting.

Then my purse starts blaring the Dixie Chicks. My mobile phone—again.

"I hope that isn't 'Cowboy Take Me Away,'" Kimberly cries, sounding disgusted. "Why don't you just wear a sign that says 'I'd rather be barefoot and pregnant'?"

"Sorry—it's my phone," I say, rummaging around in my purse. I don't get to my phone before it kicks into voice mail. When I try to redial, I can't get a signal. What is it with this town?

"Kevin," whines Lucy in a warning tone. "Can I speak to you a minute? *Alone?*" She drags him off to a back corner of the store.

"Don't they just make a darling couple?" asks Maggie.

Neither Kimberly nor I say a word.

"Those two are prom king and queen of Dixieland, that's for sure," Maggie says. "Lucy couldn't have done better. She's the prettiest girl in town and Kevin is the richest guy so it works out."

"Richest?" Kimberly asks.

"He sold his farm to Hormel," Maggie tells us. "Word is he got a six figure deal."

Only in Dixieland would six figures equal independent wealth, I think.

"Not to mention, all the ladies love Kevin," Maggie says.

"They do?" Kimberly asks, aghast.

"He's a charmer, that one," Maggie tells us. "If Lucy knows what's good for her, she'll keep a close eye on him. The ring she needs to put on him shouldn't go on his finger."

Kimberly and I look at each other.

"Maggie!" I exclaim, shocked.

"I only speak the truth," Maggie says, winking.

Twenty-three

Nobody perfect.

—Mr. Miyagi, *The Karate Kid II*

1987

By the start of eighth grade, was still wishing that I could be like Baby Jessica and fall down a well, because I was still smarting from the humiliation of the cheerleading tryouts.

I had two things to look forward to every day—the daily debate with my friend Amy about which Corey was cuter (Haim or Feldman) at lunch, and watching the new seventh graders fumble with locker combinations and trying to find their way around the school. On the weekends, I went to the new East Town Mall, built between Dixieland and Little Rock, where Kimberly worked overtime shifts at *The Limited*. She divided her paycheck between buying stirrup pants and oversize sweaters and sending cash donations to Amnesty International.

East Town was the closest city to Dixieland with a mall

and it was twenty minutes away on the Interstate. While we were years away from driving, Kimberly would sometimes give us a ride in the back of her maroon 1977 Honda Accord hatchback.

Even though we had no money, Amy and I would walk through the then-new Gap with its endless stacks of pastel V-neck sweaters.

We would often dream up reasons to walk by the arcade, where Kevin Peterson, then the reigning champion at Centipede, hung out.

It was on my thirteenth birthday that Amy and I pooled what money we'd saved from skipping lunch for the last week and wandered over to Center Stage, the in-mall recording studio where for five dollars you and your friends could record your own karaoke versions of whatever song you wanted on cassette tape.

Amy and I chose to sing "Eternal Flame" by The Bangles, which I silently dedicated to Kevin Peterson.

I decided that while maybe I had not thrived in the country music setting, back those many years ago, *maybe* my true calling was to be a pop star. After all, the way they manipulated voices in the studios these days, it's not like you really had to have any talent (See Tiffany and Debbie Gibson); maybe I did have a calling as a pop star.

Sinead O'Connor and The Bangles became famous because of songs that Prince wrote for them. All I needed, I decided, was for Prince to write me a song, too, and I'd be all set.

I wrote him a letter, telling him about Kevin Peterson.

Dear Prince,

   I realize you are very busy because you are a musical genius. But I was hoping you could write a song that I can sing. I am at least as talented as The Bangles.

   I want to impress a boy named Kevin Peterson, and I figured being a pop star might be easier than being a cheerleader (since I can't do backflips).

   If you could find time to write me a hit, something in between "When Doves Cry" and "Manic Monday," I'd be totally in your debt. Like, forever.

                              Your greatest and most devoted fan,
                                   Jen Nakamura Taylor

   P.S. I've enclosed the $15 fan membership fee, along with my self-addressed stamped envelope.

After I sent the letter to the Prince Fan Club P.O. Box, I checked our mailbox regularly for what I'd hope would be a cassette tape, or at the very least, a sheet of music. I still couldn't read music, but I could definitely find someone who could. Then I imagined I'd be in malls across the country just like Tiffany. Only I'd have a Prince song, which would be a million times better than "I Think We're Alone Now."

Prince did write me back, eventually. Well, not Prince exactly, but someone on his staff. There was no cassette tape. No sheet music. No single.

But there was an eight-by-ten glossy of Prince standing astride a motorcycle, and his stamped autograph (stamped, not original) along with a form letter that thanked me for joining his fan club and gave me a list of concert dates.

Kimberly, who spent her free time carefully ripping holes in her brand-new Guess jeans, told me that I'd be better off being her assistant, because she was either going to be the president of Greenpeace or she would direct music videos for a living, but only ones with social messages, like "We Are the World."

Ironcially, her favorite band at the time was Bon Jovi, who, as far as I know, did not dedicate themselves to any causes other than having lots of sex. She was a big fan of "Wanted: Dead or Alive" and would play it at the start of her local PETA chapter meetings she'd hold in our garage every month. Only two of her high school classmates ever showed up, and they were just two guys who were in love with her and trying to get her out on a date.

"How can you think about fame when there are people starving in Ethiopia?" Kimberly asked me.

Of course, Kimberly's new sensitivity to the hungry populations of third-world countries did not prevent her from throwing away any meat Vivien put on her plate.

"It's about sticking to your principles," she'd said when I asked her about how wasting food helped the starving masses in Ethiopia.

Twenty-four

Sometimes better to be bothered on full stomach than empty one.

    —Mr. Miyagi, *The Karate Kid III*

When we get back to Vivien's house, Old Red is parked out front and the entire place reeks of fish. There's also a trail of muddy water that leads from the porch to the kitchen. It seems the boys are back from their fishing trip.

"BUBBA!" shouts Vivien, stomping up the porch steps and through the front door.

On Vivien's nice dining-room chairs sit Riley, Matt Chang, and Bubba, all shoeless and drinking cans of Budweiser.

"I leave you alone for four hours and you already trash my house," Vivien shouts.

"Calm down, darlin', we're just relaxing a bit after our fishing trip," Bubba says. "We brought you some sushi."

I check in the sink and, sitting on ice, there are four big bass and one tiny one.

"The small one is Riley's," Bubba says.

"AND the biggest one," Riley points out.

"Matthew Chang, you had better not have fished," Kimberly says, putting her hands on her hips.

"Worry not, sugar," Bubba says. "Your boy didn't fish on account of his principles or some such nonsense."

"I swear," Vivien says. "You're just like a cat. Always bringing back useless dead animals, thinking we're going to eat them. Just *what* am I supposed to do with these fish?"

"Fry 'em?" Bubba suggests.

"The three of you had better have this kitchen *spotless*. You know very well, Bradford Alexander Taylor, that your *parents* are coming," Vivien points out. She never uses Bubba's full name unless she's really angry.

"You know my parents love a good fish fry," Bubba says.

"I'm going upstairs, and when I come down again, I'd better not see one fish," Vivien says between clenched teeth. She stomps up the stairs, leaving the rest of us in the kitchen.

"I hope you had fun," I tell Riley.

"Dead right," he says.

"Your limey Brit did all right," Bubba says, clamping Riley on the shoulder. "He only fell out of the boat twice." Bubba loves rocking the boat to see who falls out.

"Bubba—you didn't," I say. I can feel my face start to burn. Bubba is always doing embarrassing things like this. It's no wonder I never want to bring home boyfriends. He was, after all, the one who answered the door causally holding a hunting rifle the night my prom date came to pick me up. He likes to remind me it wasn't loaded, but my date sure didn't know the difference. The entire night, he barely said two words to me.

"It's all right," says Riley. "I can swim like a fish."

"Hope you're stronger than one," Bubba says, handing Riley the beer cooler. "This needs to go to the garage."

I follow Riley as he heads to the backyard. "I'm so sorry you got stuck with my dad. He can be a little odd." God knows what else Bubba said or did while they were on the lake. "And I know you must be thinking we're all backward here. My family means well, but they're not very sophisticated."

"There's nothing boring about your family, that's for sure," he says. "But I don't think there's anything to be embarrassed about either."

"I don't believe you," I say, doubtful.

"Let me tell you a story." Riley sits down on the overturned cooler and motions me to sit next to him. "My dad . . ." he starts.

"The bankrupt earl?"

"Brother of that earl," Riley corrects. "Anyway, my dad was obsessed with being proper. You know, the British, stiff upper lip and all that. He never hugged me. Never told me he loved me. The only time I realized I meant something to him was when he came to one of my rugby matches when I was a lad and watched us win the championship and he actually started crying. He couldn't stop and it was a bit embarrassing. He'd been bottling up his emotions for years. He doesn't know what to do with them, so they just come up at times like that, and he's overwhelmed."

I nod, not quite sure what this has to do with my crazy relatives.

"Families are always going to find a way to embarrass you," Riley says. "You can have people who spend all their time trying to be proper, or you can have relatives like yours who aren't afraid to show how much they love you, even if it means dunking their daughter's date in the lake a few times."

I'd never thought about it that way before. I feel a sudden, instant relief.

"Point is, your family loves you dearly, and that's the important thing," Riley says. "And they make you unique."

"Even if they are insane."

"I think the proper term is sanity-impaired."

I snort, and I feel closer to Riley than ever. He's looking every bit The Colins, and I want badly to wrap my arms around him and pull him to me, even if he does smell like lake. My knee is touching his, and I realize that there's an electric energy between us that is hard to ignore. When I look up, Riley is staring at me with a serious look on his face.

"Riley, I need to tell you something."

"I know."

"You do?"

"Well, you're going to tell me that you're mad for me and all that talk about one-night-stand stuff was just bollocks."

My mouth drops open. This is pretty much what I had planned to say.

"And do you know what I was going to tell you?" he asks me.

I shake my head.

"I was going to tell you that you're the most beautiful, smart, and engaging bird I've ever met, and I'm mad about you, too," Riley says. "Now come here and kiss me, yeah?"

Our kiss is interrupted by the sounds of Dixie blaring from an RV horn.

I look up to see Bubba's parents—my paternal grandparents—waving to us from the front seat of their RV. Grandpa and Grandma Taylor spend their time traveling around the country to watch Brooks & Dunn concerts. They jump from the front cab and I can see they're wearing matching T-shirts that read, "Idaho: The Potato Lover's State," nylon fanny packs, and plastic rainbow visors. These are the same grandparents who disapproved of their son's marrying a "geisha" all those years ago. Since then they have evolved—a little—in their thinking.

"There's our little Jen!" they cry, when they see me. Grandma Taylor puts me in a vicelike grip. She, as usual, smells like stale smoke and Oil of Olay. Grandpa Taylor hikes up his Bermuda shorts (worn with black knee-high socks, complete with the garters) and gives me his patented one-arm side hug that quickly progresses into a headlock.

"This old man still has the moves!" he shouts, rapping his knuckles along my skull.

They then present a balloon-themed gift bag to me. "It's a belated birthday gift," Grandma Taylor says.

My birthday gift is a bright pink beer cozy that reads, "I'm always beautiful when I'm drunk" and a key chain that says, "My other car is a piece of sh*t."

"We got them in Oklahoma," Grandpa Taylor says proudly. At one of their favorite gift-buying locations, I'm sure—the roadside truck stop.

"Uh, thanks," I say.

Riley takes them in with interest.

"So you must be The Boyfriend," Grandpa Taylor says, shaking Riley's hand.

"Would people please quit calling him that?" I ask, but am ignored.

"We've heard a lot about you," Grandma Taylor says. "Here—we brought you a bumper sticker."

It reads "If you're close enough to read this, back the f*ck up!"

Riley takes one look and laughs.

When introduced to Kimberly's would-be boyfriend, Matt Chang, Grandpa Taylor says, "We have a great respect for your people. We just visited Little Tokyo in San Francisco and it was so neat, wasn't it, honey?"

"Actually, grandpa, he's Chinese," Kimberly corrects.

"Oh, well, they're good people too. They make a great plastic," he says. "And they sure do make some cheap T-shirts. Were you born near Hong Kong?"

"Pasadena," Matt Chang says.

"Why there's one of those in California!" exclaims Grandma Taylor.

"What's that you were saying about family?" I ask Riley. He just smiles.

Later that afternoon, we head to the church, where the wedding rehearsal takes two hours, largely because Vivien keeps trying to interrupt, and Vivien and Teri both argue incessantly about who should be standing where. Grandma Taylor keeps insisting that Lucy and Kevin wear their matching "groom" and "bride" baseball caps that she bought in Nevada.

Kevin has changed out of his Miami Vice getup, thank goodness, and is wearing a regular suit. He's lost the boyish good looks I remember him having, but still has some of his old magnetism. This fact is not lost on the other bridesmaids (Lucy has eighteen total), who seem to pay him more than a little attention. Maybe Maggie was right about Kevin's needing a short leash.

I can't seem to shake what he said the other day. I was the first girl he wanted to kiss! *If only I had known then*, I think.

"So that's my competition," Riley says to me, as we watch Kevin Peterson entertain three of Lucy's friends with tales from the day he helped Dixieland High School win the state football championship.

"Competition?" I echo.

"He does keep looking over here at you. And it sounds like he was quite the athlete at age fifteen."

Kevin's fixation on the state high school football championship just reminds me how small-minded Dixieland can be. Your greatest accomplishments in life happen between the ages of fourteen and eighteen. I bet Kevin Peterson even gets free coffee at the local doughnut shop on the square just because people remember him from his days as a Dixieland High School quarterback.

This, I remind myself, is one of many reasons I left Dixieland. I didn't want to raise kids in a place where high school is your greatest life accomplishment.

After the rehearsal, we all pack up and head to the Catfish Parlour, Lucy's restaurant of choice, and the only one in Dixieland that uses linen tablecloths, even if they do have plastic tabletop covers. It's sandwiched between a Denny's and an Old Country Buffet out by the interstate, two restaurants that hadn't been there when I was growing up.

The Catfish Parlour boasts the "best fried catfish in five states" but doesn't specify which five states. For instance, it might not even be the best fried catfish in Arkansas; maybe it's only the best in Montana, Idaho, North Dakota, Utah, and Connecticut.

The rehearsal dinner takes up almost the entire restaurant. Everyone sits at big round tables with lazy Susans in the middle, upon which heaping plates of fried foods are placed, along with the vegetables of the meal: coleslaw and corn on the cob.

Kimberly takes one look at the fried chicken and catfish and just shakes her head. "I don't suppose I could hope for tofu," she says, sighing.

My sister, who consumes no animal products, passes on the coleslaw (because of its mayonnaise and therefore egg content), and puts a single ear of corn on her plate.

"Think of it as the Dixieland diet," I tell her.

"Even the beans have meat in them," Kimberly says, throwing down her fork in disgust. Riley offers her his corn on the cob. She accepts it with a grateful look.

"Lucy tells us you're a Vulcan," says Mrs. Peterson, Kevin's mother.

"VEE-gan," Kimberly corrects. Of course, vegans would be about as exotic as Star Trek aliens in a county known for its annual barbecue cook-off.

"I just don't know what I would do if I couldn't have my beef," says Mrs. Peterson.

Riley chokes on his iced tea and starts coughing.

When all eyes go to him, he looks about and says, "I'm not used to sweetened tea," and gives me a sly smile.

"You're not from around here, are you?" Mrs. Peterson asks Riley, who shakes his head. "Well, then, you probably don't know anything about the Taylor girls."

"Would anyone like more tea?" I ask the table. The last thing I want is for Mrs. Peterson to start talking about my family. The whole town considers us a bit odd. Kimberly thinks this is a badge of honor, but I have always felt like I lived in a fishbowl. It's what happens when you're the only Asian family in a small town and your dad played on the 1964 Championship Dixieland High football team.

"Everybody around here has been laying bets about when

those Taylor girls are going to finally find themselves good husbands," Mrs. Peterson is saying.

I want to drop through the floor. This could not get more embarrassing.

"And just what are the running odds?" Riley asks.

"When pigs fly," Kimberly mutters. I can tell from her tone that she's about to start in on her lecture straight from her women's studies thesis, when she is thankfully interrupted by Riley.

"I think the Taylor sisters are doing more than fine without husbands," Riley remarks. "Men would probably just slow them down. We're really just a lot of babies, honestly."

I send Riley an appreciative look. He simultaneously prevented Kimberly from going off on a rant while putting Mrs. Peterson in her place.

Before Mrs. Peterson can respond, our conversation is interrupted by the plunking sound of plastic silverware on glass.

"If I could have everyone's attention," says Bubba, who is standing in the middle of the restaurant and about to make a toast.

"I consider Lucy my own daughter, and I couldn't be prouder or happier for her." Bubba, who is not normally a man to show his emotions, swallows hard. "And I want Kevin to know that he'd better take good care of our Lucy or there'll be hell to pay."

A murmur of laughs and ooohs goes through the audience.

"We have a unique family, that's for sure," Bubba continues. "It's not one that just anybody can understand, and I'm glad to welcome into it Kevin, who will come to understand that to us, there isn't anything more important than family. Let's raise our glasses to Lucy and Kevin and wish them every happiness."

Everyone raises their glasses and some people applaud. It's a touching moment.

My mobile phone, in the purse on my lap, chimes in with "Cowboy Take Me Away." I look at the caller ID: it's News Four.

"Excuse me one second," I say to Riley, push myself away from the table, and answer the phone as I head outside.

"I'm so glad I finally got through," says Anne in a semi-panicked-sounding voice. "I've been calling you all day."

"The reception is patchy here at best," I say. "What's up?"

"How's Dixieland? You having a good time?" she asks me, clearly stalling.

"ANNE. What's going on?"

Anne sighs. "Okay, well, it's totally insane. You know Gary? The head anchor on the ten-o'clock news? Well, he got arrested down on North Avenue by the Edens propositioning a cop who was posing as a prostitute. But that's not the worst of it. Jen, are you sitting down?"

"No. But lay it on me."

"Ken, the producer of the evening news—he resigned. Well, technically, he had a nervous breakdown and is on some sort of extended medical leave."

"Are you serious?"

"Bob is looking for replacements. He's having everyone submit a proposal, and he wants them on his desk by Monday morning."

I'm not scheduled to even be back in the office until Tuesday morning.

"Bob's been coming by your desk every five minutes asking where you are."

"But I told him I was going on vacation."

"I know, but he keeps telling me there's no such thing as a vacation when you work in news."

I can tell Anne is near the breaking point. Having that much interaction with Bob is likely to do that to anyone.

"I'll see what I can do about coming back early. Thanks, Anne," I say.

"This could be big for you," Anne says, sounding excited.

I turn to go back inside the Catfish Parlour but as I do, Kevin comes out.

"You smoke, too?" Kevin Peterson asks me. He has a pack of cigarettes in one hand and a lighter in the other.

"Uh . . . no," I say, thinking, when did Kevin Peterson start smoking? "Just taking a phone call."

"Keep me company?" he asks me.

I hesitate.

"Come on, I don't bite." He turns on the patented Kevin Peterson charm. I can't help it. I'm drawn in a little.

"You've gotten even prettier," Kevin says, without much pretense. "I didn't think it was possible, but here you are."

"I'm sure you say that to all the girls you used to go to school with," I say.

"Hardly," Kevin says.

We drop into a small silence.

"So I keep hearing about how you're going to be the producer of the *Today* show soon," Kevin says. "Your mother talks about you all the time."

Vivien's pride in my accomplishments is endearing but also slightly embarrassing. She was the one who took the first taped broadcast of a show I produced and showed it to everyone who would sit still for twenty minutes to watch it, including the mailman.

"She's definitely my best publicist," I say.

Kevin lights his cigarette, and that's when I notice that his lighter has Chinese characters on the side.

"Where'd you get that?" I ask. It's something an AO (Asian Obsessed) blood type would have.

"This? I've had this forever," Kevin says. "I've always been interested in Asian culture."

"You have?" I say, amazed. This from the same kid who ran in the other direction at the very sight of sushi?

"Oh yeah, I couldn't get enough of it," he says. "Largely because of you. I always thought I'd marry into an Asian family. And now I am—sort of."

That is the strangest thing I've ever heard. How is my blond, blue-eyed cousin Lucy even remotely Asian?

"I have a confession to make," he says, blowing smoke up into the air. "I had the biggest crush on you."

"You did not," I squeal, like I'm thirteen again. I clear my throat and try to regain my composure. "I don't believe you."

"I swear," Kevin declares, putting his hand up like a Boy Scout.

"Why didn't you do anything about it?" I ask him, thinking about how I would have reacted if he'd told me this fifteen years ago.

"Why would someone like you go for someone like me? I was the son of a pig farmer."

"You always had girlfriends," I start. "All the girls loved you."

"All the girls except you," Kevin says. "You barely even spoke to me."

I don't tell him that it was because I was always perpetually tongue-tied whenever he came within ten feet of me.

"I didn't even think you knew my name."

"Everybody knew who you were. The smartest, prettiest girl in class."

I don't know what to say to this. I've never taken compliments well. I look at my shoes.

"Lucy reminds me of you," he says.

"Really? Lucy?" Huh? I think. *She's fair skinned. I'm dark. She's completely spoiled. I hope I'm not.*

"Well, you do share the Taylor nose," he says.

I'm still trying to process this.

"Well, I had the biggest crush on you in elementary school," I manage to admit. "Do you remember when you and Christi Collins were an item?"

Kevin thinks a moment and nods.

"Well, that bracelet she gave you was one I made. She was supposed to ask you to go with me, but instead stole you for herself. I don't think I ever forgave her for that."

Kevin laughs and taps the ash from his cigarette. "You have got to be pulling my leg," he says. He shakes his head. "I guess I missed out on the signals."

"I guess so."

He drops his cigarette butt and then takes a step closer to me. I don't move. I feel a little hypnotized.

He's right in front of me now, and he strokes the side of my face with one of his hands. I'm frozen. Completely frozen. Is he doing what I think he's doing?

He's staring at me intently, gently, and maybe a little sadly. What's that in his eyes? Regret?

"It's not fair," he says, sounding sad. "For you to get prettier."

I can't seem to move my muscles. I'm shocked he's touching me at all. And then, almost as an afterthought, he dips his head, and I realize with startling clarity that he plans to kiss me. Right here, in front of the Catfish Parlour, with his fiancée inside, along with everyone he knows. I should stop him somehow, but I can't seem to move.

His lips brush mine, softly at first. I'm completely still.

My inner thirteen-year-old girl is squealing. My twenty-eight-year-old self can't help but notice that he tastes like an ashtray. And I realize I don't feel anything. Songbirds aren't singing. My heart isn't even beating fast. In fact, it's almost like . . . kissing a relative. There are absolutely no sparks. I feel like I've finally gotten to see a movie everybody raved about for years, only to discover it's just not that impressive.

The door to the restaurant starts to open, and Kevin releases me.

Then I hear a familiar voice.

"Bollocks," Riley says, seeing me standing close to Kevin Peterson. "I didn't mean to interrupt."

Twenty-five

Wax on. Wax off.

—Mr. Miyagi, *The Karate Kid*

1988

I went without a first kiss long after most people managed to lose their lip virginity. They lost it on the jungle gym, at summer camp, in the dark rows of the movie theater. Most had done so by age eleven, and here I was at thirteen without even having done plain American kissing, much less the French version. I didn't even know if I would be capable of kissing. I read the advice columns in *Seventeen* and *YM*, but I felt sure I wouldn't be able to perform.

Even worse, in the spring of 1988, the second half of eighth grade, I got braces. This greatly diminished my kissing prospects. My full-metal-mouth grin, complete with rubber bands, was only slightly less embarrassing than, say, wearing a T-shirt that read "I AM A BIG FAT NERD."

The calamity came one week before the Tulip Festival,

which was the code name for a spring dance at Dixieland Middle School. You couldn't call it a dance outright, because the Fundamentalist Baptists—who had successfully lobbied to have evolution and *Huckleberry Finn* removed from the Dixieland school curriculum—would call for its boycott. As it was, the FBs could let the dance stand largely because while there was music, few middle schoolers actually *danced,* and more of them simply waited by the punchbowl looking unsure of themselves. So, as long as it wasn't called a dance and few people danced, they could be convinced that the festival wasn't so obviously the Devil's Work. It was our version of *Footloose.*

The Tulip Festival was the first public recognition of the fact that boys and girls should like, not hate, each other—the rite of passage during which all things of elementary school, including cooties and its vaccine, cootie spray, were left behind. It was the most important night of my life (so far, to age twelve), and I looked like James Bond's nemesis Jaws from *The Spy Who Loved Me.*

My mouth, which up until a few days before possessed simply some harmless gaps between my teeth, was now a tangled cage of wire and metal brackets that had cut a series of highways into the inner side of my cheek.

I could eat only liquid foods. Even pudding was somewhat beyond my grasp, as was soup with chunks of noodles or vegetables. Not to mention the fact that I also had to cope with the sharp pains of wire cutting into my soft, defenseless cheek whenever I talked, smiled, or sneezed. The only thing saving me from crying was a small plastic container of dental wax given to me by the kindly assistant at the orthodontist's office who said she was sorry when she tightened the wires around my teeth.

The dental wax (long cigarette-shaped sticks of white putty) easily broke off into chunks to be carefully placed over the braces wire as a barrier between them and my flesh. I struck a balance between my pain threshold and my fashion sense, managing to keep the wax concentrated at the back of my mouth, away from my front teeth. My back molars, in fact, were entirely encased in wax.

Kimberly told me that enough of her Cover Girl lipstick in frosted ice pink would disguise the fact that instead of teeth I now had barbed wire. Vivien agreed.

"No one will even notice," Vivien reassured me.

I ignored her.

I refused to speak to Vivien for, among other reasons, not being persuaded to wait two weeks until *after* the dance to take me to the orthodontist. Besides, after the Roller Rink Debacle I no longer trusted her judgment on what boys would or would not notice.

The dance was held in the gym, which was decorated with blue and white streamers, Dixieland Middle School colors. At the center of the gym, there hung a giant Trojan piñata head. The DJ was playing Frankie Goes to Hollywood's "Relax," and a few brave souls tried to dance at the center of the gym. Most of us, however, huddled awkwardly along the sidelines.

Kevin Peterson was with his current girlfriend, Debbie Jenkins, head cheerleader, who had that perfectly hot-rolled, big-hair-bangs look complemented by blue eyeliner and matching blue mascara. Debbie was thirteen but looked seventeen.

Tears for Fears' "Everybody Wants to Rule the World" came on, and I watched as they slow-danced together, Kevin slipping his hands a bit lower than Debbie's waist in a suggestive swing. The song faded, and Kevin took Debbie's hand, leading her off the dance floor toward the bleachers, where they disappeared behind the rows. It could only be assumed they planned to Make Out. No one went there for any other reason. You didn't go there to discuss music or to compare dance moves. The dark, dusty hole beneath the stands was for one purpose and one purpose only: Sucking Face.

"Hey, Jen," came the voice of Peter Deed, who was hovering beside me. In middle school, he was forever hovering. I knew he liked me. But I didn't usually take much notice, since I was busy mooning over Kevin Peterson.

In elementary school, everyone called him Peter Peed, after an unfortunate incident on the playground involving him wetting his pants during a particularly grueling game of dodgeball. Peter had only barely transcended his elementary school nickname by mysteriously disappearing for a whole school year to live with his dad in Little Rock. He returned to be with his mother at the start of middle school, brandishing a Zippo lighter, and Journey and Foreigner concert T-shirts. No one now called him Peter Peed, but when I looked at him, sometimes I still saw the boy who clutched his pants on the playground in fourth grade, crying.

"Peter!" I said, as if he were the one person I really wanted to see. "How are you?"

"Uh—fine," Peter mumbled, shocked at my enthusiasm. Usually, I did my best to discourage actual conversations. He wasn't hideous, I'd give him that. But he was no Kevin Peterson.

Peter was a little on the short and pudgy side, but he did have nice brown eyes. And his hair was okay. He had it spiked up with gel.

"I like your shirt," I told him, indicating his torn black Foreigner T.

"You do?" Peter blinked, taken aback by my compliment.

"So, uh, Peter . . ." I was desperately trying to think of something more to say. "You have a girlfriend?"

Peter snorted. "No," he said, shaking his head, as if this were a dumb question, and, in fairness, it probably was.

"Great. You want to, uh, go together or something?"

"What?" Peter cried.

"Uh, I mean, you want to go sit down?"

Peter shrugged. I didn't think he was getting what I was saying.

"Do you want to go sit over *there,*" I said, pointing to the make-out corner of the gym.

This was rash on my part, but I didn't care. I wanted to go over to those bleachers and I didn't want to go alone.

"Over there?" Peter squeaked, understanding dawning. He recovered quickly, however. "Uh, yeah, yeah, definitely, sure."

Duran Duran piped in through the speakers, and I stomped over to the bleachers to the tune of "Union of the Snake."

*   *   *

We sat in a darkened corner of the bleachers known informally as the Kissing Staging Area. Serious making out was being done below our feet, underneath the bleachers. We sat in silence during Duran Duran, and then Belinda Carlisle came on the speakers, belting out "Heaven is a Place on Earth" to a gym where there were only four people dancing.

I could see Kevin Peterson hugging Debbie, and I snuggled a little closer to Peter. At least he didn't smell, I thought. He might not have been as cute as Kevin Peterson, but I supposed I could do much worse.

I carefully smoothed out the Espirit polka dot skirt I wore, the one I had lobbied so hard for Vivien to buy. This was after we'd spent an hour in the juniors' department, with Vivien shouting out in the store, "What's the big deal about E-spirt," pronouncing it "ee-spirt" instead of "uh-spree." It was almost as embarrassing as the time she referred in public to Bono from U2 as "Bone-o."

"You want a jawbreaker?" Peter asked me, retrieving from his jacket pocket a giant red ball wrapped in cellophane.

I ran my tongue over the sharp wire on the front of my teeth. My orthodontist's instructions were clear. No gum. No nacho chips. No taffy. No caramel. Not to mention, my teeth were still sore. But I felt a little rebellious and willing to court danger.

"Sure," I said.

Peter smiled. He ripped open the jawbreaker and then popped it into his mouth.

"Hey," I cried, giving him a shove in the arm.

"I'll pass it to you," Peter said, his lips curling up into a leer.

"Gross!" I cried, understanding slowly dawning on me. He wanted to pass me a used piece of gum.

"You've never done that before?" Peter asked, incredulous. "What? Haven't you even kissed anybody before?"

I watched Kevin Peterson and Debbie in an impressive lip lock below us.

Backed into a corner, I lied.

"Yes," I said. "Of course I have."

"So, the gum thing isn't a big deal then," Peter said.

"It's still kind of gross."

Peter shrugged.

"You want to kiss me or not?" he asked me.

I considered my options. One: I could kiss him, lose my lip virginity, and then risk being passed a very unhygienic piece of gym. Two: I could tell him to shove off, and perhaps never kiss anyone ever and live through the rest of my teen years without the coveted knowledge of how to kiss a boy.

And besides, what if everyone did the gum pass? What if that was just another version of kissing, like French kissing? Maybe it had a name and I didn't even know it: Bubble Yum Kissing. I might as well sample the technique.

I nodded.

Peter visibly relaxed. He drew me to him and put his face close to mine, so close our foreheads were touching and I could smell the cherry cinnamon spice from his jawbreaker. For once, I wasn't thinking about Kevin Peterson. I was focused on Peter.

"Uh, can you take those rubber bands off?" Peter asked me, drawing back. "I had a bad experience with those."

I realized he was referring to the rubber bands in my braces. Embarrassed, I ducked my head and took off the bands.

"Better," Peter said.

My lips were slightly parted (as I've seen in all the movies, as well as in the list of "Ten Things You Should Know About Kissing," which I read in *YM*). He put his lips on mine, and at first they were nice and soft. Who knew boys' lips were so soft? And then, ever so slightly, I felt the flicker of his tongue. Then, in a sudden, swift movement, Peter pushed the wad of gum in my mouth and pulled away.

"That wasn't so bad, was it?" Peter asked me.

Tentatively, I started to chew the gum. It tasted like cherry. I smiled. My poor sore lips and teeth ached at the contact. I winced a little.

"I haven't kissed a Japanese girl before," Peter noted, absently.

"I'm only half," I reminded him.

Peter shrugged. "Same difference," he said. "Only your eyes aren't so squinty."

I was not sure if I should take this as a compliment. I glanced over at Kevin Peterson. He wasn't kissing Debbie Jenkins anymore. In fact, he was looking up at Peter and me with interest.

"Okay, now it's your turn," Peter said, leaning in.

Feeling Kevin Peterson's eyes on us, I kissed Peter, maneuvered the gum, managing to slip it back to Peter without dropping it, or doing something equally embarrassing.

It was in the split second after the pass that I realized something very sharp was poking my back cheek.

The dental wax I'd put on my back braces had come loose. Quickly, I searched my mouth. No sign of it. I had either swallowed the wax or passed it back to Peter attached to his jawbreaker.

My heart started to speed up, and my palms went clammy.

If he figured it out . . . I was doomed. Ruined. No boy would ever kiss me again. I'd be known as Wax Lips Jen, or something equally embarrassing.

The realization that something wasn't quite right with the gum seemed to be crystallizing in Peter's head. He frowned, furrowed his brow, and chewed thoughtfully.

"Pass it back to me," I pleaded, knowing that getting the evidence away from Peter would be the best defense.

Peter was slow to move. He was still chewing, his eyes focusing off in the distance as if he was trying to figure something out.

I kept silent, trying to gauge how much Peter already knew.

"There's something I should tell you," Peter said.

The gum was going to be the death of me. What if the wax had already come off? And how was he not *tasting* it?

"I think we should break up," he said.

"What?" I cried. We had only been going together for fifteen minutes.

"It's almost summer, and I'm too young to be tied down," Peter said.

Clearly, Peter had let his leather jacket and Journey concert shirts go to his head. I didn't even really like Peter. He wasn't supposed to break up with *me.*

Peter took my hand and then spit out the used piece of gum.

"By the way," Peter said. "I think something is wrong with your spit. This gum tastes funny."

I saw now, looking at the wrinkled ball of used gum, that this was where my wax went—there were braids of white mixed in with the red.

"It's kind of gross," Peter said, and then pulled himself up from the bleachers, leaving me holding his used-up gum, a red cherry pulp.

Twenty-six

No worry, Miyagi fix everything.
—Mr. Miyagi, *The Karate Kid II*

"Riley," I cry, trying to recover from the shock of having just kissed Kevin Peterson. "Uh, this is Kevin Peterson."

"We already met," Riley says, not looking at me but at Kevin.

"At the rehearsal," Kevin says.

The two men stare at each other for a beat or two.

"Kevin! Kevin, where *are* you?" cries Lucy, who comes out of the front doors next. "THERE you are. I've been looking all over for you, sugah."

Lucy's sweet southern twang sounds a little forced. Lucy takes in Riley, me, and Kevin and hesitates a moment.

"Everything all right out here? Ya'll look like you're at a funeral or something."

"We're fine," Kevin says.

"Well, come on inside, my mama wants to make a toast," Lucy says, dragging Kevin by the hand back inside the restaurant.

Riley turns to follow them but I catch his arm.

"Wait," I say.

"Look, it's not any of my business, is it?" Riley says. He sounds a bit peevish.

"But it's not what you think," I say, realizing that I sound exactly like Tiffany.

"Look, you don't owe me anything, remember?" he says, throwing my words back in my face.

"But . . ." I start again. "He kissed me. I swear I didn't want him to."

"What? Like with Paul? You're telling me that every man you run into mauls you?"

That's so not fair! I feel like I have traveled back in time. I'm in grade school again where everyone switches boyfriends and girlfriends and there's speculation on who kissed whom and when.

"Riley, wait," I say, but he brushes past me.

That night, I barely sleep. I toss and turn so heavily in bed that I wake even Grandma Saddie, who sleeps sounder than the dead.

"Ya-shee, you're like a Tasmanian Devil," Grandma Saddie says, before rolling over and falling back asleep.

I can't help it. I'm thinking about Riley, about Kevin Peterson, about the fact that even though it wasn't my fault, I may have inadvertently ruined my cousin Lucy's chance for happiness. I can't decide which I feel more: guilt for letting Kevin Peterson kiss me, or anger that he tried to kiss me at all. Isn't he the one getting married, for heaven's sake? Not to mention, I can't stop thinking about the look on Riley's face. There was surprise, and maybe hurt, but definitely disappointment.

After two hours of lying in bed and staring at the ceiling, I decide to creep down to the kitchen. I'm surprised to find the light there already on, and Lucy, wearing her pink frilly pajamas, standing by the sink and eating Cherry Garcia ice cream straight from the container.

"So you were the ice cream thief," I say. My voice surprises her, and she jumps a little. When we were kids, ice cream would always go mysteriously missing. Vivien always blamed Bubba.

"Yeah, that's me," Lucy says. Without her makeup, she looks ridiculously young. In her pink pajamas, she could pass for fifteen, not twenty.

"Mind sharing?" I ask her, grabbing a spoon from the silverware drawer.

"Sure." Lucy offers me the pint. It's the closest I've seen Lucy get to being generous. It's a sure sign she's not feeling herself and that something is bothering her. I feel that maybe I should tell her about Kevin, but I don't know how. What do you say? "By the way, your fiancé tried to make a move on me"?

"You can't sleep?" I ask Lucy.

"Do you think I'm doing the right thing?" Lucy asks, ignoring my question. "Getting married?"

"I don't know, Lucy. That's a decision only you can make."

"I know what you and Kimberly think," she says, pulling a face. "You think I'm too young. Aunt Vivien thinks so, too."

I'm silent.

"You girls, though, you're both so smart. I'm just the one who won a few beauty pageants."

"Lucy, you're smart." Just not disciplined in your studies, I don't add.

"Maybe Kevin Peterson is the best I can do, you know?"

I put down my spoon. "Lucy, no one you marry should be a life accomplishment," I say, sounding like Kimberly. "I'm not married, but I don't think marriage should be a goal or a crowning achievement. Marriage is about sharing your life with someone. But it's not supposed to be who you are."

"That's easy for you to say; you don't care about being alone," Lucy says. "You don't care if people talk about you and say that you couldn't find a man willing to marry you. I mean you're *twenty-eight*. God, if I were single and twenty-eight, I'd kill myself."

Typical Lucy.

I take a long, deep breath and try to remember that I'm back in Dixieland, where women are spinsters at twenty-five.

"Lucy, you have your whole life ahead of you, and you can do whatever you'd like. You could go to college, or travel, or anything."

"But I took two classes at the community college in Little Rock and failed them both," Lucy whines.

"Look, you can do what you want to do if you put your mind to it. How much did you actually study?"

"Not a lot," she admits.

"There you go. You can't rely on your life to be lived for you. You've got to make some decisions on your own. You've got to decide what it is you want."

Lucy thinks about this a minute. "But I wouldn't know how to live on my own."

It occurs to me that maybe Lucy wasn't simply spoiled. Maybe her whole life everyone rushed to do things for her, so she never really learned how to do things on her own. After all, she was going to go straight from living with her mother to living with her husband.

"Did you know that Kevin flirts *all* the time?" Lucy asks me, changing subjects.

"Uh, yeah, I sort of picked up on that." *I really ought to tell her,* I think.

"Other people say things about how I should put him on a short leash. I know what they say," Lucy says. "Even Billy Connor says so."

Glue-eating Billy Connor? "Billy Connor has an opinion?" I ask her. She shrugs. "About Kevin . . ." I start.

"What about Kevin?" Lucy asks me.

I look at her expectant face, and I lose my nerve.

"I'm no expert." I'm quick to add, "I just think that if you have second thoughts, maybe you should take them seriously." I hold my breath, waiting for her to answer me.

She looks up, thoughtful. "Maybe," she sighs. She's silent awhile.

"You know," Lucy says after another long pause. "I've got

some extra Biore strips if you want to do something about your skin."

"What's wrong with my skin?"

"Your pores are huge," she says, eyes wide. "And look at those blackheads," she adds, pointing at my nose.

I don't get to sleep until about two in the morning, and five hours later I'm awakened by the sound of metal clattering outside my window. It's the caterer's assistant, who has dropped a box of silverware. There's a small army of people in Vivien's backyard: caterers, florists, tent arrangers. Tables and chairs are being set up under the tent, as well as giant floral topiaries.

In the kitchen, Grandpa and Grandma Taylor are having their favorite breakfast: cigarettes and cans of Budweiser.

I take my toast outside for some fresh air and barely take one bite before my cell phone rings again. I am getting *really* tired of "Cowboy Take Me Away." I wish someone would take me away from my cell phone.

"Where the hell are you?" Bob shouts at me right off.

"I'm in Dixieland," I say. "I'm home for my cousin's wedding. Remember?"

"No matter, I need you back tonight."

"Bob, I can't come back tonight. I'm in my cousin's wedding."

"I've got the weekend producer out sick, and your assistant—what's her name?"

"Anne."

"Right, she says she can't get a babysitter, and I need someone to do the ten o'clock news tonight."

"Bob, there's no way I could get back in time."

"Look, you have to make your own decisions," Bob says. "But if you want that promotion, you'd better find a replacement, or find a way to get back here by seven thirty."

I hang up and call Anne, who tells me the same thing Bob told me. She's stuck with the kids and her husband is out of town and she simply can't find a single person to watch them. Anne is close to tears, and I tell her not to worry. I'll figure something out.

The wedding is at one. I do some quick calculations. If I skip the reception, drive like hell to the airport, and make a midafternoon flight, I might, *might* be able to be at the studio by seven. That's if there's no traffic, and the cab drives eighty miles an hour from the airport.

"Trouble at work?" comes Riley's voice from behind me. He's sitting on my parents' porch swing.

"Hey," I say to him, suddenly very glad to see him. "That seat taken?"

Riley looks up at me, and then back down. "I was hoping Jennifer Lopez would wander by, but until she gets here, I suppose you could warm the seat."

"Thanks."

I sit down. "You mad at me?"

He shrugs.

"Bob wants me to go back tonight."

"And are you?"

"You're so good at reading my mind, I figured you'd know already."

"If this were an episode of *Dallas,* there'd be dramatic music and a close-up on my face," Riley says.

"And then maybe I could wake up and find that none of the past three days ever happened."

"Would you want that?" Riley asks, suddenly serious.

I give him a look. "The only thing I want to take back is last night and that scene with Kevin," I say.

Riley considers this, a smile creeping across his face.

"Done," he says. "It was all a dream. Does this mean I have to go get in the shower like Patrick Duffy?"

Inside the house, Lucy starts screaming that Aunt Teri didn't properly transport her veil from Lulu's Bridal, because it is now wrinkled. So much for our heart-to-heart talk last night, I think.

"Ya-shee!" Vivien cries, throwing up her hands and coming out on the porch. "Bette is looking for you. She needs to do your hair. She's just got done with Lucy."

"Do I have to?" I ask Vivien.

"This is my cue to go get dressed," Riley says, getting up and leaving me alone with Vivien.

"No back talk, young lady. I've already gotten plenty from Kimberly this morning, and I don't need any more from you."

"What's she doing now?"

"Being her usual self," Vivien says. "She is *just* like her father, I swear. Bubba is as stubborn as an elephant."

"Mule," I correct.

Kimberly comes out on the porch then. "You had better not be talking about me," she snaps.

Vivien and I turn to look at Kimberly, who is all decked out in the bright pink bridesmaid's dress. Kimberly in pink anything would be funny. But pink ruffles? She looks ridiculous. Her tattoo of Buddha and her nose ring do not go with the pink frills. She looks about as happy as a cat that just fell into a tub of water.

"If either one of you even DARES to laugh, I swear, I'll take this damn thing off and be on the next plane to California," Kimberly fumes.

"You look very nice," Vivien says, but even she can't quite keep a straight face.

"BUBBA!" Kimberly shouts, stomping back into the house.

My cell phone rings.

"Don't be too long," Vivien warns me.

I expect to talk to Bob. Instead, I find Kevin Peterson on the line.

"I got your cell phone number from Lucy," he tells me. "She thinks I'm trying to set you up with one of my groomsmen."

"And that's not why you're calling me?"

"No. Well, yes and no. I've been thinking, Jen. Last night, I don't think it was a fluke. Seeing you again has brought up all kinds of feelings."

"I don't think this is the best time to talk about this." I sigh, trying to keep my voice low as I walk out to my mother's porch.

"When would be a better time? I'm getting married in three hours and I'm not sure I should be."

"You're just nervous," I say. "It's not really *me* you care for."

"Jen, I've been in love with you since I was ten years old," he says. "You can't just walk away from a feeling like that."

I sigh.

This is the exact thing I would've wanted to hear at age thirteen. Now, it all seems a bit ridiculous. There's no way I would ever be able to date Kevin Peterson now. Even if he weren't engaged to my cousin, he's your typical small-town boy. He's never been anywhere, and never plans to go anywhere.

I imagine introducing him to friends like Jason in Chicago. The minute he started talking about his state football championship, I'd be so mortified, I probably wouldn't be able to leave the house again. I try to imagine Kevin Peterson and me together, and I just can't.

"You don't even really know me," I say, my voice barely above a whisper. "You only *think* you know me. You're in love with the idea of me, not me."

I know all about this, I think. My whole life I've been chasing the dream of a guy instead of *real* guys. It's just like Riley said. I love to love ideals. Real men rarely stack up.

"I don't think I understand you," Kevin drawls. "Why do you have to talk circles around me, darlin'? You been away from the South so long that you can't speak plainly?"

"I'm not the same Jen I was fifteen years ago."

"You're right," Kevin says. "You've gotten even prettier since then."

"That is no good reason to run off with somebody," I say. "I have to go."

I never would have guessed in a million years that I would be trying to hurry Kevin Peterson off the phone. It reminds me of some fortune cookie wisdom Aunt Teri often quotes: The only thing worse than not getting what you want in life is getting it.

By noon the entire wedding party is waiting at the First Baptist Church, the site of Grandma Saddie's rebirth into the Christian faith, and where Lucy has been attending bible study since she was four.

Aunt Teri, stubborn in her Chinese superstitions, is busy putting little mirrors on the windowsills to "ward off bad luck." But no sooner does she place them than Grandma Saddie picks them up again claiming superstitions are "the Devil's work."

Aunt Teri is decked out in a pink kimono and has her blond hair swept up on her head and held in place with pearl pink chopsticks. She causes more of a stir when she tries to stick Confucius sayings into the wedding programs, including one that reads "A man with one chopstick will go hungry."

Riley is sitting in a back pew of the church arguing with Bubba about who is tougher, a rugby player or a Nascar driver. He looks particularly handsome in his dark suit, and he seems so at home with Bubba. Few of my past boyfriends made it to the chit-chat stage with Bubba. Bubba's size and the intensity at which he talks about Nascar usually scares off guys. But not Riley.

I can't help but wonder what will happen when we're back in Chicago. I wonder if his "break" with Tiffany will be permanent, and this makes me think again that maybe I should help that break along by telling him about what I saw between her and Paul.

Riley, sensing me looking at him, glances over at me. He sends me a cautious smile. I take a step toward him, but my forward momentum is stopped by the sudden appearance of Kevin Peterson. He's wearing his groom's tux, and I have to admit he does look handsome.

"Can we talk?" Kevin asks me. He looks miserable, as if he's attending a funeral instead of his own wedding.

"No."

"Give me five minutes," he pleads. "Just five minutes."

Kevin pulls me into a small room where bible study is normally held on Sundays, and takes a deep breath.

"I can't fight these feelings I have for you," Kevin says, sounding like he's quoting REO Speedwagon. "And I can't stop thinking about you," he adds. "Do you think there is *any* chance we could be together? I'm about to make a big decision here today, and I need to know how you feel about me."

The thirteen-year-old in me is definitely flattered. But the near-thirty-year-old is losing patience. He's about to *get married* and he's thinking about running off with me? What is Lucy? His backup plan?

"Kevin, I don't even know you, and you don't know me," I say.

"Just tell me this one thing. You think you would ever move back to Dixieland? You think you could see yourself as a farmer's wife?"

I sigh and shake my head. "Kevin, I've got a life in Chicago. Before long, I'll probably be living in New York. I'm not going to move back to Dixieland."

"Oh," Kevin says, looking down at his feet.

"Whatever decision you have to make," I tell him, "you have to make without thinking about me."

"I see."

The door to the bible study opens then and Kimberly bursts in.

"What the hell are you two doing?" Kimberly asks. "It's time for the groom to go up to the altar."

I hear the processional music starting from the church. I look at Kevin. He looks at me and then the door.

"I'm leaving," I say.

I walk out of the room and Kimberly follows me.

"You want to tell me what that was all about?"

"It's a long story."

In the hall we run into Vivien, who is speaking to former glue eater Billy Connor, dressed in his Arkansas State Trooper uniform.

"There you are, ya-shee, we've been looking all over for you," Vivien scolds me. "You remember Billy?"

Billy has grown since the last time I saw him and is probably four sizes bigger. He still has the look of a slightly gullible boy who would eat anything if someone dared him to do so.

"Hey, Jen," Billy says, distracted. "You seen Lucy?"

"I'm sure she's getting dressed."

"You and Billy used to play naked in the blow-up pool in the summer when you were babies," Vivien says.

Both Billy and I turn bright red.

"You missed the train on this one, Billy," Vivien says. "Jen is practically engaged now."

"Mom!" I exclaim.

"Um," Billy says, staring at the Arkansas State Trooper hat in his hands. "You seen Lucy?" he asks again.

"You'll see her soon enough," Vivien says.

He looks from right to left. "I think I'll go look for her," Billy Connor says, then wanders off.

"I told you he was strange," I tell Vivien.

"He's very nice," Vivien counters. "He rescued Aunt Teri's cat just last week. Climbed up in the tree himself to do it. Besides, he's a very nice fellow. You're just too picky!"

Vivien takes a look at Kimberly and me and then barks at us.

"What are y'all doing standing around? You're supposed to be with Lucy."

Kimberly and I wander back to the rehearsal room, where Lucy is in full wedding regalia and shouting at the top of her lungs to her bridesmaids. Of her eighteen bridesmaids, only Kimberly and I are blood relatives. The rest are "friends" of Lucy— a combination of former Miss Arkansas competitors and former teammates on the Dixieland High School Drill Team.

"I need Visine. My eyes are red!" she cries to her maid of honor, former Miss Bass County, who came in fourth behind Lucy in the Miss Arkansas Pageant.

"Calm down, I've got it," Miss Bass County says, looking around in the trunk-size cosmetic case that used to follow Lucy around to all her beauty pageants.

"Now I see who these dresses were made for," I say, looking at the four nearly six-foot-tall, rail-thin beauty contestants. They look like Barbies. I look like a Weeble Wobble.

We're given our flowers—bunches of pale pink roses—as well as drill-sergeant-like orders from Lucy that we are not—under any circumstances—to break with the stutter step down the aisle (right foot forward, then feet together, then left foot forward!). There's no sign of the doubting girl of last night. Lucy is barking commands left and right and is tackling her wedding day with the same steely determination she used to attack her flaming baton in the talent competition of Miss Arkansas.

All the while I know that I can't really let this wedding happen. Lucy has a right to know about Kevin, and I really should be the one to tell her. Or should I? Just what am I supposed to tell her? That her fiancé, the love of her life, made a pass at me in front of the Catfish Parlour? That despite her sincere hope that in the contest of marriage she'll come in first place, she's actually only Mrs. Peterson, First Runner-Up?

I keep thinking *Don't go through with this,* sending Lucy silent signals in the hope that there really is something to Nakamura Telepathy.

During a rare quiet moment, I try to approach Lucy. "Lucy," I say, trying to get her away from the other four former Miss Arkansas contestants. "Do you remember what we talked about last night?"

"Jen—please don't talk to me now, I'm trying to concentrate," Lucy says. "I'm visualizing the win. I mean, the ceremony."

"But you mentioned that maybe . . ." I can feel the eyes of the other bridesmaids following my trail of conversation with interest. "That . . ."

Kimberly sends me a look that says, "What are you doing?"

"Jen—please, I'm in my winner's zone," Lucy says, brushing me off.

"Girls! It's time," cries Aunt Bette.

The processional music goes on for what seems like forever. The church organ player, Mrs. Bradford, who is pushing seventy, starts to look fatigued by the procession of Bridesmaid number ten. I am third-to-last to go, sandwiched in between two former beauty pageant contestants and looking like their ill-formed, dwarf sister.

Stubbornly, I do not look in Kevin's direction. I wonder what I should say during the "Speak now or forever hold your peace part," since my conscience is starting to buzz in my ears like a rabid bee.

I train my eyes on Pastor Miller, who is in his late fifties and was the one who baptized me when I was a baby. He gives me a fatherly smile, and I feel even worse. How can I be a part of a wedding that I know is a sham?

I make it to the front of the church, where I turn and see the last two bridesmaids trailing behind me, and then Bubba escorting Lucy down the aisle. She's got laserlike focus on Kevin, and before I know it, they're standing in front of Pastor Miller.

"We are gathered here today to witness the union of this man and this woman," he begins.

Here it comes. I swallow, hard.

"If anyone knows of a reason why these two should not be married, speak now or forever hold your peace."

Twenty-Seven

Bonzaiii!

—Mr. Miyagi, *The Karate Kid*

1988—BEYOND THUNDERDOME

By the summer after eighth grade, I knew I had no hope of winning Kevin Peterson. Even while old couples reunited (Burt Reynolds and Loni Anderson, for instance), I had no chance with KP. I had braces, glasses, and was never going to be a cheerleader. It was also rumored, thanks to Peter Peed, that I had funny-tasting spit.

I sank into a deep depression (what Vivien called "being a moody teenager"); I slept until noon every day and refused to use sentences longer than a few words. That's the summer that Grandpa Taylor bought the RV and took Grandma Taylor on an eight-state tour of America's Finest Sights, including the world's largest ball of string.

That was also the summer that Aunt Bette, who had flunked out of junior college, tried her hand at beauty school.

She told me that what I needed to cure my depression was a perm. I agreed to let her give me one.

The fact that for most of the late eighties Aunt Bette spent three hours a day painstakingly curling and hair-spraying herself to look like all of the fans in the Hair Band videos didn't seem like a particularly serious warning sign.

Aunt Bette wore her hair sprayed high, ratted, and teased, along with skin-tight, acid-washed ripped jeans. She spent most of her time going to Def Leppard, Poison, and Guns N' Roses concerts.

"Trust me, you will look *bad ass,*" she tells me, looking at me through her heavy makeup.

The idea for my makeover, according to Aunt Bette, was to first cut layers into my bangs, then set them with a perm, which would be almost hassle-free. It would require only an hour of blow-drying with a diffuser, some strategic curling-iron use, followed by mild back-combing, and finished off with some tease and spray. Simple, Aunt Bette said. I could do it in my sleep, she said, which would be handy, since I'd have to wake up at 5:00 A.M. every day before school in order to complete this complicated beauty regimen.

My makeover began in the upstairs bathroom. "Sit still," Aunt Bette commanded, as I pushed wet bangs out of my eyes. She blared "Pour Some Sugar on Me," while periodically using her comb and brush to bang on imaginary drums.

I watched Aunt Bette's laserlike focus and wondered why she got a C in her client service class at beauty school. The layering and cutting consumed about twenty minutes, and Vivien's seashell pink bathroom was soon covered with tiny wet locks of my black hair.

"We'll clean later," Aunt Bette said. She sat me down on a folding chair in the bathroom and began the perm process. She rolled up my hair, painstakingly combing out handfuls of hair and tightening them around tiny pink plastic curlers. She then dropped my head back over the sink and applied chemicals that smelled a bit like lighter fluid.

"You sure this is what you're supposed to do?" I asked.

"Shhh. I need to concentrate." Aunt Bette looked at her watch, then at me. "There," she said, looking satisfied. "Sit just like that."

The unveiling of my perm, two hours later, was nothing if not dramatic. Aunt Bette, who had not let me see myself in the mirror yet, had blow-dried, back-combed, teased, and hair-sprayed me into what she claimed was a thirteen-year-old, half-Japanese version of Madonna in *Desperately Seeking Susan.* She had even tied one of her knit headbands around my head and poofed out my bangs.

In reality, I was less Madonna and more Orphan Annie. My hair was a few shades lighter than my natural color, and it was a giant poodle fro, held in check only by the headband, which seemed like it might burst from the pressure of holding to my head these new and aggressive curls that wanted to sprout up and out, the beauty equivalent of the Big Bang. Once it starts, the universe of my hair can't be controlled; it wants to grow out farther and farther for eternity. There should be, I decided right then and there, a special warning label on the back of all perm boxes specifically geared to Asian hair. Warning: Addition of harsh chemicals will make hair coarse beyond repair and will make you look like an Asian person who is trying not to be Asian.

I looked like I was wearing one of Tina Turner's wigs. I could be her character in *Mad Max Beyond Thunderdome*. All I needed were shoulder pads made out of chain mail.

"You like it?" Aunt Bette said, hopeful.

"I think I look weird," I said, pulling out a curl, which popped resiliently back in place. "It's kind of poofy."

"But Big Hair is *in*," Aunt Bette told me. "And besides, no one will notice your braces if they're too busy looking at your hair."

Aunt Bette would not let me go before introducing me to my "essential" hair supply tools, including: a neon pink perm "pick" comb, the diffuser ad-on to my hair dryer, a giant can of Aqua Net, and two enormous bottles of Vidal Sassoon shampoo and conditioner. She then gave me a solemn lecture on how each one should be used and the care of my perm.

While I probably looked like a cross between a poodle and Trudy during her braces phase on *The Facts of Life*, both Grandma Saddie and Vivien found nice things to say. "Ya-shee! Who's the movie star?" Grandma Saddie exclaimed when I walked down the stairs.

I think they were probably only trying to be nice, but still, by the end of the night, I started to think I looked good.

High school, I thought smugly, *here I come.*

Twenty-eight

Daniel-san, best karate still inside. Now time to let out.

—Mr. Miyagi, *The Karate Kid III*

*P*astor Miller looks at the church congregation, sweeping his eyes over us as if daring any of us to say anything.

I have to do something. I look at the audience, and I see Riley, sitting next to Grandpa Taylor, who is wearing a baseball cap that reads "I'm with the Bride!" I look back to Pastor Miller. For a second, there's complete silence in the church.

Then my mobile phone rings. It's in the tiny drawstring matching pink purse we're all holding. Frantic, I tear into my purse to get to the phone.

Every eye in the church is on me. And "Cowboy Take Me Away" is bouncing off the church rafters. I turn tomato red and finally turn off my phone.

"Sorry," I mouth to everyone. Out of the corner of my eye,

I see Vivien put her head in her hands and Grandma Saddie look at the ceiling.

"As I was saying . . ." continues Pastor Miller.

No sooner does the pastor start his sentence than my phone rings again.

"Turn that off," hisses Kimberly.

"I *did* turn it off," I hiss. My cell phone is having a meltdown. I shake it but it doesn't stop. "Sorry," I say.

In a flash, Lucy whips around, grabs the phone, and spikes it on the ground like a football. The back cover cracks and flies off, and the phone stops ringing. When it makes a pathetic whhrr sound, Lucy picks up the hem of her dress and stomps on the phone with one white kitten heel until it goes completely silent.

"May we continue now, Miss Taylor?" Pastor Miller asks me.

"Yes, sorry—yes."

"As I was saying . . . speak now or forever hold your peace."

After a beat of silence, Miss Bass County shouts: "I'm in love with Kevin Peterson."

This is followed by a chorus chime from another bridesmaid: Miss Hot Springs, who says, "But I'm in love with Kevin Peterson!"

Kevin looks a bit sheepish.

"What the blazes is going on?" Bubba cries.

"I've been having an affair with Kevin," admits Miss Bass County.

"But *I've* been having an affair with Kevin," says Miss Hot Springs.

Lucy, in a rage, whips up her veil. "You bitches!" she cries. Then she turns back to Kevin Peterson. "Is there any bridesmaid you *haven't* told you loved?"

Kevin shrugs his shoulders.

"You told me those womanizing days were behind you," Lucy cries, slapping Kevin's tuxedoed chest with her bouquet. Petals fly in every direction. "You promised me!"

I guess elementary school habits die hard. Kevin Peterson never was one to keep one girlfriend for very long. And it looks like he can still manage pretty well with women. I wonder how many of the bridesmaids he managed to seduce with his "I've always loved you" line.

"Did you sleep with her, too?" Miss Bass County says.

"And her?" Miss Hot Springs says.

"You promised!" Lucy is still shrieking, all the while batting him about the head with her flowers.

Then the doors to the chapel swing open with a thud and Billy Connor comes crashing in. "FREEZE!" he shouts. He's still wearing his Arkansas State Trooper uniform.

Everyone in the church looks back at him.

"Stop this wedding!" Billy Connor says.

"It's already stopped," Kimberly says.

"I object," Billy Connor declares. "I am in love with Lucy Lin Woo Taylor, and I want everyone to know it."

"Just what is going on?" Kevin Peterson asks.

"You thought you were the only one with side interests?" Lucy declares.

"Side interests?" Billy Connor echoes.

"Can I get out of this dress now?" Kimberly asks no one in particular.

"Lucy—come with me," Billy Connor pleads.

Lucy takes one look at Kevin Peterson and then at her two backstabbing bridesmaids. Then she gathers up the full skirt of her wedding dress and runs down the aisle toward Billy Connor. She jumps into his arms and he carries her out of the church and to the Arkansas State Trooper Bronco parked in front of the chapel.

Half the congregation moves to the front of the church to watch. I see Lucy jump into the passenger side of the Bronco, her cathedral-length veil flowing out the window. As Billy Connor picks up speed, the wind catches the veil, blows it high into the air. It does a swirling dance in the wind before landing in a heap on the ground.

Kevin Peterson trots out of the church, and picks it up, as he watches his bride throw one arm out the window in farewell.

I haven't seen a scene this awkward since Mr. T dressed up as Santa Claus for a photo op at the White House Christmas Party in 1983 and Nancy Reagan sat on his lap.

No one says anything for a beat or two.

Then Grandpa and Grandma Taylor start clapping. "That is the best damn exit I've ever seen," Grandma Taylor says. "Better than Elvis's last concert in Hawaii."

"We going to eat now or what?" Grandpa Taylor asks.

"Well, it's a shame to waste all that rib eye," Grandma Taylor says.

*   *   *

At the brideless reception, Aunt Teri downs four strawberry daiquiris and lines up the little paper umbrellas in front of her, while Vivien tries to console her by reminding her of the fact that most—if not all—of the wedding was paid for by the Peterson family.

Kevin Peterson does a successful turn on the dance floor to "I Will Survive," accompanied by four of the eighteen bridesmaids. He doesn't look like a groom who was left at the altar, but he sure doesn't mind milking the story for all the attention it will get from any female.

Kimberly, who immediately changed out of her dress, is wearing cutoff jeans and a "No War for Oil" T-shirt, while Matt Chang desperately tries to get her to the dance floor.

Aunt Bette is busy giving her Mary Kay cards out to the guests she doesn't know, and Bubba is showing off his three-foot bass to anyone willing to go into the Death Room.

This would be a perfect time for me to check my cell phone, but as it's destroyed, I have no choice but to sit and take in the scene.

"You looked like you could use one of these," Riley says.

"Thanks," I say, taking the glass.

"So? What are you waiting for?" Riley asks me. "The love of your life is a free man now."

"Kevin Peterson? No thanks," I say, making a face.

Riley laughs.

"I had to check."

"So given the little performance today, do you believe me now? Kevin kissed me. I didn't kiss him back."

"I figured," Riley says. "You should have just been honest with me."

"I was honest with you," I cry.

"Oh, right," Riley says. "Next time be honest but be honest a little louder."

I laugh.

"Speaking of being honest . . ." I say. "There's something I have to tell you. Something about Tiffany."

Riley's brown eyes are fixed on me. Waiting. I swallow. This is harder than I thought.

"You remember that night—that night when I met Paul? Well, Paul didn't come on to me in the bedroom," I say.

"He didn't?"

"No. In fact, I think he came on to . . . Tiffany."

Riley sighs and looks down in his beer. "Yeah, I know."

"You *know?*"

"Well, I didn't *know* know, but I figured. There is no way you'd let Paul corner you in the bedroom. And Tiffany told me she and Paul have been fooling around."

"Riley . . . I'm so sorry." I take his hand in mine.

He looks up at me and smiles.

"It's okay," he says. "I haven't exactly been faithful either."

"You haven't?"

"Well, even before we broke up, well, I thought about you all the time. Tiffany used to tease me that I talked about you more than I talked about her."

I don't know what to say to this.

"But I'm a little confused, I'll admit it," Riley says. "I don't quite know what I should be feeling."

"Riley . . . I . . ."

A mobile phone chimes.

"Dammit, I thought my phone was dead," I say, pulling back from Riley. It's then I realize that my phone's screen is still cracked and decidedly black. It's not my phone that's ringing.

"It's me," Riley says, fishing his phone out of his interior jacket pocket. He looks at the screen. "It's Tiffany." He pauses.

"Are you going to answer it?"

"I'll call her back."

This makes my heart jump a little. But then I see the look on his face, and I know something serious is going on.

"You packed and ready to go?" asks Bubba coming up from behind Riley and clapping him on the back.

"Go?" I echo. "Go where?"

"Give me ten minutes," Riley tells Bubba. He sends me a sort of grimace. There's something he doesn't want to tell me.

"Tiffany called a couple of hours ago," Riley says. "Her mother had a heart attack."

"Oh my God," I say.

"The Lord's name!" Grandma Saddie cries, as she walks past us.

"It looks like she'll be fine, but I think Tiffany is a bit shook up, and well, she's in town to look after her sister, and . . ."

I look at Riley and realize he's trying to tell me that he's got to go back to Chicago.

"You're flying back? Tonight?"

"I've known Tiffany and her family a long time. I think I should go," Riley says. "I wanted to wait until after the wedding, and there didn't seem a good time to tell you."

"You can go."

"We bastard nephews of royalty don't have to ask permission," Riley chides, but he's smiling.

"You do have nice strong shoulders," I say, giving him a reluctant smile. "They're perfect for leaning on."

"I hope you think more than my shoulders are nice," he says, which makes me smile.

"You know I do."

"Well *I* know that, but I wanted to hear you say it," Riley says. "We members of the royal class actually have fragile egos."

"Nigel Riley . . . are you trying to impress me with your sensitive side?"

"Only if it's working," Riley says. He hesitates, then takes my hand. "You know, I've really enjoyed meeting your family."

"Now I know you're lying."

"I'm not. It's the truth. You know, you don't have anything to be ashamed of about where you're from. This—" Riley says, indicating the buffet of fried green tomatoes and in general the South, "is only part of who you are. The nice thing about living in America is you get to decide what you want to do with your life."

I realize that Riley is right. That maybe all this time I've been afraid of coming home because of what it might say about me. That by coming home, I'd find I hadn't met some standard in my head for the person I should be.

It also occurs to me that it seems like Riley is saying good-bye. A serious Nice-Knowing-You goodbye. The sort of good-bye you'd expect from someone planning to pop back into his ex-girlfriend's life with the intent of staying.

"Are you and Tiffany still . . . on break?" I blurt suddenly.

Riley looks a little guilty. "As far as I'm concerned we are, but she did say she wanted to talk."

I feel a pang. A talk? That doesn't sound like the kind of talk where an ex wants to divvy up a CD collection. It sounds like the sort of talk where you end up having sweaty makeup sex followed by philosophic musings about how silly you were to break up in the first place.

"Oh, I see."

"I want to be honest with you," Riley says. "These past few days with you have been great. I've had the best time. But I think I have some thinking I need to do."

He needs to think? And I realize that thinking is one thing I don't need to do. I want Riley. More than anyone ever. And I understand that I should tell him so, before he gets on that plane and is back in Tiffany's size-zero arms. I open my mouth to tell him this. But instead a joke pops out.

"Since when do the noble classes think?"

Riley gives me a sly smile.

"Hardly ever," he says, winking. And then he's gone.

Twenty-nine

No need to fight anymore. Prove point.
Mr. Miyagi, *The Karate Kid II*

1989

Dixieland High School was not what I expected. I thought it would be like a John Hughes movie. I imagined myself being played by Molly Ringwald, and Kevin Peterson being played by Judd Nelson or John Cusack. I'd have a nerdy sidekick played by Anthony Michael Hall or Jon Crier, and he'd follow me around school in love with me while I pined over Kevin Peterson.

But then something would happen. I'd get Saturday detention with Kevin Peterson and it would change my life forever. I'd learn that jocks have hard lives, too, and that geeks are people with feelings, and that we're all just teenagers trying to do the best we can. Or Kevin Peterson would ask me to prom only to renege on his invite when his snooty rich friends persuade him not to take me. Of course, he'd make it up to me by apologizing at prom.

Or Kevin Peterson would be the only one to remember my birthday and by the end of it, he'd be kissing me over my very own giant birthday cake.

Yes, this is what I imagined high school would be like.

It would be me, the awkward but lovable heroine who, despite all odds, manages to land the cutest/richest/most popular boy in school.

But high school wasn't like that.

I realized this on my first day, when it became clear that high school was just another extension of middle school. Kevin Peterson ignored me; my classes were boring; and the same jocks pressured me to do their homework for them. I was still the semiawkward girl who didn't fit in anywhere—migrating from clique to clique hoping to find a sense of belonging. And hoping to win Kevin Peterson—or if not Kevin Peterson, then find a place where I fit in.

I never did. But I came to a decision. I was going to college, and I was going to leave Dixieland.

For the first time, I thought that maybe it wasn't that I didn't fit in Dixieland, but that Dixieland didn't fit me.

Thirty

Go find the balance.
—Mr. Miyagi, *The Karate Kid*

The next morning, I pack up to leave, while Vivien watches me fold my clothes. "Ya-shee, I can't believe you're leaving already—you just got here," she sighs.

"I'll be back soon."

"You always say that, but it'll be five years again," she says. "I'll be dead of a heart attack by then. You know the Nakamura women don't live long in this family."

"Now who's being the drama princess?" I ask, quoting her. But I realize that I don't feel that usual pressing panic at the thought of coming home again. This time, I know I'll probably be back sooner rather than later.

I realize that part of me feared that visiting home would somehow change me back to that awkward girl of the eighties, the one who was always chasing after Kevin Peterson, the one who never seemed to find her place. Part of me is still that girl, which is why I work so hard at my job. I want to succeed, vanquish those ghosts of the past. But I also know that you can't run from your past forever. And Riley is right. My past is only part of who I am.

"You know, you remind me of Grandpa Frank," Vivien says.

"How so?"

"Grandpa Frank, he was always thinking about the next big thing," Vivien says. "You know he was a dreamer, Grandpa Frank. That's why he didn't go back to California after the camps. He was always on the lookout for something new and better. You're just like that. You're always moving on—trying to find that next better thing."

"So you aren't mad at me for living in Chicago? I thought you hated that I lived so far away."

"Ya-shee," Vivien sighs. "Both my girls are adventurers. It's in the Nakamura blood. How do you think we got from Japan to America in the first place?"

I look down at my hands.

"Bubba and I couldn't be prouder of you," Vivien tells me. She gives my shoulders a squeeze. "And whatever you do will be the right thing for you."

Bubba drives me in Old Red back to Memphis to get my car, which is miraculously fixed, and I spend the next ten hours driving by myself straight to Chicago, thinking about Riley.

I blare the Dixie Chicks at high volume all the way up Highway 55, but I still don't feel any better when I hit

Chicago's city limits. It's two in the morning, and the Chicago skyline looks as impressive as ever. Peaceful, even.

I pull into the parking garage of my apartment building and realize that I haven't once thought of work in the last ten hours. That has to be a new record. Exhausted from the drive, I don't have the energy to worry. My phone's message light is flashing but I ignore it. I throw myself into bed and think *I'll deal with this tomorrow.*

When I wake up, it's light. I wonder if I've slept only for a few hours, but then I look at my clock. It says 5:14. I think, *five in the morning?* It takes me awhile to realize it's five in the evening—the following day. That's sixteen hours I slept. Sixteen! Granted, I haven't had a good night's sleep in weeks, but this is ridiculous.

It takes me another second to realize that what woke me up was the sound of my phone ringing. Clumsily I grab the receiver from my bedside table and croak, "Hello."

"Thank God you're home!" cries my assistant Anne. "Have I got the scoop of the century for you."

"Unless you're divorcing your husband and running off with Brad Pitt, I'm going back to sleep."

"Why are you sleeping at five in the afternoon? Wait, never mind. It's just good that you're sleeping," Anne says. "Anyway, back to the subject at hand. Michelle was fired today."

I sit up in bed.

"She was what?"

"Fired. Terminated. Escorted out of the building by security."

"No!" I gasp. "Why?"

"Remember those expense reports? The ones she kept wanting to pass on to you? Well, I did some digging. I should say that I did said digging only after she called me a worthless secretary who wouldn't know a news story if it bit me on the ass."

"Anne . . ."

"It turns out payroll has been investigating her. She expensed five thousand dollars worth of charges last year, including her four-thousand-dollar Bahamas vacation. She was sleeping with some junior accountant and he was writing checks over to her until *he* was fired two months ago."

I simply can't process this.

"Was she really led out of the building by security?"

"In front of everyone," Anne says.

"That's some kind of karmic payback."

"Amen to that, sister," Anne concurs. "And by the way, Bob has been going crazy looking for you. I think he has some good news."

"Tell me," I demand.

"Sorry—I can only leak one news story at a time. Bob's news you'll have to hear from Bob himself. Those were his orders."

After hanging up, I pull myself out of bed and see that there are five messages waiting for me on my answering machine. The first one is from Bob. "Jen, Bob here. I've been trying your cell phone but get no signal. Where does your family live? Tijuana? Call me when you get in. I want to talk about your promotion to the ten spot. Give me a call when you get back in and we'll talk details."

Promoted? He's going to promote me?

The second message is playing. "Jen—it's Bob again. I've been trying your cell phone for hours, but I keep getting your voice mail. What is it with Arkansas? Do they not have cell phone lines there? Anyway, call me about this promotion thing, okay?"

Next message. "Jen. I am beginning to think you're playing hardball. Nice job. If it's the salary you're thinking about, then trust me, we can give you a raise. We're talking 5 to 7 percent."

A raise? Bob's voice comes again on the next message. "You're a tough cookie, Jen Taylor. Okay—12 percent raise—but that's it!"

And the next: "Jen. If you're negotiating with another station, I'll match whatever they're offering."

And that's the end of my messages. None from Riley. I feel a small stab of disappointment. I call his mobile phone and get his voice mail. I leave a message saying I hope everything is all right with Tiffany's mom. Then I grab a shower, get dressed, and head to the station.

Bob is in his office, working late as usual, and when he sees me, he jumps up from his desk and sprints over as if he's going to give me a hug. Instead, he extends his hand for a shake.

"Jen Taylor, am I glad to see you," Bob says. "I take it you're here to discuss your promotion? I've been filling in for the ten o'clock shift for days, and I'm sick of it. I don't know how you deal with those anchors."

"Magic," I say, with a smile.

"So, we've got a deal then? You producing the ten o'clock spot, and your 5 percent raise."

"I think you said 12 percent," I correct.

Bob gives me a lopsided grin. "You're a tough one, Jen Taylor. You'll go far," he says.

A week passes with my new job, and I don't hear from Riley. He's made good on his promise to take his sick leave, and his desk is empty. He's also notoriously absent from IM.

My new job is everything I could have hoped it would be. I have semiregular hours, or at least, my shift ends at ten thirty most nights instead of eleven in the morning. I can finally sleep at night like other regular people, and not in the afternoon. I've got the best news stories and the biggest audience of my career, and I know I'm one step closer to a network position.

The new ten spot anchor is thankfully nothing like Michelle. She doesn't ask me to pick up her dry cleaning and she doesn't demand that our scripts be limited to words under four syllables. It's more than I could ask for in an anchor. But I can't seem to really enjoy my new job. All I can think about is Riley. He said he'd call but he hasn't.

"Just call him," implores my friend Jason, who greets me at Celtic Crossings to celebrate my promotion. Upon hearing the news he sent me a house plant and a card that read "Maybe now you'll have time to water me!"

"What do I say?" I ask Jason.

"Well, you could start by being honest," he says. "Just tell him how you feel."

"Now you know that you would never take the same relationship advice from me," I tell him. Jason, of course, is sometimes known to pretend he's an airline pilot when he meets men in bars.

"But that's how you know my advice is sound," Jason argues.

I call Riley. I don't know what I should say on his voice mail. "Hope you're not back with Tiffany"? "Why haven't you called, you ass"? I hang up without leaving a message.

I get a postcard from Lucy. It's got the Arkansas State Trooper seal on the front, and on the back she writes that she's sorry for asking me to be a bridesmaid and then running off from the wedding. "But," she writes, "I think you understand why—we independent women think alike!" and she signs it "Lucy" with a heart for a *u*. She also tells me that she's enrolled in paralegal classes at the local community college because she "has a knack for law stuff."

Kimberly calls to announce that while she is not going to get married, she is moving in with Matt Chang. She also tells me that Aunt Teri moved back to San Francisco, where she got hired at a Psychic Switchboard, reading—yes—*I Ching* coins.

The weekend after the wedding that didn't happen, Bubba catches a sixteen-pound bass—bigger even than Bud—which he calls "Ms. Bud" because it's a girl.

Aunt Bette finally sells enough Mary Kay to get herself a new pink Cadillac. Even Vivien, who still complains periodically of having a heart condition, gets a clean bill of health from her doctor who announced her cholesterol and blood pressure are well within the healthy range.

And I still have not heard from Riley.

On my desk the next day I find a Mr. Miyagi action figure. There's no note. Mr. Miyagi has one hand in a curled fist and the other flat, as if he's either about to karate-chop through wooden boards or play Rock Paper Scissors. More importantly, he's wearing tiny Elvis glasses with muttonchops. The sight of this makes me laugh. I look up and around the office for some sign of Riley. I don't find him anywhere.

I bump into Riley in the least likely of places—standing in the lobby of my building holding a bouquet of pink roses.

"Congrats on the promotion," he says, handing me the flowers.

"Thanks," I say. I want to scream, "Where have you been? Why haven't you called me?" but I manage not to do so.

"Do I have you to thank for Mr. Miyagi: Elvis Impersonator?"

"You do indeed. You quote Mr. Miyagi often enough, so I figured it was a safe bet, and I know how you love muttonchops."

I look down at the flowers.

"I was hoping we could start over," he tells me, offering me his hand. "Hi, I'm Nigel Riley."

"And I'm Jen Taylor."

"Nice to meet you. Would you like to date?"

"What about Tiffany?"

"Tiffany who?" Riley pretends he doesn't know whom I'm talking about.

"Your girlfriend, Tiffany?"

"Ex-girlfriend, actually," Riley says. "Ex-girlfriend who is living with her new boyfriend in L.A. The wanker."

"Riley, I'm sorry," I say, suddenly sad for him.

"I'm not," he says. "She did want to get back together, but it only gave me the supreme satisfaction of breaking up with her."

"Nice," I say, laughing. "How's her mom?"

"Recovering."

"That's good."

"And why didn't you call me all this time?" I ask him.

"I had to do some thinking," Riley says. "I wanted to figure some things out. I wanted to make sure of what I wanted before I went and mucked things up."

"And what did you figure out?"

"I realized on that little trip of ours that it's not Tiffany I love."

"No?"

"It's you," Riley says. "Apparently, I've been smitten with you for ages. At least, that's what Tiffany says."

I laugh. "That's got to be the least romantic way anyone has ever told me they love me."

"Hang on, there's a lot more romance where that came from, luv," Riley says.

He wraps his arm around my waist and draws me to him.

He bends down and kisses me, there in my lobby. It's a gentle but intense kiss, and when he pulls away, I feel a little breathless.

"Now, I realize since we just started dating this might be a bit forward," Riley says, tracing my face with his finger. "But, do you fancy a shag?"

I glance at my watch. "I do have fifteen hours until I have to be at work."

"Hmm." Riley pauses and pretends to do some imaginary calculations. "I guess I'll just have to make do with that," he says, pulling me closer for another kiss.

Up Close and Personal
with the Author

DIXIELAND SUSHI IS A VERY UNIQUE STORY. HOW WERE YOU INSPIRED TO WRITE IT?

Like Jen, I come from a mixed racial background. My dad is Japanese American and my mother has a mix of English and European roots, but is first and foremost proud of her Texan heritage. I grew up in Texas, and found that the culture clash I experienced as a child made for some interesting stories.

WHAT WAS IT LIKE FOR YOU GROWING UP IN TEXAS AND HAVING A MIXED HERITAGE?

Like Jen, I sometimes found it difficult to convince people that I was part Japanese. I didn't look traditionally Asian, and most people assumed I had a Latin American background. I did go through a brief identity crisis at age four. To this day, people will often ask me that dread "Where are you from?" question which is code for "Just what ARE you?" But as more people of mixed heritage—like Tiger Woods—become prominent in our culture, I think people (hopefully) will be more accepting of people with mixed heritages.

ARE ANY PEOPLE IN THE BOOK BASED ON REAL FAMILY MEMBERS?

There are no characters that are exact cookie-cutter replicas of family or friends. But as with all my characters, I do draw on experience and memory to shape many of them.

WHAT WAS IT LIKE TO WRITE ABOUT SUCH A PERSONAL SUBJECT?

I put a lot of myself into all the stories I write, but *Dixieland Sushi* in some ways extracted even more from me. Racial identity is certainly a large part of who I am, and so writing about that did require some additional soul-searching. Not to mention, there's always a challenge with any story to make it entertaining and fun, which I hope I've accomplished here.

WAS IT CHALLENGING TO APPROACH RACIAL SITUATIONS IN A FUNNY WAY?

It was difficult. Despite the progress we've made as a country in the last couple of generations, I think there are still lingering prejudices. I think as a nation, we haven't quite made peace with our racial diversity.

HAVE YOU OR YOUR FAMILY BEEN A VICTIM OF PREJUDICE?

My paternal grandparents met and married in an internment camp in Poston, Arizona, during World War II. The story about Grandpa Frank in the book losing his graduation gift of a car is a true one. And both my grandparents' families lost everything during World War II. So there's that. And like most kids, I got my fair share of taunting on the playground. Anything that makes you different, whether it's what you look like or how you speak or how you carry yourself, can make you the target of some pretty mean teasing on the playground. I'm hoping we're moving beyond that now, though.

IN THE BOOK, THERE'S SOME REFERENCES TO WHAT IT IS TO BE AN AMERICAN. WHAT DO YOU THINK BEING AMERICAN MEANS?

I think there is not one definition of an American. Right now there's a lot of discussion about how divided we are as a national politically, but I hope that we don't forget that one of the greatest things about our country is that there is room for so many combinations of cultures and attitudes. Jen's story is a unique one that could only happen in America, I think. I hope that as a nation we continue to value our diversity because I think it's our strongest attribute as a nation. The definition of being American is that there is no one definition. We are one big Benetton ad, and that's a good thing.

RILEY, THE LOVE INTEREST IN THE BOOK, GREW UP IN ENGLAND. HOW IS THAT SIGNIFICANT?

Riley, like Jen, has a uniquely American story. He was born in America but raised abroad, so he has a different accent and a different perspective, but it doesn't mean he's any less American.

YOU EXPLORE POPULAR CULTURE OF THE EIGHTIES IN MANY OF THE BOOK'S FLASHBACK PARTS. DO YOU THINK POPULAR CULTURE IS SOMETHING THAT IS SHARED BY MOST AMERICANS?

I do think popular culture can be common ground for us. Entertainment on television, radio, and on the movie screen can cut through traditional boundaries, because it's not generally divisive, but inclusive since its primary purpose is to entertain. In this book, pop culture is seen through the lens of a girl growing up with a mixed racial heritage in the South, so it's a bit different than another person's experience. For example, I'm not sure a girl growing up in Maine would dream of being a country western star, but I think they can still relate to Jen's experience.

MR. MIYAGI HAS A PROMINENT ROLE IN THIS BOOK. ARE YOU A FAN?

Of course. I don't see how you can't love Mr. Miyagi. He's a sensei who dispenses sarcastic advice and yet kicks butt. What's not to love?

WHAT ARE YOU WORKING ON NOW?

My next novel. It's top secret, so if I told you about it, I'd have to kill you, or at least extract a solemn vow of secrecy. You can look for it, however, in the spring of 2006.

Be the Next Downtown Girl
Contest Rules

1) ENTRY REQUIREMENTS:

Register to enter the contest on www.simonsaysthespot.com. Enter by submitting your story as specified below.

2) CONTEST ELIGIBILITY:

This contest is open to nonprofessional writers who are legal residents of the United States and Canada (excluding Quebec) over the age of 18 as of December 7, 2004. Entrant must not have published any more than two short stories on a professional basis or in paid professional venues. Employees (or relatives of employees living in the same household) of Simon & Schuster, VIACOM, or any of their affiliates are not eligible. This contest is void in Puerto Rico, Quebec, and wherever prohibited or restricted by law.

3) FORMAT:

Entries must not be more than 7,500 words long and must not have been previously published. Entries must be typed or printed by word processor, double spaced, on one side of noncorrasable paper. Do not justify right-side margins. Along with a cover letter, the author's name, address, email address, and phone number must appear on the first page of the entry. The author's name, the story title, and the page number should appear on every page. Electronic submissions will be accepted and must be sent to downtowngirl@simonandschuster.com. All electronic submissions must be sent as an attachment in a Microsoft Word document. All entries must be original and the sole work of the Entrant and the sole property of the Entrant.

All submissions must be in English. Entries are void if they are in whole or in part illegible, incomplete, or damaged or if they do not conform to any of the requirements specified herein. Sponsor reserves the right, in its absolute and sole discretion, to reject any entries for any reason, including but not limited to based on sexual content, vulgarity, and/or promotion of violence.

4) ADDRESS:

Entries submitted by mail must be postmarked by July 31, 2005 and sent to:

Be The Next Downtown Girl
Author Search

Downtown Press Editorial Department
Pocket Books
1230 Sixth Avenue, 13th floor
New York, NY 10020

Or Emailed By July 31, 2005 at 11:59 PM EST as a Microsoft Word document to:

downtowngirl@simonandschuster.com

Each entry may be submitted only once. Please retain a copy of your submission. You may submit more than one story, but each submission must be mailed or emailed, as applicable, separately. Entries must be received by July 31, 2005. Not responsible for lost, late, stolen, illegible, mutilated, postage due, garbled, or misdirected mail/entries.

5) PRIZES:

One Grand Prize winner will receive:

Simon & Schuster's Downtown Press Publishing Contract for Publication of Winning Entry in a future Downtown Press Anthology, Five Hundred U.S. Dollars ($500.00), and

Downtown Press Library
(20 books valued at $260.00)

Grand Prize winner must sign the Publishing contract which contains additional terms and conditions in order to be published in the anthology.

Ten Second Prize winners will receive:

A Downtown Press Collection
(10 books valued at $130.00)

No contestant can win more than one prize.

6) STORY THEME

We are not restricting stories to any specific topic, however they should embody what all of our Downtown Press authors encompass—they should be smart, savvy, sexy stories that any Downtown Girl can relate to. We all know what uptown girls are like, but girls of the new millennium prefer the Downtown Scene. That's where it happens. The music, the shopping, the sex, the dating, the heartbreak, the family squabbles, the marriage, and the divorce. You name it. Downtown Girls have done it. Twice. We encourage you to register for the contest at www.simonsaysthespot.com in order to receive our monthly emails and updates from our authors and read about our titles on www.downtownpress.com to give you a better idea of what types of books we publish.

7) JUDGING:

Submissions will be judged on the equally weighted criteria of (a) basis of writing ability and (b) the originality of the story (which can be set in any time frame or location). Judging will take place on or about October 1, 2005. The judges will include a freelance editor, the editor of the future Anthology, and 5 employees of Sponsor. The decisions of the judges shall be final.

8) NOTIFICATION:

The winners will be notified by mail or phone on or about October 1, 2005. The Grand Prize Winner must sign the publishing contract in order to be awarded the prize. All federal, local, and state taxes are the responsibility of the winner. A list of the winners will be available after October 20, 2005 on:

http://www.downtownpress.com

http://www.simonsaysthespot.com

The winners' list can also be obtained

by sending a stamped self-addressed envelope to:

Be The Next Downtown Girl
Author Search
Downtown Press Editorial Department
Pocket Books
1230 Sixth Avenue, 13th floor
New York, NY 10020

9) PUBLICITY:

Each Winner grants to Sponsor the right to use his or her name, likeness, and entry for any advertising, promotion, and publicity purposes without further compensation to or permission from such winner, except where prohibited by law.

10) INTERNET:

If for any reason this Contest is not capable of running as planned due to an infection by a computer virus, bugs, tampering, unauthorized intervention, fraud, technical failures, or any other causes beyond the control of the Sponsor which corrupt or affect the administration, security, fairness, integrity, or proper conduct of this Contest, the Sponsor reserves the right in its sole discretion, to disqualify any individual who tampers with the entry process, and to cancel, terminate, modify, or suspend the Contest. The Sponsor assumes no responsibility for any error, omission, interruption, deletion, defect, delay in operation or transmission, communications line failure, theft or destruction or unauthorized access to, or alteration of, entries. The Sponsor is not responsible for any problems or technical malfunctions of any telephone network or telephone lines, computer on-line systems, servers, or providers, computer equipment, software, failure of any email or entry to be received by the Sponsor due to technical problems, human error or traffic congestion on the Internet or at any website, or any combination thereof, including any injury or damage to participant's or any other person's computer relating to or resulting from participating in this Contest or downloading any materials in this Contest. CAUTION: ANY ATTEMPT TO DELIBERATELY DAMAGE ANY WEBSITE OR UNDERMINE THE LEGITIMATE OPERATION OF THE CONTEST IS A VIOLATION OF CRIMINAL AND CIVIL LAWS AND SHOULD SUCH AN ATTEMPT BE MADE, THE SPONSOR RESERVES THE RIGHT TO SEEK DAMAGES OR OTHER REMEDIES FROM ANY SUCH PERSON(S) RESPONSIBLE FOR THE ATTEMPT TO THE FULLEST EXTENT PERMITTED BY LAW. In the event of a dispute as to the identity or eligibility of a winner based on an email address, the winning entry will be declared made by the "Authorized Account Holder" of the email address submitted at time of entry. "Authorized Account Holder" is defined as the natural person 18 years of age or older who is assigned to an email address by an Internet access provider, online service provider, or other organization (e.g., business, education institution, etc.) that is responsible for assigning email addresses for

the domain associated with the submitted email address. Use of automated devices are not valid for entry.

11) LEGAL information:

All submissions become sole property of Sponsor and will not be acknowledged or returned. By submitting an entry, all entrants grant Sponsor the absolute and unconditional right and authority to copy, edit, publish, promote, broadcast, or otherwise use, in whole or in part, their entries, in perpetuity, in any manner without further permission, notice or compensation. Entries that contain copyrighted material must include a release from the copyright holder. Prizes are nontransferable. No substitutions or cash redemptions, except by Sponsor in the event of prize unavailability. Sponsor reserves the right at its sole discretion to not publish the winning entry for any reason whatsoever.

In the event that there is an insufficient number of entries received that meet the minimum standards determined by the judges, all prizes will not be awarded. Void in Quebec, Puerto Rico, and wherever prohibited or restricted by law. Winners will be required to complete and return an affidavit of eligibility and a liability/publicity release, within 15 days of winning notification, or an alternate winner will be selected. In the event any winner is considered a minor in his/her state of residence, such winner's parent/legal guardian will be required to sign and return all necessary paperwork.

By entering, entrants release the judges and Sponsor, and its parent company, subsidiaries, affiliates, divisions, advertising, production, and promotion agencies from any and all liability for any loss, harm, damages, costs, or expenses, including without limitation property damages, personal injury, and/or death arising out of participation in this contest, the acceptance, possession, use or misuse of any prize, claims based on publicity rights, defamation or invasion of privacy, merchandise delivery, or the violation of any intellectual property rights, including but not limited to copyright infringement and/or trademark infringement.

Sponsor:

Pocket Books,
an imprint of Simon & Schuster, Inc.
1230 Avenue of the Americas,
New York, NY 10020

Try these Downtown Press bestsellers on for size!

GOING TOPLESS
Megan McAndrew

DINNER FOR TWO
Mike Gayle

THE DEAD FATHER'S GUIDE TO SEX AND MARRIAGE
John Scott Shepherd

BABES IN CAPTIVITY
Pamela Redmond Satran

UPGRADING
Simon Brooke

MY FAVORITE MISTAKE
Beth Kendrick

BITE
C.J. Tosh

THE HAZARDS OF SLEEPING ALONE
Elise Juska

SCOTTISH GIRLS ABOUT TOWN
Jenny Colgan, Isla Dewar, Muriel Gray, and more

CALLING ROMEO
Alexandra Potter

GAME OVER
Adele Parks

PINK SLIP PARTY
Cara Lockwood

SHOUT DOWN THE MOON
Lisa Tucker

MANEATER
Gigi Levangie Grazer

CLEARING THE AISLE
Karen Schwartz

LINER NOTES
Emily Franklin

MY LURID PAST
Lauren Henderson

DRESS YOU UP IN MY LOVE
Diane Stingley

HE'S GOT TO GO
Sheila O'Flanagan

IRISH GIRLS ABOUT TOWN
Maeve Binchy, Marian Keyes, Cathy Kelly, and more

THE MAN I SHOULD HAVE MARRIED
Pamela Redmond Satran

GETTING OVER JACK WAGNER
Elise Juska

THE SONG READER
Lisa Tucker

THE HEAT SEEKERS
Zane

I DO (BUT I DON'T)
Cara Lockwood

WHY GIRLS ARE WEIRD
Pamela Ribon

LARGER THAN LIFE
Adele Parks

ELIOT'S BANANA
Heather Swain

HOW TO PEE STANDING UP
Anna Skinner

*Look for them wherever books are sold
or visit us online at www.downtownpress.com.*

Great storytelling just got a new address.
PUBLISHED BY POCKET BOOKS

11226

LaVergne, TN USA
30 December 2010
210578LV00004B/10/P